This was not happening.

Not in a hundred years.

I stared at the schedule on the computer screen in front me. The caller on the other end of the phone line forgotten.

The least of my problems.

I forgot to breathe. Or maybe I just couldn't get any air.

How many Kade Johnsons were there?

How many Kade Samuel Johnsons?

How many Kade Samuel Johnsons who were pilots?

"Hello?"

Right. I was scheduling a flight for Markus Peters. One of Skye Travel's best customers.

Shit.

"I'm so sorry Mr. Peters. There was a glitch in the phone line." There was actually a glitch in my brain.

It had been eight years since I'd seen Kade Johnson.

Eight years.

And not a day in those eight years had passed that I hadn't had at least a fleeting thought of Kade Johnson in one way or another.

SECOND CHANCE KISSES

SECOND CHANCE KISSES

THE WORTHINGTONS

KATHRYN KALEIGH

To learn more about Kathryn Kaleigh, visit

www.kathrynkaleigh.com

Kathryn Kaleigh

1

MADISON WORTHINGTON

This was not happening.

Not in a hundred years.

I stared at the schedule on the computer screen in front me. The caller on the other end of the phone line forgotten.

The least of my problems.

I forgot to breathe. Or maybe I just couldn't get any air.

How many Kade Johnsons were there?

How many Kade Samuel Johnsons?

How many Kade Samuel Johnsons who were pilots?

"Hello?"

Right. I was scheduling a flight for Markus Peters. One of Skye Travel's best customers.

Shit.

"I'm so sorry Mr. Peters. There was a glitch in the phone line." There was actually a glitch in my brain.

It had been eight years since I'd seen Kade Johnson.

Eight years.

And not a day in those eight years had passed that I hadn't had at least a fleeting thought of Kade Johnson in one way or another.

I put Mr. Peters on speaker and keyed in his information. He now had a flight to Florida with his family scheduled for Friday.

With Kade Johnson in the pilot's seat.

My little brother, Quinn, was going to hear about this. Had Quinn lost his mind?

"Thank you, Mr. Peters, for flying Skye Travels. We'll see you Friday."

I clicked off the phone and looked toward the conference room.

Fortunately for Quinn, he was tied up in a meeting for the next... I glanced at my watch... hour or so.

And by then, I'd be heading out.

It was only my first day on the job—sort of, but I'd been doing this work on and off, since I was a senior in high school.

A questionable perk of being the boss's daughter.

My father, Noah Worthington, believed his children should work like everyone else.

He didn't want us growing up soft, living off his money. And all five of his children had careers.

The only questionable one, though, was my little brother Quinn.

He'd gotten his business degree, then somehow slid right into the company as vice-president.

He claimed to be following in our father's footsteps, but I seemed to be the only one who noticed that Quinn had never flown an airplane.

Our father, however, was a well-known and respected pilot and had formed his company, Skye Travels, based on that reputation.

I could see the tarmac from here. Close enough that the office carried the comforting scent of jet fuel. But right now even that wasn't enough to calm my nerves.

I had to get through the next hour. Then I could figure out

what to do about this Kade Johnson thing.

I straightened up what was going to be my workspace for the next three months and checked my phone messages.

I had one text from my best friend Emily.

EMILY: *Are you off yet?*

ME: *Not yet. One hour left.*

EMILY: *Drinks at the Skyhouse?*

She completely read my mind. I'd only been back in town a few days and hadn't seen my best friend yet.

ME: *OMG. Yes.*

EMILY: *See you there.*

My fingers hovered over the keys. But I set my phone down. I wasn't ready to tell her about Kade. I was still processing it myself and I didn't need Emily's opinion tossed into my brain just yet.

Quinn stuck his head out of the conference room across the hall.

"Madison? Would you make some copies for us?"

"Of course." I put a big fake smile on my face for the benefit of the two men who were meeting with Quinn as I took the envelope from him.

The men were from a big marketing firm and Quinn was meeting them to set up a contract. I had to give Quinn credit. He was good at schmoozing.

But seriously. Quinn was taking advantage of me.

I should have a nameplate made for the receptionist desk.

Dr. Madison Worthington.

I squared my shoulders. I'd done it to myself. I was the one who'd volunteered to help out until he could hire someone for the summer. And then I'd be the one to train the new person.

The receptionist they'd had for years had retired last week. I had trained her myself during the summer before I left for graduate school. I seriously think she waited until she knew I was coming in for the summer before she announced it.

I didn't blame her. This way I was the one doing the training.

My father's work ethic was firmly cemented in my psyche.

I didn't begrudge it. That work ethic was what had gotten me through undergrad in three years. Then graduate school.

After getting my license to practice psychology, I'd done some teaching at Houston Community College and discovered that I liked it. Okay. Loved it.

At first, I couldn't believe they were paying me to do something that was so much fun.

It hadn't taken me long to land a full-time teaching job.

In Denver.

I had three months before I had to show up for new faculty orientation.

Since I already had my apartment secured, I had some time on my hands.

The copy room was at the other end of the office suite. Past the elevator.

Just as I stepped past the elevator, it dinged.

Skye Travels was known for not only its efficiency, but also its Houston hospitality.

I turned, holding the brown envelope Quinn had handed me against my chest and prepared to greet whoever stepped off the elevator.

But also, Quinn was waiting.

I took a step backwards.

The elevator doors opened.

And I froze.

Kade Samuel Johnson stepped off the elevator.

I was having that breathing problem again.

Maybe I should see a doctor about that.

But I already knew it was full-fledged anxiety.

And I knew how to treat it. I was a psychologist after all.

Take a deep breath.

Kade stepped out of the elevator. Stopped and looked right at me.

It was almost like he'd known I was standing there.

He wouldn't have known, of course.

Couldn't have known.

He looked at me blankly.

He didn't even recognize me.

We'd been together for three years and he didn't even recognize me.

I clamped down every thought that came to my head.

Kade worked here now.

My stupid, inconsiderate, clueless brother had hired him.

So I just turned around.

I turned around and continued to the copy room.

I wasn't about to let Kade Johnson know that I'd thought about him every day when he couldn't even have the decency to recognize me.

Sure. It had been eight years.

Sure. Instead of actually breaking up, we'd drifted apart.

But still.

I stepped into the copy room and opened the envelope.

My hands were shaking too much for me to do the simple task of pulling the papers out of the envelope and my eyes wouldn't focus.

Damn it.

This was not going to get the best of me.

I yelped as the envelope sliced across my right index finger giving me a paper cut.

I dropped the envelope onto the copier and stuck my bleeding finger in my mouth.

When I'd gotten up this morning, I'd had no idea that this would be the day I'd see Kade Johnson again.

And all the psychological training in the world was useless.

2

———

KADE JOHNSON

I recognized Madison immediately, of course.

But I swear my body knew she was there before I did.

As soon as the elevator dinged and the door opened, it knew.

I'd always liked the scent of jet fuel, but it had never been a turn on.

Not like that.

It was definitely Madison.

By the time my brain caught up, she'd turned around and walked away.

My first instinct was to follow her. And I even took two steps forward before my logical brain reminded me that my instinct was eight years out of date.

She'd always been pretty. With a quick smile.

But the Madison who'd just walked away from me was not pretty. She was drop dead gorgeous.

Long, brunette mermaid hair. That perfect heart-shaped face. Lips that naturally turned up at the corners.

And a tight black skirt that did everything to remind me what I knew about that body beneath it.

She was wearing a white button-down shirt tucked into that skirt, revealing her narrow waist.

I bet I could still wrap my hands around that waist.

But I worked here now. And she was the boss's daughter.

I had to keep it together.

And keep it in my pants.

I needed a minute before I walked down to reception to meet up with Quinn.

The last thing I needed was to walk into my new office with a hard-on.

I'd only met Quinn Worthington once and during the interview calls, neither one of us had mentioned my previous relationship with his sister. It was possible he didn't even remember me from back then.

Not likely. But certainly possible.

He was younger than I was. Five years? Maybe more.

And when I'd been with Madison, Quinn had been away at a boarding school or some such to prep him for college.

It occurred to me then that Quinn might have hired me without telling Madison.

And if Madison worked here…

I thought she'd be far away from here by now.

I'd seen enough social media updates—not stalking—to know that she'd finished her degree in psychology.

She'd finished it just like she'd set out to do.

Madison completed everything she set out to do. It was one of the many things I admired about her.

Unfortunately, though, it had been the end of our relationship.

We'd decided not to do the whole long distance thing.

I don't know what she'd been thinking, but I always sort of thought we were on a break.

I'd dated, of course. It had been eight years after all and a man had needs.

But I'd never let myself get serious with anyone.

Was it because of Madison?

Not that I would ever admit it.

I turned left and went toward what looked like a lobby. All my interviews and discussions had been via FaceTime. My reputation was good enough to get me a job anywhere in the industry.

But life happened and I needed to be closer to home.

There was no one at the receptionist's desk. Quinn was in the glass-walled conference room on the other end of the lobby with two men.

I took a seat on one of the little sofas in the spacious lobby. This whole side of the office had floor to ceiling windows overlooking the tarmac.

I had an involuntary little sense of excitement. This third floor office space was perfect.

I should have known Noah Worthington would do it right. The man had gone from being a commercial pilot—like me—to owning a fleet of small jets. He had started out in Dallas/Fort Worth, but for some unknown reason, he'd moved his main office to Houston.

Rumors suggested it had something to do with his wife Savannah. And apparently they were living in Houston now.

The receptionist must have already left for the day. Not a problem. I didn't have anything else I had to do today.

I stretched out my legs and pulled out my iPad. Scrolled idly through my emails.

But. Damn it. I couldn't concentrate.

Madison was somewhere in this office. I know she recognized me, but she'd turned walked away.

At the sound of feminine heels coming toward me from the elevator area, I looked up.

And watched as Madison walked straight toward me.
I stood up. Bad idea.
All the blood had rushed to my center.
Then she smiled and I nearly came undone.

3

———

MADISON

Kade Johnson had gotten even more handsome with age. But it was like that with guys.

He was wearing black slacks and a white button-down shirt. Basic pilot attire. Same basic outfit I was wearing except that I was wearing a skirt and heels, of course.

Was that why I had butterflies in my stomach? Just because we were wearing the same kind of clothes?

Of course not. Sometimes I put too much into all the psychological theories that had been hammered into my head.

He recognized me now. I could see it all over his face.

It had certainly taken him long enough.

I afforded him the same hospitality I'd give anyone visiting my father's company.

Only, he was doing more than just visiting. And since I was going to be working here for the next three months, I had no choice but to be cordial.

We'd parted as friends and promised to stay in touch.

That promise had been made eight years ago and I hadn't heard from him since that day we'd said good-bye in the parking lot of our favorite taco pub.

"Hello Kade," I said.

"Hello Madison." He smiled back.

I was impressed by how quickly he'd recovered from not recognizing me.

"You're working here now."

"What are you doing here?"

We both spoke at the same time.

We'd always had an uncanny kind of sync.

Was that how his first day and my first day were the same?

But no, I was being fanciful. I'd worked here on and off as needed over the years and this was the first time Kade had shown up.

It was just a weird quirk of chance.

Unless…

I narrowed my eyes in the direction of the conference room.

Had Quinn orchestrated this?

"Quinn didn't tell you, did he?" Kade asked, echoing my thoughts.

"No," I said. "But I saw your name on the schedule."

"Quinn moves fast," he said.

"We don't like to waste time here at Skye Travels." I held the envelope with the copies close to my chest. Like a shield.

"It's good to see you," he said. "But, seriously, what are you doing here?"

"Working," I said. "If you'll excuse me, I have to get these to Quinn."

I turned and walked straight for the conference door.

Quinn met me there and took the papers off my hands.

I went back to the reception desk, took my seat, and put the headset back on.

I did all this without glancing at Kade one single time.

I could do this.

I could be around him and not focus on him.

I was very pleased with my progress so far.

"Why aren't you somewhere straightening out lives?"

I jumped back, stifling a yelp.

Kade was leaning on the counter, smiling at me.

In my efforts to not look at him, I hadn't seen him move over to the reception desk.

Maybe this was going to be a bit harder than I thought.

4

KADE

"What makes you think I'm not straightening out lives here?"

I laughed. "I'm sure you straighten out lives wherever you go."

Maybe coming over here hadn't been the best idea.

Although I had admired her from a distance, I wasn't quite prepared for looking into those green eyes of hers up close.

She had the oddest expression on her face. I couldn't quite tell if it was curiosity… or amusement… or desire.

Being a man, I opted for desire.

"I thought you were supposed to be in Denver," I said.

"Denver. How would you know that?"

How would I know that indeed? "I read it somewhere." Ok. I'd given away my hand. So now she knew I'd kept up with her, at least enough to know that.

"Have you been cyber stalking me?" she asked, narrowing her eyes.

I pulled back with a feigned wounded look. "You know," he said. "If you'd keep your accounts a little more updated, I would have known that you were here and not in Denver."

She shrugged. "I—"

The phone rang and she deftly tapped a key on the computer.

"Skye Travels. This is Madison Worthington. How can I help you?"

She was using her maiden name and she wasn't wearing a ring. Two things social media had gotten right.

I put my elbows on the counter and watched her work.

I liked the way her face flushed, knowing I was watching her. It made me think of other things that made her flush.

Then the conference door opened and Quinn followed the two men out.

I nodded at the two men in fancy suits as they passed, noting that they wore that satisfied expression men wore when they felt like they'd gotten a good deal.

Quinn stepped up to me.

"Nice to meet you in person," he said, holding out a hand.

I shook his hand and didn't tell him that we'd actually met one time before.

It explained why he hadn't told Madison about me.

Madison was watching our interaction as she finished up her phone call.

Quinn glanced at his watch. "Instead of meeting in my office, why don't we have a drink? There's a little bar across the street called the Skyhouse."

"Sure," I said. "Is the Skyhouse part of Skye Travels?"

Quinn looked blankly at me for a moment. "No," he said. "Just a coincidence. Wait here while I close up my office."

"Take your time," I said, then turned my attention back to Madison.

She'd taken off her headset and was shutting everything down for the night.

"Come with us," I said.

Her fingers froze as she met my gaze. "I can't. I already have plans." Then she looked back down, pulling out her handbag.

"Another time then," I said.

Before she could answer, Quinn was coming back toward us.

"All ready to go?" he asked, not even noticing that he was interrupting.

My gaze locked with Madison's and held.

She hadn't said no outright.

I took that as a good sign.

5

MADISON

I was a heartbeat away from canceling.

And I would have, too, if Emily hadn't sent me a text right before I walked out the door.

EMILY: *I got us a great table off to the side. Our favorite one.*

I had ridden the elevator down with Quinn and Kade. I'd just left them to go to my car when the text came in.

My fingers hovered over the keys as I watched the two men get into Quinn's car.

Going to the same place was not a good idea.

But Quinn was driving Kade over to the tarmac before going up to the bar, so I had time to get in and *maybe* get out before they showed up.

ME: *I'm on my way.*

The Skyhouse was close enough that I could have walked, but that would have meant crossing six lanes of Houston traffic. Never a good idea.

Driving across six lanes of traffic was bad enough. Fortunately, Texas was u-turn friendly, making it not so bad.

It had been about six months since I'd seen Emily. Way too long.

The Skyhouse wasn't crowded tonight. There were just enough people to give it a little buzz of energy. Mostly businessmen waiting for their flights or having airport meetings.

I recognized one pilot sitting at the bar. Probably just landed.

Emily waved when I walked through the door. But she was right. She was sitting at our favorite table. It was off to the side giving us a perfect view to people watch.

I gave her a quick hug and we picked up like we'd just seen each other yesterday.

"You cut your hair," I said.

Emily might not be a natural blonde, but the color suited her perfectly. Her straight hair swept her shoulders.

"Thanks," she said, turning her head to show off her hair's healthy bounce. "You like?"

"I like very much."

Emily looked good no matter what she wore or how she wore her hair.

But she looked especially good tonight.

Where I was still wearing work clothes, she wore her red dress. The one that showed off her slim figure perfectly.

"And you've been growing your hair," she said.

I nodded. "I know you remember what happened when I tried going short."

Emily scrunched up her nose. "Couldn't forget. It looks good," she said as the bartender set our drinks down. "I ordered for you."

"Thanks." I slid the dirty martini with extra olives toward me. One thing about Emily. I could always count on her to tell me the truth about everything from hair to clothes to boys.

I glanced toward the door. "I can't stay long," I said, hating the disappointment that swept over Emily's features.

But she shrugged it off. "Got a date?" she asked.

"No," I said. "I don't have a date." I had the opposite of a date. I was in avoidance mode.

And I should probably just tell her because she'd figure it out anyway.

I sipped the drink. The Skyhouse had THE best martinis. Hands down.

"There's something I should probably tell you," I said.

"Hey," Emily said, peering past me toward the door.

My stomach dropped.

I knew what she was talking about before she even said anything.

"Is that…?" She looked back at me with a look of accusation that should have been humorous.

But I had a hand over my cheek, my head turned away from the door.

I didn't say a word, but I didn't have to.

"It is," she said in a stage whisper, though no one could have heard her anyway. "And you didn't tell me."

I laughed. "Emily," I said. "I just got here and I was just about to tell you."

Emily sat back, holding her drink in one hand. "You didn't know, did you?"

God. That's what happened when you stayed best friends with the same person from Kindergarten all the way to age thirty.

It was like we shared brain waves.

She took a quick sip of her drink and leaned forward. "So… catch me up."

I waited as Quinn and Kade took a seat at the bar. I wasn't watching them. Wasn't going to watch them.

"There's nothing to tell," I said.

But Emily watched the men.

"Stop it," I said. "They're going to feel you watching them."

She waved a hand. "That's not a thing. You can't feel someone watching you."

I narrowed my gaze at her. "Are you really going to go toe-to-toe with me on this?"

"Alright," Emily said with a smile. "Dr. Worthington. If you say it's a thing, it's a thing."

But she kept staring.

And just as I predicted, Quinn turned around and looked in our direction.

I turned my face away. "See. I told you."

Emily held up a hand in greeting. Something had happened between her and Quinn, but oddly enough, she'd never told me about it.

And I didn't press her, because, well, he was my brother and I wasn't sure I wanted to know.

She put both hands on the table. "So what's up with you and Kade Johnson?"

I shook my head, but Kade was looking this way.

6

———

KADE

he Skyhouse was an upscale bar right across the street from the Worthington's private terminal.

It wasn't very crowded. According to Quinn, that was typical.

It was baffling to me that Quinn didn't know who I was.

That I'd dated his older sister in college.

But—and I dealt with his type all the time—he was more focused on meeting and greeting than anything else.

Hell, if I hadn't known better, I would have thought he was a politician.

He knew a third of the people in here. Mostly men.

He was in mid-sentence, saying something about training schedules that I was more familiar with than he would ever be, when he stopped talking.

He was staring over at a private booth I hadn't noticed before.

There was a woman with short blonde hair sitting there. She held up a hand in greeting.

Quinn, just finished off his drink and shoved the empty glass aside.

Then I saw the other woman.

It was Madison.

Just seeing her seemed to set my whole system on fire.

It was like she had some kind of magnetic pull on me.

I still didn't know how I'd just let her walk away eight years ago.

The stupidness of youth.

Now it seemed that fate had brought us back together.

But she wasn't looking at me.

Her friend was. Her friend looked at me and said something to Madison.

Madison shook her head.

So that was her previous engagement?

"Who's Madison's friend?" I asked.

Quinn, who had been so talkative and open about everything else just shrugged. "Nobody. Look," he said. "I need to head out. Can I give you a ride across the street?"

The Worthington building was just across the street, but with traffic like it was, I could see why they didn't walk. That was unfortunate.

It would have been fitting if Noah had put this *Skyhouse* on the top floor of his building. It made me wonder…

"Sure," I said. "Just give me a minute."

If Quinn left without me, I'd find my way back to my car.

Crossing a few lanes of traffic was nothing for a seasoned pilot like me.

But he just shrugged and ordered another drink.

"Want one?" he asked.

"No. Thanks. One's my limit. Gotta drive."

I kept my eyes on Madison as I walked toward the girls' table.

That's when I realized I knew that blonde.

It was Emily. Madison's childhood friend.

Unlike Madison, Emily had changed a lot. She looked...
jaded.

But she wasn't my concern.

I stopped at the table.

Madison straightened and looked right at me.

"Hi." She smiled, looking a bit guilty. Or maybe I just
imagined it.

Either way, that innocent smile nearly took my breath
away.

"Hi," I said. "Hello Emily." I added, acknowledging
Madison's friend.

Emily didn't say anything. Just sat back and watched.

I started to ask Madison for her phone. But a phone was too
impersonal, no matter how modern.

So I asked for her hand.

Pulling a pen out of my inside coat pocket, I held out my
hand.

I clicked the pen with a little smile.

She just looked at me.

I smiled. "Your hand. Can I borrow your hand?"

"You—" But she stopped herself and held out her hand.

I held her hand palm up. I hadn't prepared myself for the
feel of her skin against mine.

For the onslaught of memories that my whole system had
to deal with. Not the least of which was the hardness that
reminded me of so many other things. Right on cue.

Using careful pen strokes, I wrote my phone number across
the palm of her hand.

Still holding her hand, I grinned at her. "In case you need
private tutoring," I said.

7

———

MADISON — BEFORE

*M*ath wasn't my favorite subject.

Sure. I could do it, but it just seemed like a waste of time.

That's what calculators were for, after all.

I sat in one of the computer labs in Wiley Tower at Louisiana Tech University.

The sun was coming in through the eighth floor window, sending dust sparkles through the room, but the sun did nothing to decrease the musty scent of the older building.

The building always smelled like ink. Ink and old books.

I had about two more pages of homework to do, then I could get out of here. Get something to eat before class.

But I was having trouble with my concentration.

The guy sitting next to me was tapping on a keyboard. The keyboard tapping didn't bother me. It just blended into the background.

But about every five minutes or so, he'd stop and click the top of his pen for a few seconds.

Every time he did this, I lost my train of thought and had to start over.

This time, his pen clicking for a few seconds was turning into at least a minute.

I tapped my fingers on the desk. Looked at the math problem again, but my brain couldn't pick the threads back up.

"Do you mind?" I blurted.

"What?" he asked, but the clicking stopped.

"I'm trying to concentrate."

I took a deep breath and went back to the beginning of the math problem and started over. But I already knew it was futile.

The clicking started again.

I slammed my book closed. There was no use in even trying to get this done. My thoughts were scattered.

"Oh," he said. "You meant this." He clicked his pen again. Twice.

"Yes," I said, still not looking at him.

I waited for him to apologize, but he didn't.

I was just about to open my book and give it one last try. The homework was due in four hours, so I couldn't put it off much longer.

But he clicked his pen again.

"Okay," I said, grabbing my backpack and tossing my books inside.

He laughed and I turned to look at him for the first time.

As a freshman, I knew he was at least a sophomore. Maybe even a junior.

Freshmen could tell those things.

He was wearing blue jeans, clean white sneakers, and a blue t-shirt with Tech splashed across it in red ink.

And he was smiling at me with a devilish crooked grin.

My eyes locked onto his and I all but forgot to breathe.

His eyes were a stunning blue. Like a perfectly clear blue sky.

He was absolutely handsome. But unfortunately, he knew it.

I zipped my backpack.

"You know," he said. "I'm actually really good at math."

"Okay," I said. "I'm glad to hear that."

He leaned back in his chair with obvious confidence. But I had to admit he was charming.

Dangerously charming.

"Maybe I can help." He nodded in the direction of my backpack.

"I don't need help. I just need quiet time to concentrate."

"I'm sorry," he said. "At least let me make it up to you."

I looked at him sideways. Shook my head. "I'll just do it later."

"Come on. At least let me help you with that word problem."

While I thought he'd been working, he'd been watching me.

I wondered if that was weird.

It didn't feel weird.

Follow your instincts, my grandmother always said.

I glanced at my watch.

"It's due for my 1:00 class."

He motioned with his hand. "It's an easy one."

I didn't answer.

"Come on. I owe you one."

It was his fault I wasn't getting my work done.

"Okay," I said. "But I do know how to work math problems."

"I always found math more interesting as a team sport."

I snorted, then laughed. "Math a sport?"

But I pulled out my book and my notebook.

"You are obviously going about math the wrong way."

"Obviously," I said to myself.

I'd never thought about math homework being fun. It was just something to get done and out of the way.

He started out by reading the math problem out loud and drawing some stick figures next to his version of a train.

He had me laughing.

Then he leaned back and looked at me.

"So?" he asked. "What's the answer?"

I looked down at his drawings with a smile I didn't seem to be able to stop.

I gave him a number.

"All right." He held up a hand for a high-five and I pressed my palm ever so briefly against his. "Easy, huh?"

"Actually, yes," I said.

"Let's do the next one."

It took me a minute to focus. Now, it wasn't his pen clicking that had me distracted. It was my fingers. They were tingling from his touch.

Forty-five minutes later, we had all my homework done. I probably could have done it in thirty minutes—in a quiet room. But I was entertained by his animated drawings as he went through each problem.

"Thank you," I said as wrote down the answer to the last problem.

"The pleasure was mine," he said.

I looked at him from beneath my lashes. Not something a typical college student would say.

"I'll let you get back to doing whatever it is you're doing," I said, tucking my books into my backpack again.

His computer had gone to screensaver mode, so I had no idea what it was he'd been doing.

"Can I borrow your hand?" he asked before I had time to stand up.

"Excuse me?"

He was wearing that crooked grin again.

"Your hand. May I?"

I held out my hand and he turned it over palm up. Then with his other hand, he picked up his pen, clicked it twice, and started to write some numbers on my palm.

Finished, he released my hand and winked at me.

"In case you need private tutoring."

8

MADISON

I watched as Kade walked back to my brother. Quinn was waiting impatiently.

I could tell by the way he was tapping his foot and looking in our direction. I was surprised he wasn't glaring at us, but he was watching Emily.

Emily didn't seem to notice.

But when Kade turned and started back in his direction, Quinn put a smile on his face and stood up.

Emily sat forward and waved her hand in front of her face.

"OMG. Madison."

"What?" I asked, but my gaze was still on Kade and my hand still tingled from his touch.

"Kade was cute in college, but he's smoking hot now."

I watched them until they walked out the door.

Kade didn't look back. I was a little disappointed, but my brother was rushing him along.

I looked down at the numbers on my hand.

"He's done this before," I said, thinking out loud.

Emily looked at my hand, then smiled slowly.

"I remember," she said slowly. "And how long was it before you called him?"

"I didn't." I smiled a little. "I didn't have to."

Emily picked up her glass, but it was empty. "Kade always was resourceful."

Then Emily picked up my phone and held it front of my face to unlock it.

"What are you doing?"

"I'm putting his number in your phone," she said, glancing from my palm to the phone. "I know how stubborn you can be."

"I'm not stubborn."

She held the phone up. "Double check the numbers."

I did. And, of course, they were right. *409-753-7593.*

Emily took two mints out of her handbag. Handed one to me.

"You have to call him," she said.

I took a sip of my drink, but I'd lost my taste for it. I shoved it aside and ate the mint instead.

"Actually," I said. "I don't."

Emily made an exasperated face at me.

I just smiled. "I don't. Because Kade just went to work at Skye Travels."

I didn't hear Emily's response.

All I could hear was the blood pounding in my ears as I realized the significance of what I'd just said.

I would be seeing Kade every day at work all summer.

"That explains why he's with Quinn," Emily said, her words finally penetrating my dazed brain.

I picked up my handbag, dropped it over my shoulder. "I have to go."

Emily was distracting me.

I needed some time alone.

Time to think.

9

KADE

*B*ack at my hotel room, I dropped my keys and wallet on the table just inside the door.

Shrugged out of my jacket and hung it in the closet.

I should have gotten an apartment already, but I wanted to wait.

Get a feel for the area before making that kind of commitment.

Now I had to either find a place in the next three days before my first flight with Skye Travels or live in the hotel and take my time looking for a place whenever I could find the time.

I untied my shoes and kicked them off.

But right now all I wanted to do was think about Madison.

When I'd taken this job with Skye Travels, I'd known it was possible that I would see Madison.

One day.

I hadn't expected it to be today.

Later.

Seeing her brought so many memories rushing back.

It had been love at first sight.

Something that had never happened to me again.

The two of us had been inseparable for three years.

Then graduate school had separated us.

I remembered the conversation well. We'd sat at our favorite taco pub, discussed our options, and calmly made the decision that we should pursue our own separate careers. Aviation for me. Psychology for her.

Grad school for her. A flight internship for me.

Different directions.

She was moving to Austin and I was moving to Auburn.

I'd been a year ahead of her, but somehow she'd managed to catch up and we'd graduated undergrad at the same time.

I distinctly remembered sitting there, calm on the outside while my heart was breaking.

I'd decided right then and there that I wasn't going to push her. She deserved to focus on graduate school without me holding her back.

I would not call her.

And I hadn't.

It had been hard at first, but over time it had gotten easier.

I'd folded that first Christmas eve. I'd been sitting with my family when I'd stepped outside and dialed her number.

A stranger answered—a man—and I hung up.

That had been that.

God, I'd missed her.

And now.

Wow. Now I couldn't even begin to believe how sexy she'd gotten.

I wanted to untuck her shirt. Slide my hands up and slip my fingers beneath her bra.

Torturing her would be so sweet.

Then I'd unbutton her shirt with my teeth. Was that even possible?

I'd unhook her bra and lick her nipples until they were hard.

While I'd suck on her nipples, unbutton my shirt.

Then I'd have her out of that sexy as fuck skirt. Wrap my hands around that plump ass and slide right inside.

Oh hell.

I looked down. I was straining against the zipper of my pants.

Just thinking about Madison had always gotten me hard.

But the grown-up Madison was making me come undone.

I unzipped my pants, freeing myself.

I wrapped my hands around my length and cupped my balls.

Still thinking about Madison, hot and wet, it only took a few strokes before I came all over my pants.

Damn it. How was I going to explain this to the dry cleaner?

10

MADISON

I jogged down the familiar path at Memorial Park, taking the long way around.

It was a beautiful spring morning. Not a cloud in the sky.

It would be a good day for flying.

Daddy had me behind the wheel of a Cessna before I could even walk.

He would have loved it if I'd taken to flying.

But it didn't take and my sister Ainsley had been the one to grow up in our father's footsteps.

One of the best pilots in the country and only one of his five children took to flying airplanes.

I felt bad for Daddy. But me. I took after Momma. Though she'd gotten a bit of a late start, Mom had been a top-notch psychologist. Still was. Part time.

Now that was something that intrigued me. She'd been the one whose footsteps I'd followed. It had come so easy for me.

Didn't mean I still wasn't Daddy's favorite.

It was an ongoing argument between me and my sisters.

Noah insisted that he loved us all equally.

But I knew that I had to be his favorite since I was most like Mom.

The sun was warm on my skin, but the breeze was light.

I was wearing a baseball cap, my hair pulled high in a ponytail in the back. I had on tights and a little skirt.

It was early, but I wasn't the only jogger out early.

Today was Saturday and I had the weekend off.

I hadn't seen Kade at work yesterday, but I hadn't expected to.

He didn't start work until Monday.

That hadn't kept me from watching for him. It had been quite distracting.

Fortunately, we hadn't had any visitors and the phones had been relatively quiet.

I looked down at my hand. At the numbers Kade had written on my skin. Little shivers ran through my system.

I'd been careful not to scrub the ink off, but it had faded a little anyway. By tomorrow, there would be no evidence left.

When I thought about how he'd so seamlessly replicated that first day we'd met, my eyes misted over and I had to wipe my eyes with the back of my hand.

I would have bet he didn't even remember how we'd met, but he must have remembered as clearly as I did.

I kicked a pinecone off the path, sending it flying out of the way.

But he'd let me go.

I'd be stupid to just fall back into his arms.

Besides, I was leaving for Denver in three months.

I'd thought about going early. Getting settled into the city.

It would have been the smart thing to do. To get ready for my new job.

But nope.

I had to come back here.

To spend the summer with my family.

At my old job.

A job I certainly didn't need.

I was a psychologist now. Not a student.

Dr. Worthington.

It had taken me eight years of school to achieve that. After undergrad.

It should have taken me six, but I'd done an extra postdoc, then a year of training at a neuropsych institute.

Every one of my supervisors had tried to convince me that I needed to practice psychology, not take a job as a professor.

But they didn't understand. It was a goal I'd set in undergrad and once I set a goal, I went for it.

I veered left and sprinted the rest of the way toward my car.

A man with a beautiful black lab was jogging toward me.

My heart skipped a beat. Just for a moment, I thought it was Kade.

But then he ran past me and I knew it had just been my imagination.

This was going to be a difficult summer.

But there was one thing I was happy about.

I was happy that I'd decided to spend the summer here in Houston.

Even though I was still mad at him, I felt like the stars had somehow aligned to put us back in the same place at the same time.

11

———

KADE

$\mathcal{M}$y weekend had started with me finding a dry cleaners near the airport.

Not one of my finest moments, but the man—thank God it had been a man and not a young girl—had quietly put a sticker on the front of my pants like it happened everyday.

And maybe it did.

But not to me.

Madison was going to drive me crazy if I had to see her every day for three months.

I'd barely seen her at all and already she was driving me insane.

I figured that since most of my time would be spent in the air, I could mostly avoid her. Even though I had a designated office there in the Skye Travels Building, I could do my paperwork on my own iPad and avoid the office.

It would be best.

I turned off of San Felipe and onto another small road. One more left and I pulled into the gated community. The guard was expecting me, but I showed him my identification anyway. I wanted the staff to get to know me well enough that they would feel comfortable talking to me when they needed to.

I parked the car and looked around. Everything looked clean. And secure.

Those things were very important.

When I knocked on the door, it took a few minutes for someone to come and open it.

I recognized the girl immediately. Her name was Susan and I'd hired her myself three months ago.

About the same time I'd made the decision to move back to Houston.

"Come on in," Susan said with a smile. "She's in the sunroom."

Susan was not only capable, but she was one of the most positive people I knew. She always had a smile and something good to say.

I followed her through the house. It was clean and uncluttered. I paid someone for that, too, to keep it that way.

I stepped into a bright sunlit room with walls of glass. Just outside the window there was a birdfeeder, birds fluttering all around it.

There was also a hummingbird feeder. Hummingbirds were her favorite. One buzzed the window just as I walked through the door.

My mother was sitting in a recliner, her feet up, her eyes glued to her iPad. She didn't know I was there, but she glanced up at the hummingbird.

Trying not to startle her, I walked around to stand in front of her so she could see me.

"Kade?" Her face lit into a smile and she closed the cover on her iPad. "I thought you weren't coming until tomorrow."

"I couldn't wait any longer to see you."

I went over and gave her a huge, long hug.

It had been two years since I'd seen her. Two years too long.

I'd vowed to myself never to do that again.

Work was important, but not as important as family.

Unfortunately, I hadn't known how much care she needed until she'd fallen and broken her leg.

"It's so good to see you," she said and I heard the tears in her voice.

"I'm sorry, Mother. I'm here now."

"Yes, you are," she pushed me back and I straightened. "So let me look at you."

My mother had aged in two years. I could see it in the lines around her eyes that weren't so obvious on facetime calls.

But she was taken care of now and I would be able to see her often.

Never again would I let two years keep me away from my family.

Not for work.

Not for anything.

"Sit down," she said. "I want to hear all about Madison."

12

MADISON

By the time I got to the office Monday morning, I'd already finished half my venti latte, skinny of course, with extra vanilla.

I wasn't supposed to be happy about seeing Kade. Not while I was still mad at him.

He would have to come in to the office this morning to sign some papers and get set up.

His first flight wasn't until morning.

I could tell myself not to be happy about seeing him all day long.

But I couldn't fight it.

I'd fought it all weekend and I was battle weary.

All I had to do was to admit to myself that I was happy to have the opportunity to catch up with him.

That was my story and I was sticking with it.

Just because I was happy to see him did not mean that we were getting back together.

In fact, there was no way I would get back together with Kade.

Not a chance.

He'd let me just walk away and then he hadn't had the decency to even call me. Not even once.

And that was after we said we'd stay in touch.

I pushed the button on the elevator and rode up to the third floor.

Ok. I'd spent a little extra time on my makeup this morning. And my hair.

And I'd worn my red blouse beneath my standard black jacket. I was wearing my favorite black skirt—the one that hugged my curves just so and I'd even worn my shoes with the red bottoms.

Basically my standard outfit—the best one, but I just felt good today. Like I had something to look forward to.

Just knowing that Kade was going to be there put a lightness in my step that I hadn't felt in a long time.

I made it to my work station ten minutes early. Flipped on the computer and the phone.

If someone called early, they'd get me, not the machine. I was here, so why not.

I tucked my handbag in the large drawer at the bottom of the desk and watered the ivy that the last receptionist had left behind.

I'd taken a liking to it even though I'd never been much of a plant person.

It looked like a good hardy plant, so I had high hopes that I wouldn't kill it.

There. I stood back and looked around.

Everything was ready for the day.

There was something satisfying about having a job to do and knowing that you were good at it.

That's what the latest psychological research was showing. Life is all about work and relationships.

People need a purpose and they need to feel like they're making a difference.

I'd be making a bigger difference when started teaching at the end of August, but for now I was determined to make my family's company the best it could be.

Just as I sat in my chair and put on my headset, I heard male laughter coming from the office area.

I froze.

I knew that laugh.

It was Kade Johnson.

How had he gotten to work before me?

And what was I supposed to do with the sudden rush of adrenalin that shot through my system?

Before I could come up with any ideas, the office phone buzzed.

But it wasn't a customer, it was Quinn.

"Can you come back here for a few minutes? Kade and I need your help."

13

KADE

*S*o much for best laid plans and all that.

I'd planned on avoiding Madison until I figured out exactly how I was going to approach her.

But Quinn was relentless. We'd had breakfast at five a.m. In the office by six thirty.

If Quinn worked this hard all the time, I understood why Noah had put him in charge.

Apparently Quinn had a flight out mid-morning and needed to get me set up before he left.

"Which plane do you fly?" I asked as he turned off the speaker he'd used to call Madison.

Maybe talking about flying airplanes would distract me from thinking about Madison.

Quinn, sitting on the corner of my desk answered quickly. "I don't fly," he said.

I thought I might have misunderstood. "You mean today?"

Quinn looked at me, then back to the computer. "No. I'm not a pilot."

Before I had time to process how a man carrying Noah

Worthington's genes did not hold a pilot's license, Madison walked in.

So instead of using Quinn and talk of airplanes to distract me from Madison, the opposite happened.

One look at Madison and I forgot all about the mystery of how Quinn Worthington had managed to not learn to fly an airplane.

She was wearing a tight black skirt, falling tastefully to just below her knees, medium high heels, and a black jacket. Underneath the jacket, she wore a bright red blouse that highlighted her red lips.

She saw me, flashed a smile, then turned her attention to Quinn.

Since all the blood had rushed below my belt, I paid little attention to whatever technical thing they were talking about regarding a computer program.

Then Madison was leaning over into my space, putting her fingers on my keyboard.

She smelled like vanilla honeysuckle crossed with jasmine.

It wasn't a heavy perfume, but simply her soap and maybe her hair products.

Her hair brushed against my cheek for a half second. Long enough to envelope me in her scent.

It was almost more than I could handle. I was a breath away from excusing myself to go to the restroom when she stepped back.

"All done." She straightened. Then looked into my eyes with a little smirk. "Any questions?"

Her green eyes pulled me in and took me deep. I wanted to kiss that smirk off her lips.

And if Quinn hadn't been sitting there on *my* desk, I would have pulled her into my lap and done just that.

But instead, I just looked away. "No," I said. "No questions."

That was a lie. I had lots of questions. The most salient being what exactly were her and Quinn talking about.

"Good," she said. "you know where to find me."

She turned and walked out of my office.

I watched her walk away. I couldn't help it.

Even with Quinn sitting there, I couldn't not look at her.

But Quinn seemed clueless as to how hot his sister was.

Probably a good thing.

Now all I had to was figure out how to use the scheduling program Madison had just demonstrated.

14

MADISON

I sat at my desk and stared out at the tarmac as the crew brought one of the small jets around. This was the plane that was going to take Quinn to Dallas. He had a meeting with Daddy later today.

That explained why he'd been too distracted to notice that Kade and I weren't strangers.

In my mind, it was rather obvious.

I got a text from Emily while I was sitting there waiting for my pulse to calm down to some semblance of normal.

EMILY: *Have you seen him yet?*

I knew perfectly well who she was talking about. Kade Johnson.

ME: *Yes.*

EMILY: *Yes? That's all I get? I need details.*

ME: *Nothing to tell. Just work stuff.*

EMILY: *I hope it gets better.*

I laughed, but didn't write back.

While I was staring at my phone, a message came in from Momma.

MOMMA: *Good morning, sweetheart.*

ME: *Good morning.*

I tried to remember what I'd forgotten to do. Momma never texted me this early in the morning. This was her work time and she was relentless about keeping to her schedule.

MOMMA: *Don't forget we have family dinner this Sunday at your sister's place.*

I blew out a breath. At least I hadn't forgotten to do anything.

ME: *I remember. It's on my phone.*

MOMMA: *Well, write it down on the paper calendar. You know how things get lost in cyberspace... and don't forget to pick up a present for your sister's birthday.*

ME: *I'm already on it.*

MOMMA: *What are you getting her?*

ME: *Still finalizing my ideas... I won't forget.*

MOMMA: *Ok. Get back to work.*

I just stared at my phone. Momma had a funny sense of humor. But she was happy that she had all her children in one city for the summer.

It hadn't happened that way in a very long time.

I didn't blame her for being excited.

I sat back in the chair and turned slowly from side to side.

Allowed my thoughts to circle back to this morning's interaction with Kade.

He was a hard one to keep up with.

This morning he was acting distant and cold.

Of course, he was with my brother, so I had to give him a break.

Maybe he'd taken the weekend and decided that a summer office romance with his boss's daughter—who happened to be his old college girlfriend—wasn't the best of ideas.

Well. I agreed wholeheartedly.

I could acknowledge that it was nice to see him. And leave the rest alone.

Right. When pigs sprouted wings.

Quinn would be leaving in about two hours for his flight, leaving me and Kade alone in the building. Surely Kade had something to do. Errands. A lunch.

Something to get him out of here.

He was setting my nerves on fire just by being in the same general proximity.

I just had to be strong.

We'd dated once.

Now we worked together.

People did it all the time.

It didn't have to be hard.

15

KADE

Quinn finally got the hell out of my office.

I could figure computer programs out myself. If I could fly twenty different types of airplanes, I could figure out a simple computer program.

I was just settling in to my office when I got a text from Susan.

SUSAN: *Sorry to bother you at work.*

My stomach dropped. And my thoughts flashed to a hundred different things that could be wrong. Mother could have fallen again. She wasn't supposed to be walking, but she was too stubborn to do what she was supposed to do.

Actually, I think maybe she was forgetting that she wasn't supposed to be walking.

Unfortunately, Susan confirmed those fears.

ME: *Not a problem. What's wrong?*

SUSAN: *Nothing serious. She seems more forgetful today. Keeps talking about Madison.*

ME: *Madison?*

Mother had asked about Madison during our visit, but I thought—hoped—it was a fleeting thing.

I seriously thought she'd been joking with me since I'd talked a lot about Madison when we were together and Mother knew she lived here in Houston.

If she remembered.

ME: *Can you schedule her a doctor's appointment? With the neurologist?*

I'd expected to do more for Mother. To see her on the weekends. Help with things around the house.

I didn't count on being needed for day to day things. It was starting to sink in just how much there was to be done for her.

Just yesterday, Mother had called me and asked me to come over and change the bandage on her leg.

She didn't seem to remember that she had twenty-four seven caregivers for that sort of thing.

It had taken me a good half hour to find out who was staying with her and get them on the phone.

I now had a detailed schedule on my iPad. So now I was a caregiver scheduler.

That was going to be a full-time job in itself.

Damn it. I was going to have to hire someone just to keep up with the caregivers.

SUSAN: *I'll schedule something and let you know when it is.*

I stared at my phone.

I was going to have to take off from work to take my mother to the doctor.

Maybe Susan could do it. She seemed to be the most reliable of the caregivers.

But right now I had to figure out this paperwork program for Skye Travels.

Without depending too much on Madison.

Another text came in from Susan.

SUSAN: *I got her scheduled for tomorrow morning. Can you take her?*

16

MADISON

I was on the phone with a client—an upset client—doing some fancy schedule juggling while managing to calm the client.

Would I be bragging to say that I was good at what I did?

Between my experience with juggling schedules *and* my experience with emotional people, I was having a good morning.

I was wearing my headset, so I couldn't hear anything outside the phone call.

It was almost lunch-time and I'd made myself comfortable.

I had kicked off my shoes and propped my feet up on the counter.

I had one hand on the keyboard and the end of an ink pen in my mouth.

"Yes, Mrs. Bailey. You're all set."

She was worried about making sure everything was in place. Apparently she'd had schedule mix-ups before.

"Yes, Mrs. Bailey. Be here on Saturday. Our pilots will get you there safely."

I'd told her my name when she answered, but she asked me again.

"D—Madison Worthington," I said.

I hung up the phone and tossed my pen to the counter. That had been a most trying phone call. And on top of it all, I'd almost called myself Dr. Worthington. Habit. And I had a feeling that Mrs. Bailey would have kept me on the phone with that revelation.

"Hi."

I jumped, my feet slamming to the floor.

Kade was leaning against the counter, a smile on his face.

"You scared me half to death." I put a hand on my chest. "I forgot you were here."

That was a lie of course. I was acutely aware of Kade's presence here.

That we were the only ones here.

He feigned a wounded expression. "You really know how to boost a guy's ego."

"Like you need your ego boosted." I said.

He just grinned. "Want to go to lunch?"

"Can't," I said. "No one's here."

Another lie. I could close up for lunch if I wanted to.

But lunch with Kade would be taking things to a whole other level. And I wasn't ready for that.

He pulled out his cell phone.

"You still like cheese pizza?"

"Of course," I said.

I shoved my feet back into my heels.

While he ordered the pizza, I ran a finger over my palm.

If I looked carefully, I could still see a shadow of the numbers he'd written on my palm.

I didn't know what to make of him.

He was being charming.

And when he was being charming, he was dangerous.
The charming version of Kade was my undoing.
Every time.

17

KADE

"Please tell me you didn't schedule Mrs. Bailey with me," I said.

Madison smiled. "I can't imagine why you wouldn't want to have her on your schedule. After all, she's bringing her twelve-year-old nephew and her two dogs."

I groaned. "Now I seriously hope you didn't put me with her."

Madison laughed. "You're not on the weekend schedule." She pulled her keyboard toward her and looked up at me from beneath those thick, dark eyelashes. "But I can change that for you." She rested her fingers on the keyboard.

Now she was teasing me. I could tell by that smug expression on her face.

"Unfortunately, I have other obligations."

She nodded. "Part of your deal with Quinn?"

"You bet." I waited a moment. She wasn't my boss and I didn't report to her. But she was in charge of the schedule. "Do you have me down for a flight in the morning?"

She clicked a few keys on the keyboard.

"Somebody does. It wasn't me. But you're down for a ten o'clock flight."

Damn.

I did not need to ask for a schedule change the first day on a new job.

I would just have to reschedule Mother's appointment.

It wasn't anything life-threatening and, besides, I hadn't expected to get her in so soon.

My phone chimed telling me the pizza was five minutes out.

I pulled up my texts to Susan. Started typing a request to reschedule.

"You know what," Madison said. "I misread. You're actually all clear tomorrow."

I stopped typing my text, my fingers hovering over the keys. "Are you sure?"

"Positive," she said. "You've got an ethics training thing to do online before you can take anybody in the air."

"Alright," I said. "Any particular time?"

"Totally up to you," she said. "The first couple of days are flexible. You know. For people moving into town. Having things to take care of. Besides basic paperwork and training."

I had things to take care of.

And it was generous of her to offer that, but I had a feeling I was going to need more than just flexibility tomorrow morning.

I wasn't sure what I was going to do about it all, just yet.

But I did know that I'd figure it out.

I was here now, so I at least I was close enough to know what was going on with my mother.

"You okay?" Madison asked.

I forced a smile onto my lips.

"I'm good." But I'd forgotten about how impossible it was to hide anything from a psychologist. Especially Madison who already knew me pretty much inside and out.

We'd both changed some, though.

I'd like to know the grownup Madison better. To see what how, exactly, she'd changed.

"The pizza's here," I said and the elevator dinged.

Just in time to save me from further inquiry.

18

MADISON

Kade and I sat on the sofa in the lobby of Skye Travels, the pizza box between us.

Other than me wearing a skirt suit and him wearing a suit, it was just like old times.

Those college days when we'd eat right out of the pizza box.

Since there was no one else around, that was exactly what we did.

There was something going on with Kade. I just didn't know what it was yet.

He'd been on the schedule for tomorrow.

But I'd changed it for him.

I knew he wouldn't ask. He couldn't very well ask for a schedule change his first day on the job.

Fortunately for him, he had me to take care of it for him.

"Does Noah ever come around?" he asked. "I see that he has a really nice office here."

And I also knew that whatever was going on with Kade, he wasn't ready to talk about it.

"Sometimes," I said, answering his question. "Daddy still has his old office in Dallas/Fort Worth."

I took a big bite of cheese pizza. I should so not be eating this. Unlike the college days, my body couldn't metabolize junk food like it used to.

"But mostly he works from home," I added.

Kade was already on his second piece of pizza. He must work out. He had to. He was in better shape than he had been in college.

"But they still live here, right?" he asked.

I nodded, chewing another bite of the evilly good pizza.

"Yep. Moved here not long after they got married, liked it, and stayed."

A small jet landed on the tarmac. It wasn't one of ours.

"The competition," Kade said.

"Something like that. I think of it as more like overflow."

My daddy, Noah Worthington, had somehow turned a passion into an empire.

Other small companies came and went, but he just kept steadily growing.

He jumped on opportunities before most people even knew they were coming.

Noah Worthington, the legend, had no fear.

Noah, my daddy, had four daughters with Momma and another daughter with his first wife. Every one of us had him wrapped around our fingers.

But not like Momma. Daddy worshipped the ground Momma walked on.

They'd dated in college, then drifted apart for awhile…

Just like…

I stopped chewing and looked over at Kade.

He winked at me and opened a bottle of water.

Just like me and Kade.

I realized in that moment that I wasn't mad at him anymore.

I'd tried to stay mad at him over the years, but it had been a futile effort.

I couldn't do it.

I'd never stopped loving Kade Johnson.

19

KADE

’d missed sitting around eating pizza with Madison.

I’d missed other things, too, of course, but just hanging out with her had been just as important to me as the making out had been.

Well, almost as important.

We’d been good together.

I still didn’t know why I’d let her go.

Probably never would. It was just one of those things that happened.

Seemed like a good idea at the time.

Young and dumb.

I had all kinds of excuses.

I was the one who should have called, but I honestly didn’t know what I would have done if she’d shown up on my doorstep after we moved apart.

I went a little bit wild after I moved away from her.

I didn’t have to be a psychologist to know that it had been my feeble attempt of getting over Madison.

It hadn’t worked.

I’d never stopped thinking about her.

It hadn't been fair to the other girls I'd dated—a term I used loosely—so I never let things get serious.

Madison was watching me closely. She was trying to figure out what was going on with me.

But I wasn't ready to tell her.

"How's your mom doing?" she asked.

Damn it. How did she do that?

"Good," I said, taking a big bite of pizza to avoid expanding on my answer.

"Quinn said you wanted to move back to be closer to family. That's why you were giving up your job with the major airline."

"Apparently I told Quinn too much."

She laughed.

"That's what you're supposed to say, right?" I asked. "when you get tired of the big rat race."

She shrugged. "I guess."

It was funny. I was stepping down from the job of a lifetime. Most pilots would kill to have the job I had. But I'd already been there and done that. The novelty had worn off.

And Madison was just now starting her major career.

All that time I'd spent working already, she'd spent in school.

So it was strange that we'd ended up in the same place.

It was Kismet.

"She still living at home?" Madison persisted.

"For now," I said. If I wasn't careful, she was going to get it out of me before I even had time to it figure out myself.

Fortunately, for me, the phone rang and Madison, always the responsible one, took the call and went back over to her station.

All I had to do was to hang in there. I'd know more tomorrow what I was dealing with.

If I told Madison, things would become more real.

And I wasn't ready to deal with real just yet.

Madison smiled at me from across the room as she spoke into her headset.

She was the exception.

I wouldn't mind getting real with Madison.

20

———

MADISON

*H*aving pizza with Kade was like sliding back into our college years.

But we weren't the same.

Eight years had passed since we'd even spoken.

The years didn't just wash away like they'd never happened.

We'd had eight years of life between now and then.

But being with him felt so right.

Like it had always been meant to be.

I'd been busy at the desk for the last couple of hours. Kade had cleaned up all evidence of the pizza and disappeared back to his office.

It would have been so easy to just walk into his office and wrap my arms around him.

To rest my cheek against his chest.

To feel safe with him.

I'd always felt safe with Kade.

He'd never done anything to hurt me.

Not until that day we had agreed to… do what? Break up? Take a break?

We'd never really given it a name, so I never knew exactly what had happened.

I'd just put my head down and focused on graduate school.

The years had slipped past and after a while, I stopped checking for messages from him.

I'd even had to get a new phone that first December and a new number.

That's when I knew he wasn't going to call. He couldn't.

He didn't know where to find me.

Fortunately or unfortunately, depending on the moment, I had memorized his number.

I actually dialed it once.

A woman answered the phone and I'd immediately hung up.

I didn't want to know.

For all I knew, he could have a girlfriend.

He could have even been married and I wouldn't know it.

He could have a child.

That thought held me up for awhile.

I was thankful that it was a busy day in the scheduling department.

The work distracted me from my own thoughts and kept me from walking into Kade's office and doing something stupid.

I ran a finger over the palm of my hand.

He had a different phone number, too, now.

Too much time had passed for us.

I had some papers I needed to take to Quinn's office, but I'd been putting it off.

I had to walk past Kade's office to get to Quinn's.

Deciding to just get it over with, I gathered up the papers and headed down the hallway toward the offices.

I walked past Kade's office without even so much as even glancing in his direction.

I was rather proud of myself.

After dropped the papers off on Quinn's desk, I turned around and came face to face to Kade.

He was leaning against the door, watching me.

His eyes were hooded, like something was bothering him.

This was where I had to tread carefully.

Comforting Kade Johnson had gotten me into trouble before.

21

———

KADE — BEFORE

I'd spent all my free time in the computer lab in Wiley Tower for the last two days.

Yes, I had to admit, I'd been stalking Madison.

I only knew her name because I'd seen it written on one of her papers. I didn't have a last name though, so that made it a bit more difficult.

If she didn't show back up to the lab soon, I'd have to resort to more active methods of stalking.

I wasn't sure what that was going to be just yet, but I'd figure something out.

Louisiana Tech was a big school, but not that big.

I knew what time her math class was, so I could find her.

I just preferred that she either show back up or even better, she could call me.

I could have made everything more simple by getting her number, but I hadn't wanted her to say no.

As long as she didn't come right out and tell me to get lost, I figured I stood a chance.

Unfortunately, I did get a phone call two days after I'd met Madison. Just not the one I was wanting.

My mother had called to tell me that my father was in the hospital.

So I had to get from here to Houston as soon as possible.

I had a car, but driving would take too long.

I needed to fly.

What I didn't have was an airplane.

Going on instinct and sheer adrenaline, I raced back to my dorm, threw a few things into my overnight bag, and drove to the airport.

I didn't have a plan.

Not exactly.

Somehow I thought that if I just showed up at the airport, something would work its way out.

As I parked my car at the little airport, I noticed a Learjet sitting there that I hadn't seen before.

Tech had a nice fleet of prop planes, but the university didn't own anything like this brand new jet sitting on the tarmac.

I went inside the office and checked the schedule.

Bobby was sitting behind the desk.

Bobby was in charge of keeping up with the planes.

He was a nice guy, but he'd washed out of the aviation program early on. The boss had let him keep his job. It was supposed to have been for just a little while, but Bobby had been there since I'd been become a student.

"Hey Bobby," I said. "Any planes available? I need to get to Houston."

"You know I can't approve you taking a plane. You don't have the hours yet."

He was right. I didn't have the flight hours yet that would allow me to take a plane out on my own.

"The boss around?" I asked. I was feeling desperation start to well up in my gut.

"Nope," he said. "Sorry."

I walked to the window. Looked out. That was one fine looking Learjet.

"Whose plane is that?" I asked.

Bobby knew exactly what I was talking about.

He shrugged. "Just showed up."

Maybe driving was my best option yet.

I hated spending all those hours on the road when I needed to be at the hospital.

A pilot, wearing a pilot's cap, stepped out of the Learjet and looked toward the office.

He was waiting for someone.

I'd be like him someday.

I needed to leave, to get on the road.

But I was fascinated by the Learjet.

It was curious that I hadn't seen it here before.

I heard someone, a girl, talking to Bobby.

At first I just ignored it, but something about her voice caught my attention.

I turned around.

It was her.

It was Madison.

She hadn't seen me.

She looked… different.

She was wearing a tight pencil skirt that showed off her figure and an emerald green silk blouse. She was wearing low heeled pumps.

A completely different girl than the college student I'd spent the afternoon doing math problems with.

"Thank you, Bobby," she said as Bobby took her luggage and carryon bag, both a high end, high quality brand.

Maybe it wasn't her.

Maybe it just looked like her.

I took a step forward so I could see her better.

"When are you coming back?" Bobby asked.

"Not sure." She seemed preoccupied.

And didn't look up as they headed toward the door leading out to the tarmac.

The phone rang just as they were about to go outside.

She stopped. "You should get that."

Bobby shrugged. "They'll leave a message."

But she didn't budge. "It could be important."

Bobby frowned, but turned around and went back to the desk to answer the phone.

Madison turned around and looked right at me.

She just blinked as though she wasn't sure she knew me.

I grinned.

Of all the gin joints…

"Hello Madison," I said.

"Hi," she just looked at me. "It's kinda odd. I have your phone number, but I don't know your name. Yet… you know my name, but not my number."

I shrugged. "That's what I get for trying to be smooth."

She smiled then. And I saw the girl who'd captivated me in the computer lab.

"Going somewhere?" she asked, glancing down at my beat-up bag.

"I have to get to Houston," I said. "Family emergency."

She had a funny expression on her face.

"How odd," she said. "I'm headed to Houston, too."

"That is odd," I said. And quite unbelievable how this girl suddenly kept showing up in the places I frequented. "What about class?"

"I'm out until Tuesday."

"You only have Tuesday Thursday classes?" I thought back, putting together the time line. Made sense.

"And Wednesday."

"Huh." I waited for her to explain.

She was obviously about to get on that Learjet.

The question was why.

"I work in Houston on the weekends."

I nodded.

My thoughts swirled with possibilities.

Maybe she was a flight attendant.

Or a call girl.

She didn't look like either.

She looked like a wealthy as fuck young lady.

But she was a college student just like me.

I decided to go with flight attendant.

It suited her better.

And it suited me better.

Her brow was furrowed as she looked at me.

"I should get on the road," I said, suddenly remembering why I was here. I needed to get to Houston. To the hospital.

"You're driving?" she asked.

Bobby came back. "You ready?"

She held up a hand and Bobby stopped where he stood.

"Are you driving?" she asked again.

"Looks like it," I said, with a quick glance toward Bobby.

"Do you want a ride?" she asked.

Out of the corner of my eye, I saw Bobby's jaw drop.

I just grinned.

"You're kidding right?"

She just shrugged.

"Up to you."

22

KADE

*I*t was funny, really.

I could see so much of who Madison was now in who she had been all those years ago. Ten years ago or so when she'd first walked into my life.

When I first met her, I thought I'd have the advantage.

I was the aviation major. I was the one who was going to have the good job.

I came from a privileged family in Houston. My father was the CEO of a Fortune 500 company.

My parents were still baffled as to why I'd chosen Louisiana Tech. But all that mattered to me was that it had a top-notch aviation program.

Besides, I liked it. Go Bulldogs.

I'd liked the small-town feel. It had been nice to get away from the city for awhile.

To a place with a slower pace.

Not that my life was any slower.

I was always busy. I took after my dad in that way.

But it turned out my privileged family had nothing on Madison Worthington.

Her father owned Skye Travels. An aviation empire.

All new pilots anywhere near the Dallas area aspired to work for Skye Travels and Noah Worthington.

I soon learned that Madison worked for her family on the weekends.

Turns out Skye Travels was a closely held family corporation.

And it still was. The fact that she—Dr. Madison Worthington—was still helping out her family in the day-to-day operations spoke to that.

Most young ladies of her status would be out doing social charity work or whatever it was my mother—before she broke her leg—and sister—before she moved to Europe—did all day.

But not Madison. She was in the trenches. Answering the phones. Doing scheduling.

And she was quite good at it.

But she was here temporarily.

It had never been a career for her.

She was following in her mother's footsteps.

Savannah Worthington was a renowned psychologist.

I wondered, as I often had over the years, what it must be like to have such successful parents.

My parents had been successful, too, but just not on the same level as the Worthingtons.

And with my father gone now, I was left to take care of my mother.

My sister had moved to Europe, leaving me to handle everything on my own.

I didn't begrudge her happiness. But I did sometimes wonder how she was ever going to make this up to me.

Right now, the grown-up version of Madison Worthington was looking at me the way she'd looked at me back in college.

As though I'd somehow hung the moon.

And she wanted to console me for having done it.

"What?" I asked.

"Something's troubling you," she said.

God. She was already in tune to me. And now with her being a psychologist… I didn't stand a chance.

My phone rang. It was Mother calling.

"I need to take this," I said. "I just need a minute."

"No problem. I'll get us some coffee." She lifted an elegant eyebrow, waiting for my consent.

I nodded.

"Be right back."

I watched her turn around. A girl like her wearing a skirt like that should be illegal.

23

MADISON

I went into the break room to make two lattes. Pulled out two white mugs with the Skye Travels logo plastered across them in a tasteful blue and set them on the counter while the lattes heated.

I was going to miss being here.

I'd spent all my summers and holidays working here for as long as I could remember. And a lot of weekends, too. Daddy would simply send a plane for me and I'd come home.

And somehow I always ended up here. My home away from home.

But taking an academic job was going to change all that. I was going to be busier than I'd ever been.

Being a professor wasn't just presenting lectures. I was going to have class preparation. Papers to grade. Committee meetings.

Then there was research. And supervision of practicum students.

Thinking about all of that gave me butterflies. I was excited, but overwhelmed at the same time.

I took my time making the coffee.

I was having to constantly remind myself that Kade had a life that didn't involve me.

It was hard to not just slip back into the way we were before.

With two lattes in hand, I made my way back toward his office.

I heard him talking as I approached his office. I walked lightly, keeping my heels from making noise on the wood floor.

His tone was kind. Gentle even.

I stopped just before I reached his door.

I wasn't trying to listen in to his conversation. I was just trying to give him the space to finish his phone call.

"Alright," he said into the phone. "I'll see you tonight."

There was a brief pause.

"I love you, too."

I stood frozen, my hands absorbing the warmth from the coffee mugs.

This was not what I'd prepared for.

I took a deep breath.

I'd known it was possible he had other relationships. Girlfriend. Wife. Child.

All those things were normal.

Just because I didn't have a husband or a boyfriend or a child, didn't mean he couldn't.

I lifted my chin.

It didn't matter. I would be gone in no time.

Starting a new life. In Denver.

I had all sorts of things to look forward to that didn't involve Kade Johnson.

Maybe even a husband and child of my own.

Walking into his office, I let my heels tap normally on the wood floor and I plastered a smile on my face. I wouldn't ask him about it. It wasn't my business.

He was standing at the window, looking out over the tarmac. He turned when he heard me walk in.

"Everything okay?" I asked, handing him one of the mugs.

"Yeah," he said, looking at me with an odd expression. "Everything okay with you?"

I let my smile relax. He was the one person who could tell when my smile wasn't genuine.

I dropped into one of the chairs in front of his desk.

"Quinn didn't tell me anything about you," I said.

He sat down in the leather chair behind his desk. Leaned forward with brows furrowed.

I didn't like having the desk between us. It didn't feel right being separated from him like this.

"What is it you think Quinn should have told you?" he asked.

I shrugged and sipped the hot coffee, careful not to burn my tongue.

"I don't know. Eight years is a long time. Things happen."

"Madison," Kade looked at me sideways. Glanced at my hands. "If you've found someone, you can tell me."

My stomach dropped.

He didn't care if I was with someone else.

He'd truly moved on and expected me to do the same.

I didn't want to tell him that none of my other relationships had compared to what we'd had. That I'd dated some, but no one had ever grabbed my heart like he had.

I dropped into psychologist mode. It was what I knew best.

"It's not about me," I said. "I was asking about you."

He nodded slowly.

"Some things have changed," he said.

My phone buzzed in my pocket. I pulled it out and scowled at it. It was Daddy.

I always answered Daddy's calls and texts. Sometimes he only had a minute and it could be important.

But it was only a text. I relaxed a bit.

DADDY: *Everything ok down there?*

ME: *Everything is going great.*

DADDY: *I'll be home tonight. Meet for dinner?*

I glanced up at Kade. He was glaring at his computer.

ME: *Sure.*

DADDY: *Have to run. I'll text you later.*

I slid the phone back into my pocket.

"Your computer do something to offend you?"

"What?" He glanced at me. "Nothing other than being difficult."

I realized that I wasn't ready to leave Kade's office. There was a lot I didn't know about him. But there was so much more that I did know.

And one of those things was that I enjoyed his company.

We'd figure the rest of it out as we went.

"I could offer you private tutoring."

24

KADE

Madison was trying to help.

But her leaning next to me was not helping.

"Hold on," I said. "I need to get you a chair."

"I won't—" She started to protest, but I was already heading down the hallway to grab another chair.

Minutes later, we were sitting side by side. Much better.

I was having trouble paying attention to what she was trying to show me on the computer.

I was good with computers. I'd figure out what I needed to do.

But when she'd offered to help, I'd jumped on the opportunity to spend more time with her.

I'd figure out the computer program later. On my own.

In the meantime, Madison was driving me a little bit insane.

She was being professional, but distant.

Not really paying me much attention.

The way she was acting, I could be just one of her students.

Nothing personal.

I intended to change that.

I sat back a bit and relaxed my knees, bumping against hers.

It was a brief touch, barely noticeable.

Though there was a hiccup in her sentence, she didn't move away.

I took that as encouragement.

A few minutes later, I went to pick up my pen under the pretense of making a note and my hand brushed against hers.

Again, a barely noticeable hiccup in her sentence.

But again, she didn't move away.

She had one hand on the mouse and the other resting on my desk.

I moved my hand closer to hers.

She stopped talking and turned to face me.

"Are you listening?" she asked.

"I'm hearing every word," I said. It was completely a lie. I did hear her.

I just wasn't listening.

She looked into my eyes.

Looking into those mesmerizing mermaid green eyes tipped me over the edge.

My lips curved slowly as I smiled at her.

"You're not paying attention," she said letting go of the mouse and sitting back.

"Sorry," I said. "You've got to admit…" I nodded toward the computer. "There are more interesting topics."

She shook her head and obviously resigned herself to the fact that today's lesson was over. "Like what?"

"Tell me something about you I don't know."

She scowled at me. "You know too much already."

I leaned back, warming to the topic. "I know that you like cheese pizza. That you've been a psychology major since the day you set foot on the Tech campus. I know that you're loyal to your family and would do anything for them."

"See. I told you you know too much."

"Oh no," I said. "that's just the surface. I also know that

you're no longer that same college student I knew years ago. I know you've changed."

"You're saying you've changed," she said.

I just grinned. She was going to make a damn fine psychologist. Just like her mother.

I ignored the statement. I knew what she was doing. I knew she was trying to turn it back around to me.

"I don't know where you live," I said.

She seemed to think about her answer before responding.

"I'm currently living with my sister Ainsley," she said. "until I move to Denver."

That reminder that she would be leaving soon caught me right in the gut.

As long as I didn't think about how little time we had before she left for Denver, I didn't have to deal with it.

But it was obviously something at the front of her mind.

"Denver's going to be a whole lot different from Houston," I said. "or even Dallas/Fort Worth."

I knew she'd spent her share of time in the Dallas area, with her daddy having an office there.

"I know," she said. "I can adapt."

"I have no doubt about that."

We just looked at each other for a few minutes. It was hard being this close to her and not being able to touch her.

My gaze drifted to her lips.

She had a slightly pouty expression. Not enough that anyone who didn't know her well would notice.

But I knew her expressions well enough to know that I was making her just a little uncomfortable.

I also knew that she wouldn't let me keep the upper hand for very long.

"How's that going?" I asked.

"How's what going?

"Living with your sister?"

She shrugged. "She has a nice place. It's plenty big. I hardly ever see her."

I couldn't tell if not seeing her sister was a good thing or a bad thing.

She'd learned to control her expressions. I had to give her that.

"How about you?" she asked. "Do you have a place to live yet?"

"Nah," I said. "I haven't had time to look yet. Got a hotel down the street."

The old Madison would have offered to help me find something. Something, though, was holding her back.

Maybe she had a boyfriend. It wouldn't be unusual for her to have found another psychologist to connect with.

They'd have a lot in common. A lot to talk about.

She and I had never had trouble talking.

At least not until right now.

I backed off. I was pushing too hard.

"When's the last time you went for a burger?"

She knew exactly what I was asking. Getting a burger had been one of our favorite things to do.

We'd pick a destination. Fly there. Grab one of the complimentary cars they kept for pilots, then dash to the nearest burger place.

After a quick meal, we'd get back in the plane and fly home. To Louisiana Tech.

I'd logged a lot of my flight hours that way.

And it had come with the added bonus of getting to spend time with Madison.

Between the time spent with her father and the time spent in the plane with me, I was pretty sure she could fly a small plane if she had to.

But it didn't interest her.

She was as passionate about psychology as I was about flying. And that said a lot.

Thing was, I'd also been as passionate about her. But I'd never really let her know that.

My question seemed to catch her off-guard.

"I don't know… I guess it's been awhile. I usually have somewhere to go when I'm flying."

So she no longer flew for fun. That told me something new about her. It told me she wasn't dating a pilot, for one thing.

"Getting dinner is going somewhere."

She shook her head. "Not the same thing."

"No," I said, watching the play of emotions on her lovely face. "No. I guess it isn't quite the same."

25

MADISON

I wasn't sure I liked how this was going.

Kade was getting there, teetering on the edge of asking me some hard questions.

I was used to being on the other side of that particular table.

He was distracting me just by sitting here next to me.

That's what I got for offering to help him.

We'd always worked well together. Me studying psychology and him studying aviation.

But we played even better together.

Lots of breaks in there when we studied.

"Let's go," he said.

"What?" He jarred me out of my trip down memory lane. Probably a good thing since I was starting to think far too much about some of that playing we'd done.

"Let's go." He sat up straight. "Remember that little place in Lafayette we used to go to?"

I knew exactly the one he was talking about. It was a little restaurant bar not far from the Lafayette airport. They had great fried seafood.

I'd heard they also had great martinis, but flying and alcohol didn't mix, so we'd never tried them out.

"I remember," I said.

Kade stood up. Held out a hand.

"Let's go see if it's still there."

I put my hand in his and allowed him to pull me to my feet. I straightened my skirt.

"We can't just go right now."

"Why not? It's almost closing time. There's nothing going on today."

"The phone…" I couldn't just leave the phone unattended.

He looked at me sideways. "Who's answering the phone right now?"

"It's going to…" I squinted my eyes at him. "voicemail." He was good. He knew exactly what he was doing.

He grinned. "Exactly. You can come in tomorrow. Return all the phone calls."

I shook my head. Poked him in the stomach with my finger. "You, Kade Johnson, are a bad influence."

He just shrugged. "I guess that's my lot in life. To bring fun to your life."

I bit my lip, trying not to smile back at him.

But it was hopeless.

I didn't know if it was his lot in life or not, but he certainly did a good job of it.

Entertaining me and skirting the edge of danger.

He was really good at skirting danger.

It made me wonder just how bad he really could be when he wasn't being a responsible pilot.

"I have fun," I said, but it felt like a lie.

I tried to remember the last time I'd done something spontaneous. Just for the fun of it.

I couldn't think of anything.

All that came to mind was exactly what Kade was asking me

to do right now. Close my textbooks and jump on an airplane with him.

"Don't you have somewhere you need to be?" I asked.

He seemed to consider for a second. Shook his head. "Not 'til morning."

"Yes." I said. "You do."

I distinctly remembered the phone call I'd overheard. He'd told the person on the other end of the phone that he'd see them tonight and that he loved them.

I turned away. Not my business.

"Right," he said. "Plenty of time to do that after we get back."

I squinted at him.

I would not ask my ex-boyfriend if he had a booty call scheduled for later.

Nope. I would not ask him that.

"Something could happen," I said, instead, mostly to distract myself from thinking about Kade and booty call in the same sentence. "We could end up being out later than you think."

He raised an eyebrow at me. "I like it that you're open to possibilities."

Something about the way he said it along with the appreciative way he was looking at me reminded me of our early days. When we were first getting to know each other.

Back when he was trying to convince me to go out with him.

Was he trying to convince me to date him again? Either way, I couldn't stop my gaze from dipping to his lips. He kissed better than anyone I knew. That was something a girl would never forget. Not that many years had gone by.

"You're trouble," I said.

"Only if you let me be."

I pulled my cell phone out of my pocket. He was right. It was late and we rarely got any calls this late in the day that couldn't be returned the next day.

There was an option on the voicemail menu that routed urgent calls to my cell.

So I wouldn't be abandoning my post.

Only for the short time we'd be in the air.

Damn it. How was Kade so good at convincing me to do things I wouldn't otherwise do?

"Ok," I said. "But we have to be back in time for your date."

He looked at me like I had suddenly sprouted an extra head.

"I'll make sure of it," he said, smiling broadly. "Which plane should we take?"

Now I understood. He was just getting itchy to fly.

"How long since you were in the pilot's seat?" I asked.

"A week. Maybe two."

I waited while he gathered up his things.

"I see what you're doing. You're just needing to scratch that itch to get in the air."

We walked out of his office together.

"Flying with you is never just scratching an itch."

I didn't say a word as I gathered up my handbag and closed down the desk. He waited while I turned out the light and locked up.

We went to the elevator and waited.

Kade Johnson was going to get me into so much trouble.

But in the moment, I was never able to resist.

26

KADE

*W*e boarded a sweet little Cessna Skyhawk and got clearance for take-off in no time.

It felt good to be back in a small jet.

I ran down the checklist, keeping thoughts of Madison firmly in the back of my mind.

At least for now.

She had on her own headset. The girl definitely knew her way around an airplane.

"Ready?" I asked.

"Born ready," she said with a big grin.

This was scary familiar. And comfortable.

The two of us here in a little airplane together. Setting off on a spontaneous adventure.

I taxied out to the runway waiting for the go ahead to take off.

Madison was watching me with a strange expression.

Something tickled the back of my memory.

Then, just as the permission to take off came through my headset, I remembered.

Anytime I flew with Madison, I always kissed her before taking off.

How long I kissed her depended on how long we had to wait to take off.

I looked over at her and I didn't try to hide my indecision about this quandary.

She must have remembered our little ritual even before I did.

She frowned at me, then turned gaze forward.

Pilots, by nature, were superstitious people, and I was no exception.

Granted, I didn't have someone to kiss before every take off. In fact, she was the only person I'd had this ritual with.

But she was sitting there and we were about to take off.

If she wasn't going to kiss me, I was going to turn this airplane around and cancel the trip.

Well, not really, but the thought did occur to me.

"Madison," I said.

She pursed her lips and shook her head.

That only made me want to kiss her all the more.

I could out wait her.

I sat there while the controller repeated the permission to take off.

"We have to go," she said.

"We can't."

She turned and looked at me. "You can't be serious."

I just shrugged with a little grin.

I was having fun now. Torturing Madison like this was always entertaining.

"It's not my fault," I said. "It's our ritual. And I think you started it."

Her eyes widened. "I did not."

I knew she hadn't, but I didn't tell her that.

"Well, you were there."

She crossed her arms. "You are a rogue."

"A rogue?" I chuckled. "I don't think anyone's ever called me that before. Incorrigible. Charming. But never a rogue."

"You do know that charming and incorrigible aren't synonyms, right?"

"Really?" I pretended to be surprised. "Are you sure? Because I've been called both. In similar situations. Even by the same people."

"I don't need to know about your other girlfriends," she said.

"I never said they were girlfriends."

She turned and looked at me sternly, but I could see the smile playing about her lips.

"You might as well kiss me and get it over with," I said.

"Well, that's roman—"

I leaned over and pressed my lips against hers.

And now I wanted to turn the plane around and go back to the office.

And it had nothing to do with luck.

And everything to do with getting her out of that tight skirt.

27

———

MADISON

Kade pressed his lips against mine and my world tilted.

From the moment we stepped onto the plane and belted ourselves in, I'd been thinking about the way he always kissed me right before taking off.

I didn't think he remembered.

He flew for the love of the flight.

Taking me along was just an extra benefit. At least, that was how it always seemed.

I didn't blame him for it.

I'd been around pilots my whole life. I knew how they were.

Passionate about flying.

Not a single one of them could hold a conversation for more than a minute that somehow didn't involve an airplane.

And in all truthfulness, psychologists were pretty much the same way.

We all ate, slept, and breathed psychology.

It made us who we were.

His love of flying made him who he was.

With his lips against mine, the years disappeared.

But he was different.

He'd been a boy in college.

He was a man now.

He had little lines around his eyes that made him irresistible.

His lips were… different. More intense.

When the flight controller came on for the fourth time with the go ahead to take off, he pulled back and smiled into my eyes.

"Affirmative," he said into the headset.

Then he began the process of getting the plane into takeoff mode.

I looked straight ahead, but couldn't keep from watching him out of the corner of my eye.

I'd thought he was cocky and confident when he was younger, but now… He was just hands down competent.

His moved with the sureness of years of experience.

It made me think about his hands in other places.

There was that moment when the plane first left the ground that our eyes met.

He still wore that self-assured grin.

He winked at me.

And I knew I was in trouble.

Kade Johnson still had the same effect on me that he'd had eight years ago.

And it might possibly be even worse than it was then.

We were grown up now and our worlds had become more complicated.

But that didn't change how I felt about him.

How I'd always felt about him.

I'd warned myself that I needed to keep my distance.

But here I was. Right back in his world again.

And I couldn't even begin to think about what that might mean.

28

KADE

That moment the plane hit ground effect, that little thrill that I never failed to experience at takeoff coalesced with my feelings for Madison.

It was a good thing that getting a plane in the air was something I could do in my sleep.

My thoughts were preoccupied with the woman sitting in the passenger seat.

She was staring straight ahead, but I could tell she was deep in thought.

I left her alone.

We'd be landing before long and I'd have plenty of time to torture her again.

I'd missed talking to her.

There was a time when we'd told each other everything.

I hadn't had that with any other woman.

And in all truthfulness, I hadn't really tried.

Maybe that was part of the reason I'd taken this job.

Unconsciously, of course.

Madison would have a field day with that one.

Psychologists were always looking for unconscious explanations for things.

Sometimes the reason wasn't unconscious.

Sometimes we just did things because we wanted to.

That's why I'd kissed her.

I'd been wanting to since I'd seen her standing at the elevators.

It had just taken me a minute to figure out a good excuse.

Now all I had to do was come up with another excuse.

Right now, my blood had settled into my pants and I didn't trust myself to make any rational decisions.

Any blood flow I had left over had to be oriented toward making sure this plane stayed in the air.

I put on my sunshades as we flew away from the sunset.

The effect was like flying into the darkness.

Twilight was a magical time to be in the air. Not quite day and not quite night.

I hadn't planned it this way, but we'd left Houston in the light of day and landed an hour later, at Lafayette, in twilight.

As we landed, everything looked old-timey, tinged with sepia.

The bright colors of day had faded and it wasn't quite dark.

"This is my favorite part of the day," Madison said as we taxied down the runway.

"Yeah? Why is that?" This was something she'd never told me.

She smiled a little. "It's how I imagine everything looked in the 1920s. I know it's not, but it's how I imagine it."

"Like an old movie," I said.

"Exactly. That's probably why."

She didn't have to tell me that she loved old movies.

I already knew that about her.

We had no problem grabbing a car and making it to the restaurant.

I pulled up in front of it and stopped.

"It looks the same," I said.

"It does," she said. "but it's not quite how I remembered it."

"Things look different from the perspective of a college student than they do as an adult."

"Most things do," she said and I knew she wasn't talking about the restaurant anymore.

But I didn't mind.

I wasn't afraid of anything Madison could throw at me.

29

MADISON

We sat in the back of the noisy restaurant.

Kade slid into the booth next to me.

When I raised an eyebrow at him, he just grinned. "Hard to have a conversation in here with a table in between us."

He was right, but the noise was part of the restaurant's charm.

Maybe it was from growing up in the city, but I liked being in a place like this.

We were surrounded by people, yet we were alone. Ensconced in our own little world.

If we leaned close we could hear each other. Everyone else faded into the background.

And no one else could hear us. And even more, no one cared what we talked about.

"Do you want a cocktail?" he asked.

I shook my head automatically. When I traveled with pilots, I didn't drink.

It didn't seem fair to drink around people who couldn't because they were working.

"I don't mind," he said. "Honest."

"I can't. It goes against everything I've always known."

"I know," he said, drinking from the glass of water the server had dropped off. "It's like you're one of us."

I smiled. "I am one of you."

"Yet you don't pilot."

I ran a finger down the side of my water glass. "I have flown."

He leaned back. "I know the stories of your daddy taking all his girls up at some point or another. But I mean actually flying a plane."

I smiled. "I have."

He looked at me sideways. "Right… there was that one time with me."

The server came to our table and we ordered fried shrimp po'boys and French fries.

"There were other times…" I said as I handed my menu back to the server.

"Who did you fly with?"

I blinked my eyelashes. "A girl never flies and tells."

He looked at me blankly for a moment. "You continue to delight and impress me, Dr. Worthington."

I laughed, but lowered my eyes and looked away. "That's my job. To delight and impress."

I played with the straw in my glass. He was watching me. But I'd told him more than I'd intended.

Kade had always had that effect on me. He could pull the truth out of me with frightening ease and he could get me to try anything. At least once.

"Have you been water skiing lately?" I asked, grasping at anything to get him off the subject of who I'd been flying with.

"Actually, no," he said. "I sold my boat after I took the job with the commercial airline."

I nodded. I wasn't surprised. That's how pilots were. Even when they tried to stray into other interests, the other interests tended to not hold for long.

"Don't tell me you water ski now," he said with obvious skepticism.

I shuddered.

"Surely you jest."

Even ten years after it happened, I still found it hard to believe that I'd gotten in a lake while Kade tried to show me how to stand up on a pair of water skies.

I wasn't an outdoorsy person to start with. And second, who'd want to get into water when you couldn't see beneath the surface.

There could have been snakes all around. And alligators. And God knows what else.

The fact that I'd gotten into lake water while wearing a swimsuit spoke to the level of my infatuation for him.

But that had been a long time ago. Back when I was young.

"So already I've learned two new things about you and we haven't even gotten our food yet." Kade was grinning at me like a Cheshire cat. "You've taken up flying airplanes and you gave up water skiing."

I wrapped my lips around my straw and looked up at him.

The little gesture was enough to wipe the silly grin off his face.

It kind of backfired on me though. Now he was looking at me with an intensity I hadn't seen in a long time.

Fortunately, our food arrived and we ate in silence for a few minutes.

About halfway through, he nudged me.

"Do you have plans for this weekend?" he asked.

Of course I didn't. Especially not if he was asking. But I didn't tell him that.

"Nothing definite yet. Why do you ask?"

"Just curious."

Now it was my turn to look at him with skepticism.

He just shrugged. "I'm not sure yet, but I might need a favor."

30

KADE

I'd thought I wasn't afraid of anything Madison could throw at me, but I might very well have been wrong. Slightly wrong.

When she put that straw in her mouth and looked up at me like that, I nearly lost it.

She was so damn sexy.

And it was even sexier that she didn't even know it.

I dipped a French fry in ketchup and bit into it.

I'd planned on waiting until after I took Momma to the doctor tomorrow before I brought up that favor I might need.

But now that I'd spent more time with Madison, I wanted to spend even more time with her.

I wanted to lock in some time this weekend even if was just taking a walk in the park.

I didn't care.

I just wanted to be around her.

And if it happened to lead to more, I wouldn't be opposed.

"What kind of favor?" she asked.

"A family thing," he said. "I'll know more tomorrow." I knew that she wasn't going to let it go until I told her what the favor was, but I could distract her away from it for a little while anyway.

"So was this an overnight flight you did or just a day trip?"

"Kade! Stop it."

"What? I'm just curious. I'm trying to get a feel for what you've been doing."

"Mostly studying and working." She pushed her plate aside. "I had an internship in Salt Lake City."

I didn't know if I'd pushed her too much and she'd lost her appetite. Didn't know her that well anymore.

"Internship?"

"I had to do a year of internship at a hospital. It was a neuropsychiatric hospital."

"So… you lived there? In Salt Lake City? For a year?"

She tucked her hair behind her ears and turned slightly in the booth so she could look straight at me.

"I know," she said. "Hard to believe, isn't it?"

"A little, yes. Though I'm not sure why."

I shrugged. "Probably you know I'm a Texan through and through and when I'm not being a Texan, I'm a Louisiana Tech bulldog."

I hadn't been lying when I'd said she continued to delight me.

We'd gone to most of the Tech football games and a whole lot of the baseball games.

Thinking about her living in Salt Lake City for a year made me think about her moving to Denver.

But there was an upside in all this.

With me being a pilot and her being the daughter of Skye Travels, I could see her as often as if she lived on the other side of Houston.

The downside was that I was going to miss seeing her every day.

31

MADISON

I bit my bottom lip and watched as Kade paid the server.

Yes, I decided. He had definitely gotten more handsome than he was in college.

He'd asked me about this weekend. But it was just a favor. Not a date.

I wanted to ask him what it was about, but I'd learned, in my training as a psychologist, to give the other person time. He'd tell me when he was ready.

And if not, I'd eventually ask him again.

But not yet.

I still didn't know much about him.

And. He still had that date tonight.

I was giving some thought to asking him about it again when he turned and looked at me with that inquisitive look he had.

"Why Denver?" he asked.

Why indeed.

I shrugged and picked up my water glass.

"I applied and they offered."

With the straw between my lips, I looked up at him from beneath my lashes.

It was one of my flirty moves, but he didn't seem to notice.

"So you applied," he said.

"I applied to a lot of places."

"How many offers?" he asked, not skipping a beat.

This was beginning to feel like an inquisition.

I straightened and set my glass down.

"Three."

When I didn't expound on my answer, he lifted an eyebrow with the unspoken question.

"One was in South Carolina. And the other was California."

"Those are all nice places to live."

"So is Denver," I said, fighting off a gut reaction of defensiveness. He was just making conversation anyway.

"Besides," I said, deciding to give him a break. Denver was the only one in a city. The others were in small towns. I wanted to be close to an airport."

"That makes sense," he said, looking around the restaurant.

I was about to assure him that all my decisions made sense, when his phone chimed.

He glanced at it. Then said. "Ready to head back?"

"Sure," I said. His date must be ready for him.

He slid out of the booth, then held out a hand to help me slide across.

I put my hand in his and tried to ignore the way his touch set off all kinds of thoughts of what his hands felt like on my skin.

He kept his hold on my hand as we walked through the crowded restaurant toward the door. I saw the way women looked at him. A couple of them looked from him to me before looking away.

Kade was a handsome man. He might have a hookup later, but I was the one he'd taken on a flight to dinner.

But... he'd taken me out of state.

I didn't need to read into it. It was something we used to do.

But... if he was in a relationship, it would explain why he'd taken me out of state.

We stepped out of the noisy restaurant into the quiet night and walked to the car in silence.

I was trying not to think about the possibility of Kade being a serious relationship. One serious enough that he didn't want to risk anyone seeing us together.

He opened my door and I slid inside.

I was thinking too much. It was what I did.

And while I was busy thinking too much, I was ruining the moment.

I forced a smile on my face when he climbed into the car on his side.

"What?" he asked, looking at me with that suspicious expression.

"Nothing."

Apparently Kade Johnson had developed an immunity to my charm.

32

KADE

I needed to get Madison back to Houston before I did or said something that would frighten her away.

I wanted to play it cool so she'd hang out with me this weekend.

But, damn it, she was hard to resist.

First she'd done that thing with the straw in the restaurant. Not just once, but twice.

And looked up at me through those lashes.

Then she'd given me that smile that I could never resist.

I was deep in my own thoughts on the way back to the airplane.

It was going to be late when we landed. But I'd promised my mother I'd stop by.

I'd give her a call when we landed to make sure she was still up. Last I'd heard, she was in bed by eight. Nine at the latest.

I glanced at my watch. I wasn't going to make it before her bedtime. But I'd see her in the morning anyway.

We made it back to the airplane in no time and I helped Madison get onboard.

But instead of just closing the door, I fastened her into the four-point harness. Not that she didn't know how to do it herself, but it was sort of holding the door for a lady. A gentlemanly thing to do.

I leaned over her to snap the belt in place.

She smelled like... a concoction of femininity. Vanilla honeysuckle crossed with jasmine. Whatever it was, it was a scent distinctive to her.

Before closing the door, I smiled at her.

I wasn't being very successful at resisting her charms.

I'd been around the country a thousand times. I was used to women coming on to me.

It was true what they said about women being attracted to a man in uniform.

So I'd learned how to resist some of the best.

Not that I always resisted, but this was different.

This was Madison.

As I walked around the plane to get in on my side, I stopped and looked up at the stars.

The thing was I didn't have a logical reason to resist Madison.

I was unattached and so was she.

There was no reason we couldn't get... reacquainted.

Even her moving away in three months wasn't a good reason.

We could have a helluva summer romance, then we could see each other long distance.

Long distance wasn't a problem for pilots.

But with Madison a summer romance would never be enough.

We'd drifted apart once. I didn't think we could do that again.

I didn't think I could let her go a second time.

This was a second chance.

We taxied out to the runway.

I knew I shouldn't kiss her again.

Pilots were superstitious people, but I like to think that I had some self-control and some common sense.

The clearance to takeoff came through my headset.

Determined not to succumb to a long-ago superstitious behavior, I began to prepare for takeoff.

Then Madison put a hand on my arm.

She was looking at me with a little smile. "Aren't you going to kiss me?"

It was all I needed.

Leaning over I closed the distance between us. I pressed my lips against hers. But with the way she leaned into me, her lips parted, it wasn't enough.

I needed more.

My tongue swept across her lips. Still not enough.

My tongue pressed forward and she responded by opening her mouth and sweeping her tongue against mine.

Oh. My. God.

I couldn't get enough.

It was a good thing we were harnessed in and the controller kept talking into my ears.

After the fifth time he announced our clearance, I pulled away from her and prepared for takeoff.

33

MADISON

*A*s the plane entered ground effect, I felt that little thrill that I always felt when the plane left the ground.

I'd never wanted to *be* a pilot, but I'd been around airplanes all my life.

Airplanes and pilots.

In a way, airplanes were as commonplace as automobiles to me.

In another way, they were special. Not just anyone could get into a cockpit and safely fly a plane.

There was something unique about being in the air. Something exhilarating.

But right now my head was spinning for an entirely different reason.

And my lips tingled with the aftereffect of Kade's kisses.

I knew logically, in my head, that this didn't change anything.

That we were still just two people who'd drifted apart and bumped into each other again.

It was curiosity. Everyone had thoughts about what it

would be like get back together with a high school or college sweetheart.

We just happened to be in a place where we had the opportunity to find out what it might be like.

And now that we had, we'd go our separate ways. Again.

The thought was saddening.

And I really didn't want to think about it.

I watched the lights of civilization passing along below us. I recognized Interstate 10 and knew that we had pretty much a straight flight path to Houston.

And once we got back, Kade had something else he had to do.

That was probably the worst part.

It wasn't that I was going to be moving away to Denver in three months. I had time to deal with that.

It was that he had scheduled a hookup on the same night he took me on a dinner flight.

Something that used to be our special thing.

I sat up straighter. It was silly to be worried about it.

Even if we stood a chance of getting back together, I wasn't sure I wanted to.

The flip side of being around pilots all the time was that I knew how they liked to play.

Not all of them. Not Daddy.

Noah Worthington had the reputation of being madly in love with his wife.

But I'd heard enough stories to make me wary.

Kade was the only pilot I'd ever dated and he'd been a student at the time.

It had been crazy to come out with him.

But he'd always had the ability to get me to do things. And despite my misgivings, I'd had a good time.

It had been like being with an old friend.

Kade and I could be friends.
Right?

34

KADE

I probably shouldn't have kissed her like that.

But damn, I was glad I did.

I'd had wet dreams about kissing her like that.

And in my dreams, those kisses always led to so much more.

She was staring out the window.

Not unusual. But she wasn't looking at me either.

I'd probably messed up by kissing her too soon.

But damn it, she was the one who'd asked to be kissed this time.

I was definitely calling my mom to cancel whatever it was she was wanting tonight. Since it wasn't an emergency, it could wait until tomorrow.

It was time for Madison and me to really get reacquainted.

We'd waited too long.

It was my fault. I could have gotten in contact with her if I'd wanted to.

I'd been stupid to just let her slip out of my fingers like that.

And I'd be crazy to let it happen again.

But I'd have to figure it out as I went.

Some things required planning, but some things, things like Madison Worthington had to be handled with white gloves.

I would have to stay on my toes and stay alert.

Otherwise, we'd end up with a repeat of eight years ago. Or worse.

As we neared the runway at the Houston airport, I became fairly certain that Madison was going to need some time to process what had happened between us.

I had no problem giving her that kind of time.

But I still needed that favor from her.

Perhaps in a couple of days, I'd be able to ask her.

And it would take me a couple of days to get over that kiss. Maybe longer.

The hell of it was, I didn't want to get over it.

I wanted more.

There was never going to be enough Madison Worthington for me.

She was like an addiction.

One I did not want to give up.

Back in Houston, we made a smooth landing and taxied back to our area.

"Are you ok?" I asked, pulling off my headset after I'd turned off the motor.

"Or course," she said, starting to unbuckle her harness. "I have an early morning, so I'll see you at some point tomorrow."

"I'll walk you to your car." I said.

She nodded. She'd let me. Madison was nothing if not sensible.

But I wouldn't be getting any more kisses tonight.

It was probably a good thing.

I wasn't sure I'd be able to stop at just kisses.

35

———

MADISON

I loved casual Fridays. I had on a pair of blue jeans and a blazer. And flat boots. That was probably the best part. Not having to tromp around in heels.

During my internship, we hadn't even been allowed to wear heels. Or open-toed shoes. Or jewelry.

I turned on all the lights and made sure all the magazines were arranged just so on the end tables in the lobby.

Markus Peters and his family were on their way in. They would wait here until Kade was ready for them to board.

It was Kade's first flight at Skye Travels. I'd made sure of it. In the interest of allowing him to settle in and learn our computer system.

And in the interest of keeping him as far away from me as possible.

That meant that for three days, I'd pretended to be deep in conversation every time he walked past. My eyes glued to the computer.

All that pretending hadn't kept my heart from tripping every time I caught a glimpse of him or even heard his voice.

It wasn't that I didn't want to see him. To talk to him. Just the opposite. It was that I wanted to see him and talk to him too much.

So much that I could hardly bear it.

I put a plate of fresh baked cookies from the bakery next to the pot with fresh coffee.

Mr. Peters would drink coffee. His wife liked bottles of cold water. And his grandson liked sugar cookies.

And that was just pre-flight.

Everything else they required—champagne, salted cashews, bottles of water, among other things—was already stocked on the plane.

I'd stocked the plane this time. Kade would have to do it next time.

I just hadn't been ready to face him. So I took care of everything.

I could only imagine how much fun my fellow graduate interns would enjoy analyzing my issues with Kade.

I hadn't even talked to Emily this week. I knew she'd get it out of me that Kade had kissed me…. Or rather we had kissed. And I wasn't ready to talk about it, much less have my friend analyze it.

I hadn't even finished absorbing it myself.

So I'd put my head down and stayed under the radar.

I greeted the Peters as they stepped off the elevator and escorted them to the lobby for their morning snacks and coffee.

Mrs. Peters gave me a quick hug. "It's good to see you again, Dear. I heard you were back, but you won't be staying. Dr. Worthington."

I laughed. "I'll always have time to stop in even if it's just to see you all."

Mrs. Peters patted my arm. "For now maybe," she said. "Until you meet a young man who sweeps you off your feet."

"Well, I don't see that happening anytime soon. So I'll be seeing a lot of you."

"We'll see." Mrs. Peters was old enough to be my grandmother, so she could get away with saying just about anything. "A girl as pretty as you won't be single long."

I directed her to the snacks and got her distracted away from my love life.

After getting them settled, I turned around with plans to head back to the reception area. I wanted to be seated behind the safety of the computer before Kade came in.

But when I turned around, I found myself face to face with Kade Johnson.

My heart did all sorts of gymnastics and I had to remind myself to take a deep breath.

He'd been standing there watching my interaction with Mrs. Peters, but I wasn't sure for how long.

If the elevator doors had opened, I would have heard them. I was quite in tune especially knowing that Kade was on his way up.

He must have been on the same elevator as the Peters. But he'd hung back. Waiting until they were settled.

"Good morning," he said.

"Hi," I said, taking a step toward my station.

He took a step to block me so I was forced to stop and talk to him.

"Quinn said you got everything ready for the flight," he said. "Thank you."

I shrugged. "It was just easier. I've known them a long time, so I knew what to do. I'll get you up to speed later."

He scratched his clean-shaven cheek. "Might be hard to do if you keep avoiding me."

My eyes widened. "I wasn't avoiding you."

"Okay," he said, his eyes twinkling.

I took another step to move around him, but he stepped in front of me again.

I gave up and crossed my arms.

When Kade Johnson had something to say, nothing would stop him.

"I never got to talk to you," he said. "To ask you for that favor."

"You have my number," I said.

"Actually, I don't have your cell number and the favor is personal."

"Oh," I said. Since I had his number, I'd forgotten that he didn't have mine. Besides, I was sure he could have gotten it if he'd wanted to.

"Fair enough," I said. "Can you tell me what it is now?"

He glanced over at the Peters family. And I knew Kade wasn't going to tell me with them in possible earshot.

"Do you have tomorrow open?" he asked.

"Which part of tomorrow?" I held my hands together to keep them from trembling.

How was it he still had this effect on me after all this time?

"All day," he said. Then quickly added. "Starting in the morning around ten."

I could have said no. But the truth was I didn't have any plans for the weekend and I was curious about what his mystery was. And on top of that, I wanted to spend time with Kade, no matter how much it scared me.

"Great," he said. "I'll pick you up at ten."

Grinning he turned around.

"Wait," I said. "Don't you need my address?"

"I have it."

"But... you said you don't have my number."

"I don't have your number, but I know where you live."

He winked at me and walked down to the hall to his office. "Just wear something breezy," he said.

As I walked to my station, I wondered if he'd figured out how to log into the system.

But even more important, I wondered what Kade had planned for me tomorrow.

And what the hell did he mean by *something breezy?*

36

KADE

I was as nervous as a schoolboy.

And I didn't even bother trying to tell myself that I shouldn't be.

Hell, how many men got a second chance with their college girlfriend?

A real chance.

Of course, I was getting ahead of myself. I didn't know if this was really a second chance or just a dalliance for her.

In her studies and training to be a psychologist, she would have had the chance to work through any lingering issues related to our relationship.

Including the shitty way I'd ended it.

I was lucky she would even talk to me.

My phone chimed indicating a text message.

SUSAN: *Your mother is asking me how long before you get here.*

I'd just parked my car at Madison's apartment building. Technically, it was her sister's apartment. But for the summer, it would be Madison's, too.

And technically it was a condo since Ainsley owned it.

ME: *Just picking up Madison. Tell her I'm on the way.*

SUSAN: *Thank you.*

Mother's doctor's appointment hadn't gone quite like I would have wanted it to.

The trauma of breaking her leg had somehow triggered an acceleration of her light dementia.

The doctors claimed that it wasn't uncommon. They weren't sure if the experience of the trauma actually made the dementia worse. Or it was just a marker that we could use to measure it.

Didn't really matter how they wanted to make sense of it. The bottom line was that Mother's dementia was getting worse.

They had given her a couple of new medications, but said we had to wait from two to six weeks to really know if they were going to help slow it down or even possibly reverse it to some extent.

They suggested we keep things as familiar for her as we could. That meant keeping the same caregivers around as much as possible.

She especially seemed to like Susan. So I'd bumped Susan's hourly wage up to make sure she didn't go anywhere. I'd offered her a room in Mother's house to make her full time, but Susan had a teenager and wasn't willing to give that up.

It was understandable, of course.

Going over to the private elevator, I pressed the call button.

I'd barely even pressed it and didn't even have to say anything before the elevator door opened. Cameras. Of course.

The elevator took me straight up to what I knew was floor thirty.

The elevator door opened into the living room.

And an awesome view across the city.

Even as a pilot, I was impressed.

Madison stood waiting for me.

I'd told her to wear something breezy. And to be honest, I didn't even know what that meant. To me it meant something relaxed and comfortable. She was wearing a relaxed dress, belted at the waist with short sleeves and vee-neck that dipped to places I'd like to explore.

The skirt, white with yellow lemons splashed across it, was long and relaxed, falling to just below her knees.

She wore flat strappy sandals and a straw hat.

It was absolutely perfect.

Even though I hadn't known exactly what breezy meant when I'd suggested it, she apparently did and she'd nailed it.

"Is this breezy enough?" she asked, turning to illustrate how her skirt flowed.

"You look beautiful," I said. And I wasn't about to admit that I hadn't even known what breezy meant when I'd said it.

"Do you want to sit for minute?" she asked. "Or do we have an appointment?"

I smiled to myself. I knew how much restraint it must be taking for her to appear so nonchalant about our plans.

Madison was a planner. She liked to know the wheres and the whens. That attention to detail had made her hard as hell, according to Quinn and everyone else I'd talked to, to replace her at Skye Travels.

But she couldn't stay there forever, no matter how good she was at keeping up with all the scheduling and other details required to make the clients happy. And the pilots, too, for that matter.

"An appointment," I said.

She raised an eyebrow, but instead of commenting, just picked up her handbag and joined me at the elevator.

As we rode down in silence, I admired her in the mirror. Her hair was breezy, too.

It fell straight around her shoulders with a little flip at the ends.

Her look, altogether, was rather retro. She could have easily been a stylish lady of the 1940s on her way to a Saturday lunch date.

When she caught me watching her in the mirror, I just winked at her.

She quickly looked away and I caught the little flush that spread over her cheeks.

I opened the car door for her and after she'd settled into her side of my BMW sedan, I went around to the driver's side and got in.

She was already buckled up.

"Ready?" I asked.

She smiled and looked at me sideways. "That depends," she said.

"What does that depend on?"

"Depends on how well you drive in Houston traffic."

I laughed. "Good point."

Other than the short ride to the restaurant in Lafayette, the last time we'd ridden in a car together had been in Ruston. Not much traffic in a small Louisiana university town.

"I think I can manage," I said.

Especially since my mother's house wasn't far from here.

"When are you going to tell me where we're going?"

"I guess now's a good enough time." But instead of explaining, I focused on navigating the traffic.

She sat back and waited quietly.

We turned right on Memorial.

"We're going to see your mother?" she asked.

Startled, I glanced over at her.

"Has anyone ever told you that you have an extraordinary memory?"

"All the time," she said. "So... you must have a reason for taking me to see your mother."

I turned left onto a side road.

Not only was her memory extraordinary, but so were her powers of perception.

"She's been asking for you."

MADISON

I had fond memories of Kade's mother. I'd spent some time at Christmas with them the year before Kade and I had gone our separate ways.

Kade had grown up in the privileged old town area near Rice University.

His parents had a large brick house. Gated. Old money.

I'd always found it odd that we'd found our way from Houston to the small university in Louisiana.

His was for the aviation program. Mine was mostly rebellion. At least at first.

After I'd spent some time there, Louisiana Tech had quickly become my second home.

It hadn't hurt that I had Kade there.

Kade's father had been living then. Still working as a corporate attorney.

He'd seemed aloof.

His whole family, in fact, had seemed a bit overly formal. That was in retrospect, of course.

And now his father had passed and his mother was asking for me.

He pulled into the driveway and parked the car.

"Kade," I asked. "Why would your mother ask for me?"

Kade sighed and turned to face me.

"She thinks we're still together."

My eyes widened. "Surely you told her we'd… broken up."

I still didn't think of us as breaking up. Just drifting apart. And now we seemed to be quickly moving back into our old patterns.

The years we'd been apart were starting to fade.

He laughed. "Of course," he said, taking a deep breath. "My mother has some dementia and she's somehow gotten it in her head that we're still together."

"Oh God, Kade. I'm so sorry."

I hadn't realized Kade was going through this.

It all made sense, though. Now I understood why he'd given up his job and moved back here.

Kade had a sister, but she lived in Europe. That left Kade with all the responsibility for caring for their mother.

I was fortunate that I had four siblings. And all of us took care of each other.

I was the one, it suddenly occurred to me, who was moving away to make a life in another city.

I was going to be like Kade's sister. Leaving my sibling to care for my elderly parents.

The realization made me uncomfortable, so I put it away to think about later.

Right now I needed to focus on Kade and his mother.

He'd brought me here to make his mother happy.

"What do you need me to do?" I asked.

"Just um…" He ran a hand through his hair. "Just sort of pretend that we're still together."

I didn't say anything. It wouldn't do any good.

It was just like Kade to throw this at me without any warning.

It was how he operated. Asking him to be any different would be like asking for summers in Houston to be less hot.

Wasn't going to happen.

"Sorry I didn't warn you," he said.

"They say admitting you have a problem is the first step," I said, looking out the window at what used to be manicured beds of pansies and other flowers. Now it was just a plain lawn that someone came and mowed every week. Just like all the other houses on the block.

"What?"

"Nothing," I said. So I'm supposed to be your fake girlfriend."

"You don't have to be fake," he said. "I mean… just be like you always are."

"I don't even know what that means," I said. "but okay. I'll figure it out."

"Thank you," he said.

"I haven't done anything yet."

He placed a hand over mine. "You're here, aren't you?"

With Kade's hand over mine, I could almost forget that I wasn't still his real girlfriend.

He had no idea what he was asking of me.

And I hadn't either until right this minute.

He was asking me to pretend to be the person I'd never stopped wanting to be.

38

KADE

We sat in the sunroom with the air conditioning blaring.

It almost felt more like a fall day than a summer day.

Of course, the flowers in the backyard and the green lawn were a constant reminder that it was actually a beautiful warm day.

Mother had given up trying to keep up the whole yard a long time ago.

Now she had a gardener who just kept up a section of the yard outside her sunroom window.

It was where she spent most of her days and the money spent on the gardener was more than worth the money.

Mother had given me full access to her accounts and I had full power of attorney. Fortunately, she had enough money to take care of all her needs.

Caregivers. Gardeners. Physical therapists.

All sorts of people coming in to take care of her.

My life had gotten a lot easier since I'd given Susan the job of scheduling.

It had only been a few days, but so far, she was doing an

excellent job. She had bought one of those big calendars and posted it in the kitchen.

Madison noticed everything. But she didn't say anything.

She graciously accepted the cold tea and cookies that Mother had someone leave out for us.

I knew for a fact that Madison hated cold tea.

But she smiled and sipped it anyway.

"It's so good to see you," Mother told Madison. "You look lovely as always."

"So do you, Mrs. Johnson," Madison said. "How have you been?"

"Oh, I've been just wonderful. Staying busy."

"You have a lovely view back here. Very relaxing."

Mother beamed. "It is, isn't it?"

"Do you do some reading? Some letter writing?"

"Of course," Mother said.

I glanced around. I didn't see any sign of books or letter writing. In fact, I didn't see anything that indicated Mother did anything other than sit and look out the window.

"What do you like to read, Mother?" I asked.

"A few magazines and I read some novels."

"What novel are you reading right now?"

"Oh," Mother said, with a wave of her hand. "I've forgotten the name. They all run together, you know."

"It's okay," Madison said. "You know what. I have the same problem sometimes. I do good to keep up with my favorite authors."

Mother put a hand over Madison's. "I'm so glad you came, dear. You make Kade so happy."

Oh no.

"Mother," I said, drawing her attention to a little plant on the coffee table. "When did you get this new plant?"

Mother looked up at me. "Don't you remember? You brought that to me last week?"

I felt sick. Deep in the pit of my stomach. I'd never seen that plant before. And I certainly hadn't given it to her.

"Of course," I murmured, not sure what to say.

I was in over my head and the doctors were unfortunately right. Mother's cognitive functioning was slipping.

But she quickly moved on and looked from one to the other of us.

"So..." she said. "Have you two set a date yet?"

39

MADISON

Kade hadn't warned me about the severity of his mother's condition.

I hadn't been with Kade in eight years and it had been longer than that since I'd seen Mrs. Johnson.

A whole lot of things ran through my head and Mrs. Johnson sat there looking at me expectantly, a smile on my face.

I quickly tucked away the pain in my heart at seeing her this way.

I'd taught myself to do that. It didn't mean I didn't care. It just allowed me to keep my emotions at bay so I could help people.

But Kade hadn't brought me here in a therapeutic role.

He'd brought me here so I could make his mother happy by pretending to be his girlfriend.

I wasn't sure that was the best thing for her. But it wasn't for me to decide.

So I just smiled and reached for Kade's hand. "Not yet."

"Well, don't wait too long. You're not getting any younger, you know."

Her statement inadvertently struck me as being far too accurate for comfort.

I'd been so focused on school and training lately, that I hadn't given much thought to starting a family.

None of my siblings, in fact, were married and none of us had children.

I hadn't given much thought to that either, even though I was the oldest.

Momma and Daddy had never pressured us one way or the other to have children.

It was interesting because they had gotten together a little later in life.

Our stepsister, Danielle had two children, and she seemed to keep the focus off of the rest of us, at least for now.

"You'll be the first to know, Mrs. Johnson," I said.

"Well, Kade needs someone to keep him in line. And you seem to be the only one who can do it."

I looked over at Kade questioningly and smiled. "Is that so?"

Mrs. Johnson actually had her son squirming.

"It's a hard job, but somebody's got to do it."

Mrs. Johnson beamed. "I'm so glad Kade has you."

We spent another thirty minutes visiting with Mrs. Johnson before his caregiver, a younger lady named Susan brought her some medicine.

"If you'll excuse me," Mrs. Johnson said. "I think I'll go lie down now for a while. You two enjoy yourselves out here."

With Susan's help, Mrs. Johnson navigated her way from the sunroom, leaving me and Kade there alone.

"Thank you," he said.

"No need to thank me," I said. "I've always liked your mother."

"She's always liked you, too," he said, staring at the empty doorway. "I didn't realize she'd gotten this bad."

"Dementia can be difficult," I said. What I didn't say was

that dementia was difficult on family members. "Do we need to wait for her?" I asked.

"She'll sleep for two hours easy. Besides…" He stood up. "She'll be content for a while now that she's seen you."

I didn't tell him that he could be wrong. She might very well wake up from her nap and forget that I'd ever even been there.

I didn't need to tell him that. He'd figure that out soon enough.

He held out a hand to help me up. "Do you want to get some lunch?"

"Kade Johnson," I said, our hands still linked. "Was this your way of getting me to have lunch with you?"

"What? Why would I do that? If that were the case, I could have just asked you to lunch."

So he said. But I wasn't sure I believed him.

At any rate, Kade was going to need a friend to get through this difficult time.

I'd help him all I could.

He kept his hand linked with mine as we left his mother's house. He didn't have to do that. No one was watching.

He'd parked on the street, just out of sight of the house.

When we got to the car, he went around to open my door, but instead of opening it, he leaned an arm across the door, blocking me in.

When I turned to face him, I found my back pressed against the car door with his hands on either side.

I looked over his shoulder.

"Kade," I said. "No one can see us now."

"I know." He leaned forward and I knew what he was about. There was something in his eyes.

This wasn't a superstition kiss.

This was going to be a real kiss.

His lips pressed firmly against mine.

Then he pressed against me and whispered against my lips. "Do you know how sexy you are when you're working?"

"I wasn't working."

He shifted closer. "Looked like work to me."

"Not really," I protested.

He smiled into my eyes. "Just because something comes easy to you doesn't mean it isn't work."

"Sort of like you flying an airplane?"

"Sort of. Yes."

Then his lips were on mine.

And if anyone was watching us, neither one of us cared.

His tongue swept across my bottom lip, then he sucked it. As he sucked my bottom lip, I sucked his top lip.

Oh my.

He teased my mouth open with his tongue and touched the roof of my mouth with the roof of his tongue.

He was the only one who'd ever kissed me like this and it made me weak in the knees.

Fortunately, he had his arms wrapped firmly around me.

Anyone walking past would have seen two people who looked like they couldn't get enough of each other.

And in my case, that was dangerously true.

It was going to be hard to keep my heart safe with him kissing me like this.

The only problem was. I didn't want him to stop.

40

KADE

I shouldn't have kissed her like that.

Madison sat in the passenger seat as I drove toward a little sandwich shop that we used to go to.

Her lips were already swollen and she wasn't making eye contact.

Besides that, she was being quiet. She'd been quiet most the day today. Except when she'd been talking with my mother.

I owed her big time for that.

I'd meant what I said that she was sexy when she was working.

But just because she was my ex-girlfriend and possibly even my current love interest, didn't mean I could just put her to work helping me with my ailing mother.

I pulled into the parking lot of the little sandwich shop, parked, and looked around.

"Is this the right place?" I asked.

"It's not here anymore," she said. "I think they closed down."

"That's too bad," I said. "They had the best sandwiches."

"They really did. There's a similar place around the corner

if you want to try it. My sister got us takeout from there a few days ago."

"Sure," I said. "Why do all the good places have to close down?"

I pulled back into traffic and followed her directions to the other shop.

Before turning off the motor, I turned and looked at Madison.

The air conditioning fluttered her hair and with her lips swollen from my kisses, she looked like a goddess.

And why did all the good things have to end?

Not staying in touch with Madison was the stupidest thing I'd ever done.

But from the way she'd responded to my kiss told me that there might still be something salvageable from the wreckage I'd created.

"Ready?" I asked.

She nodded. And she waited while I came around and opened her door.

It was something I'd always done for her since the very beginning. And that she seemed to remember, warmed my heart.

I could only imagine that Madison Worthington was quite capable of opening her own car door. It was a privilege that she let me do it for her.

It spoke to the ingrained history that we shared.

We walked into the crowded sandwich shop and took a table near the window.

I watched her as she settled into her chair.

She and I had a good foundation. A firm foundation.

Something we could build on.

But she probably didn't trust me yet.

And she was making plans to leave in three months.

Three months would fly by and there was nothing I could do to stop the flow of time.

The passing of time was like a wound that wouldn't stop bleeding.

I wanted to wrap her around me like a bandage and ride out the flow of time with her.

"Madison," I said, taking her hand.

She looked into my eyes.

I didn't even know what I wanted to say to her.

I just wanted her to look at me. I wanted to be part of her world. Hell, I couldn't kid myself. I wanted to be at the center of her world.

"What can I get you?" the server, a young man holding a pencil and pad asked, stopping next to our table.

"We haven't even looked at the menus," I said, releasing her hand. "Can we have a minute?"

"Sure thing," the server said. "take your time."

Madison picked up her menu and smiled at me.

"What are you hungry for?"

I picked up my own menu and stared at it, but I couldn't focus on the words.

Her innocent question sent my brain down a path I was certain she hadn't intended.

It would be awhile before I could stand up without embarrassing myself.

I had to get control of myself. We weren't college students anymore.

41

MADISON

omma's office was as large most people's living rooms. And her desk was big. Executive level big.

There was a table with four chairs on one side of the room.

And on the side with the floor to ceiling windows, there was a chair and a love seat.

That was Momma's chair. The love seat was for the patients.

But today Momma sat behind her desk, perky reading glasses perched on her nose. The notebook computer was open in front of her and she was concentrating on the notes she was writing.

But when she saw me, she closed the computer lid, and stood up, grinning.

"Madison," she said. "I didn't expect you today."

"I know, Momma." I gave her a quick hug. At least quick by Momma's standards. She was always glad to see her children and she showered affection on us.

Unlike with Daddy, the girls didn't argue over who was her favorite. She loved all her girls equally.

Besides, we all knew she loved Quinn the best.

He was not only the only boy of five children, he was youngest.

It was only natural that she'd love him best.

And he was a spitting image of his father. Us girls didn't stand a chance and didn't even try.

"I was hoping we could grab some lunch," I said, sitting down in one of the two chairs in front of her desk and dropping my handbag into the other chair.

Momma sat back down in her chair and leaned forward, her elbows resting on the table.

"Sounds good," she said. "But you're sitting down."

I smiled. Momma was quick as lightning.

"While I was here, I was hoping you could give me a quick consult." In my training, I'd worked with young adults and middle-aged adults. I didn't work with children and I had limited experience working with the elderly. I knew just enough to know that they required special care that I wasn't equipped to handle in any depth.

"A patient?" she asked.

"Sort of," I said, deciding to maintain confidentiality and not tell her I was asking about Kade's mother.

"So… my patient is older… geriatric."

Momma sat back and instinctively slid a pad of paper over in front of her.

"Hospitalized?" she asked.

"No. She's still living at home, but she has caregivers. She has a broken leg, but otherwise she's doing okay physically."

Momma nodded. Waiting for me to continue.

"She has some dementia. And until quite recently she'd been hiding it with confabulation."

"Not unusual."

"She's been hiding it from her family." I laced my fingers

together. "Do you have any experience in working with adult children in a case like this?"

"How old are the children?"

"Around my age."

"It must be really hard on them."

"It is," I said. Talking to Momma always seemed to make things better. Less stressful.

"When you're young, you don't think you'll ever get old. You understand the concept, but it doesn't seem real. It's not something that you think will really happen."

Momma drew a line across the piece of paper in front of her.

"Until it does."

I didn't say anything. I waited for Momma to explain where she was headed with this.

"And it's the same with children and their parents. We think they're always going to be there. Until they aren't."

"You're worried about Grandma?" I asked.

Momma nodded and smiled a little.

"Of course," she said. "But your father and I aren't getting any younger." She took a deep breath. "There's no easy answer to your question. It's something we all have to go through at our own pace. Just try to encourage patience."

"Easier said than done."

"Isn't everything?" Momma asked.

I nodded and picked up my handbag.

Momma stood up, too.

"How's Kade?" she asked.

Seriously, how did Momma do that?

She knew exactly who I'd been talking about, but she hadn't said a word.

A flush crept over my cheeks and I knew that Momma would notice. There was very little that she missed.

Oddly enough though, she seemed distracted and didn't seem to notice.

As we left her office, I watched her carefully.

"Are you okay, Momma? Is something bothering you?"

She brushed off my question. Sort of. "I will be," she said. "Everything will work out."

I wasn't sure I believed her. Or worse that she believed her own words, but I let it drop.

If something was bothering Momma, she'd keep it to herself until she felt like someone needed to know. Which could be never.

Fortunately for me, it kept her from asking me questions about Kade.

42

KADE

I landed back in Houston early Monday morning. I'd had an early flight, but it had been an easy one.

The passenger was a middle-aged business man who didn't ask for anything special. Other than bringing his dog.

And since it was a Skye Travels policy that pets were family, I had no complaints. I wouldn't have anyway since I agreed that pets were family.

It was just a complete change from the commercial restrictions I was used to.

I liked it.

As the wheels touched the runway, I found my thoughts going down a familiar path.

Would Madison still be at the office?

If so, how could I talk her into going over to the Skyhouse for a drink? I didn't have a flight until day after tomorrow, so my twenty-four hours bottle to throttle rule was intact.

I knew Madison was taking it easy on me. Giving me time to settle in before she put me in the air every day.

Or maybe she was just messing with me. She had to know how much I loved flying.

Just some of the things I wanted to find out.

I hadn't seen her since Saturday when I'd dropped her off at her sister's apartment.

And she'd dashed off before I could kiss her again.

I taxied down the runway after a smooth landing and made my way toward the hangar.

I found my gaze drawn to the windows of the Sky Travels offices.

The clock was ticking down that would take Madison away from here.

And I didn't like that one bit.

I'd spent most of the day at my mother's house yesterday. I went over her medication with one of the new girls since it was Susan's day off and helped Mother order some things on the Internet.

It quickly became evident that she was lonely.

And I found myself wondering if I was doing her a disservice.

As much as I didn't want to put her in an assisted living community, I felt like I was depriving her of social interactions with her peers.

Mother had always liked being around people.

Now she only had the help, all women much younger than she was.

Maybe after her broken leg healed, I could have a conversation with her.

Not that she was in any condition to make any serious decisions about her help.

That had been driven home to me yesterday when Mother asked when I was going to bring Madison by to see her.

Said it had been ages since she'd seen her.

She didn't even remember Madison coming by Saturday.

And yet it was all I could think about.

Four hours in the air. Two hours layover while my

passenger attended a meeting. Six hours altogether free for me to think.

And that was just today. It didn't include the last two nights.

I'd had to wash my sheets twice.

Turns out my body had an excellent memory of everything Madison.

I secured the plane and headed up the elevator to my office.

Madison's laughter was the first thing I heard when the elevators doors opened.

First of all, Madison was one of the most serious people I knew. It was hard to make her laugh. To really laugh.

And second, her laughter was mixed with male laughter.

And it wasn't her brother Quinn or her father Noah.

As I rounded the corner so I could see the lobby area, including the reception area where she sat, I quickly took in the scene.

Madison was standing up behind the desk.

There was a man, about our age, leaning against the counter. He was dressed in a suit and tie. And I knew instantly that he wasn't a pilot.

That was a relief quickly followed by a new worry.

What is this was one of her psychology friends? One of those people whose language she spoke.

It was hard to know which she would choose. A pilot like her father and the men she'd grown up around. Or somebody she'd been through graduate school with.

I'd heard that Ph.D. programs were a lot like boot camp and friends were made for life.

I hadn't been prepared for the shot of jealousy that shot through my system.

And Madison was laughing so hard, she didn't even see me come up.

I instantly disliked the man. For no logical reason. I hadn't even met him.

I kept walking toward my office, deciding to let them be.

Sitting down hard in my leather chair, I nursed a foul mood.

I knew Madison had a life outside of my world.

We hadn't so much as talked for eight years.

Of course she knew people.

Had friends and colleagues.

Men who made her laugh.

I logged into the computer and tapped a few keys.

I still hadn't taken the time to learn more than the basics of the system, so it took me twice as long to enter my daily records than it should have.

With that done, I slammed down the computer lid and leaned back in my chair.

This day was not going the way I'd imagined.

Then to top it off, I got a text from Susan.

Pulling my phone out of my pocket, I unlocked the screen and stared at the message.

SUSAN: *Your mother tried to walk. Fell down. Ambulance is on the way.*

I didn't even write back. I grabbed my car keys and headed out the door at a breakneck speed.

Why did the woman have to be so damn stubborn?

I'd just reminded her yesterday that she wasn't ready to start walking.

As I dashed through the lobby, I dialed Susan's number.

With one glance at the elevator doors, I took the stairs.

"How bad is it?" I asked.

43

———

MADISON

I'd completely forgotten that my friend Garth was coming by tonight.

We'd set up a plan to have drinks at least two weeks ago and I'd completely forgotten.

Once again, Momma was right.

She was always telling me to *write it down on your paper calendar*.

It was a bit irritating that she was always right.

I wasn't sure how Kade had gotten past me, but I'd seen him dash out, his phone to his ear.

"Who was that?" Garth asked.

"I…'um…one of our pilots," I said absently. But Kade wasn't just one of our pilots.

I wasn't quite sure what he was, but he was far more than one of the company's pilots.

"Do you have Emily's number?" I asked.

"Sure. Why?"

I logged off my computer and started gathering up my things.

"I have to run," I said. "But I bet Emily will be excited to see you. You should call her. And—"

I pulled my handbag out of my desk and slipped my phone into my pocket. "I'll have to take a raincheck for tonight."

I dashed toward the elevator, hoping to catch Kade, but he must have already been on his way down.

I pushed the elevator button and paced impatiently as I waited for the door to open.

If I weren't wearing these heels, I'd take the stairs.

Finally, the door opened and I stepped inside.

There was no way I was going to catch him at this speed.

He'd been in a hurry.

And he hadn't even looked in my direction as he walked out.

He had to have seen me talking to Garth and he probably thought the worst.

Garth had a way of making people feel at ease and laugh.

What Kade wouldn't know was that Garth had a husband at home and despite his flirty ways, when it came to intimacy, he preferred the company of men.

When the elevator doors finally opened, I dashed out and practically ran through the building toward the main doors.

Just as I reached the door, I saw the tail lights of Kade's car as he entered traffic heading away from the airport.

Damn it.

And I'd been looking forward to seeing him all day.

It wasn't my business where he was going.

Kade was a grown man and he could do whatever he wanted to do.

Since I was already headed out, I went to my car and started to back out of my parking space.

I saw a text come in front Emily and answered it while I sat in traffic.

EMILY: *What happened? You bailed on Garth?*

ME: *Something came up. Headed home.*
EMILY: *What came up?*
ME: *Not sure yet. Can you hang out with Garth?*
EMILY: *Of course. Call me if you need anything.*
ME: *Talk to you tomorrow.*

Traffic cleared and I put away my phone.

I didn't feel like going out tonight anyway.

I'd known this was going to happen.

I was getting too close to Kade again.

I ignored what was probably a booty call the other night and for all I knew, he was headed out to meet someone again.

Feeling down in the dumps, I drove straight to my sister's apartment. Parked my car, and went up the private elevator.

Since no one was home, I kicked out of my heels and poured myself a glass of pinot noir.

I flipped on the Weather Channel and just relaxed on the couch.

I gave myself the evening to wallow in disappointment.

It was supposed to be therapeutic. To help me cope with my feelings about getting reacquainted with Kade, only to be disappointed.

I took full advantage of it because I knew that when I woke up in the morning, I was going to need to have figured out a way to cope with the fact that I worked with my ex-boyfriend. Whom I still had feelings for.

And I was leaving for Denver in less than three months.

I set the glass of wine aside and, curling my feet up under me, leaned back and closed my eyes.

It was best for us to keep the relationship casual.

Anything else and it was going to be too hard to leave him.

We'd faced a similar situation eight years ago.

Practically the same situation. We both had things to do. In different parts of the country.

Left with a broken heart, I'd channel all my energy into my studies and training.

Graduated first out of the six graduate students in my cohort.

Was I going to have to do the same thing all over again?

Throw everything into my work at the university in Denver just to keep from thinking about Kade?

They were going to love me out there.

I had lots of energy. Especially when it came to getting over Kade.

I would just have to be more careful.

And I definitely had to stop letting him kiss me.

44

KADE

Fortunately Susan had overreacted.

It was better than the alternative, so I didn't fault her for it.

It was nearly eight o'clock by the time Mother got checked out and released.

She'd fallen down, but other than twisting the ankle on her already broken leg, she was unharmed.

After getting her settled in back in her house, I needed a break. And going back to my hotel room was not something I considered a break at all.

So I drove back to what I knew. I drove back out toward the airport and pulled into the parking lot of the Skyhouse Lounge.

I knew there was a possibility that Madison could be there with her friend. I wasn't sure if I wanted her to be there or not.

The bar was crowded tonight, but I saw the man who'd been talking with Madison earlier. He was sitting at a little table with Emily, Madison's friend.

Emily was laughing at something the fellow had said.

After a quick look around, I determined that Madison wasn't there.

I ordered a whiskey and sat on a bar stool, my back to the bar.

I scanned the room again, looking for Madison.

Then, with hooded eyes, I just watched Emily and the guy.

I would have bet money that Madison would be here with them.

And I would have lost.

After about fifteen minutes, Emily excused herself and started making her way toward me.

I turned around, even though it was probably too late to keep from being noticed.

I'd been right.

Emily came right up beside and sat down.

Emily wasn't the kind of girl I was attracted to. She was cute enough, but she was a bit more outspoken than I liked.

Besides, she really didn't stand a chance. Any girl I compared to Madison came up short just by the very nature of the comparison.

"Whatcha doing here?" Emily asked, ordering a cosmopolitan.

I let the whiskey burn its way down my throat before I answered.

"Just needed a break," I said, going with the honest answer.

"I sort of thought you'd be with Madison."

The bartender brought her pretty pink drink and slid it over in front of her.

I looked at Emily with surprise. "Why would you say that?"

Emily sipped her drink. Shrugged. "Just considering that she isn't here."

I found this conversation to be odd. And for the hundredth time since I'd known the two of them, I wondered how they stayed friends.

"Who's that fellow?" I asked, nodding over toward the man she'd been sitting with.

She glanced over her shoulder. "Oh. That's Garth."

I lifted an eyebrow questioningly.

She shrugged. "Garth's an old friend of ours."

An old friend. That could mean a lot of things.

If it was anyone other than Emily, I would probably probe a bit further, but Emily was hard to talk to.

And since Madison wasn't here, I suddenly felt compelled to leave.

As I paid the bartender, Emily turned, taking her drink with her. "See you later, Kade."

Though it was a relief to step outside into the fresh air, I quickly got into my car and headed toward town.

Unfortunately it was too late to track down Madison.

45

MADISON

The next morning, I got to the office early. Turned on all the lights. Opened the shades. And turned on the coffeemaker.

Instead of stopping by the café for a coffee, I made my own latte.

While I waited, I paced over to the window and looked out over the tarmac.

Maybe it was time to make a trip up to Denver.

Just to look around.

Start to get a feel for my new home.

I could get Daddy to fly me up there. We could make a day of it. It would be fun. I hadn't had the chance to spend any time with him lately.

We were all so busy, we hardly saw each other, even though we lived right here in the same city.

I expected to feel excited about my move to Denver. Wanted to feel excited about it.

But it just wasn't there.

I went back to the break room, grabbed my latte, and went to the reception desk.

I tapped my fingers against the counter.

It would be good to get a head start on things.

I opened my iPad and dashed off a quick email to the department chair. It was time I got a list of the textbooks I'd be teaching from so I could start reading and putting together my lectures.

The more I could get done this summer, the better off I'd be this fall.

Besides, I needed to get more accomplished this summer than just working for the family and spending time with Kade.

Kade had his own life.

The sooner I got mine together and stopped trying to relive the past, the better off I'd be.

I knew Kade didn't have a flight until the afternoon, but it didn't keep me from monitoring the direction of the elevators.

If he showed up early, I didn't want to miss him like I had yesterday.

And that brought me right back around to the whole problem with me hanging out here at the office all summer.

I was spending all my energy on Kade.

Quinn came in a few minutes later and disappeared back to his own office.

I heard him on the phone shortly thereafter. Quinn was always working the next deal.

I seriously thought he was trying to live up to Daddy's reputation in his own way.

But before I could go too far down that psychoanalytic road, I stopped myself. It wasn't good to psychoanalyze one's own family.

I definitely needed something constructive to do.

It was about mid-morning when I got an email response from the department chair.

From the tone of his email, he sounded pleased that I wanted to get started on my course preparations.

DR. BERTRAND: *If you'd like to come up for a couple of days, I can show you around. Go over some things with you ahead of time. We can set up an appointment with HR to get things moving. Just let me know.*

I stared at the email, wondering why I felt so off-kilter.

It was because I was getting used to being here. Back in the safe world of Skye Travels. Home.

But this wasn't my career.

ME: *Sounds like a great idea. Let me check my schedule to see when I can clear out some time.*

There. That's what I needed to be doing.

I sent Daddy a text next.

ME: *I need to hitch a ride to Denver. Thought you might want to come with. Have a couple of days open anytime soon?*

It only took a half a minute to get a response.

DADDY: *How about Thursday? I'm clear from then until next Monday. Want me to put you on my schedule?*

I smiled to myself. Daddy was like me with his schedule. He kept his appointments on his calendar, but that was mostly for others to see. Others meaning Momma. His schedule was mostly in his head.

I took a deep breath. *Just do it. Get it over with.*

ME: *Okay. Let's do it.*

Back to my email.

So within ten minutes, I'd committed myself to at least a two-day trip to Denver.

I took off my headset and sat back in the chair.

It would be good for me.

I needed to rekindle some of the excitement of moving to Denver.

While I was there, I could take Daddy to see my new apartment.

Maybe Momma would want to come, too.

ME: *Heading to Denver this weekend with Daddy. Want to come?*

MOMMA: *I heard. Sounds great. Unfortunately, I'm booked. It'll be good for you and Daddy to have some time.*

It was almost like Momma and Daddy shared a brain.

They told each other everything.

But from the way they told it, it hadn't always been that way.

Before they got married, Daddy would disappear without a word, only to show up again out of the blue. Expecting Momma to still be there waiting for him.

Apparently it hadn't taken long for her to break him of that. And now, five kids later, he hardly made a move without telling her about it.

It was actually adorable when it wasn't annoying.

Had definitely prevented us kids from ever trying to play one against the other.

Not that we would do anything like that.

With everything in place, I glanced up to see Kade coming around the hallway leading from the elevators.

My heart rate shot into overdrive.

Like it always had when I saw him.

He was wearing black slacks, black lace-up shoes, and a white shirt. He even wore the captain's hat that Daddy insisted all his pilots wore.

Daddy insisted that it gave them a respectable look. Professional.

I think he just liked the way it made them look in general.

And right now I didn't disagree with him one bit.

If Daddy was trying to attract more female clients, then the Skye Travels uniform was definitely a step in the right direction.

I wasn't wearing my headset, so I had no excuse to not talk to him.

And now that he knew I'd seen him, I had no reason to look away.

I wasn't sure I could have, even if I wanted to. His gaze locked onto mine and I lost all ability to look away.

I thought for a minute that he was going to keep walking to his office, but instead, he veered in my direction.

He smiled at me and I reflexively smiled back.

I pressed my hands against the counter to keep them from trembling.

Geez. This was just Kade. My old boyfriend.

Not my current boyfriend. Or even boyfriend interest.

At least that's what I told myself.

His kisses said otherwise.

"There you are," he said.

I lifted a delicate eyebrow. "Was I missing?" I asked.

"Actually, yes," he said.

I was about to ask him what he meant, but he moved on before I had the chance.

"Do you have plans for tonight?"

I started to tell him that, of course, I had plans. I was going to go to my sister's apartment, have a glass of wine, and read something for fun.

My sister's apartment was big enough that we could both be home and not even see each other unless we happened to go into the kitchen at the same time.

But then I remembered that he might need help with his mother. It was the ingrained psychologist training. It followed me wherever I went.

"Nothing in particular," I said, keeping my hands firmly locked on the edge of the counter.

"Can we have a coffee?"

I glanced at the schedule, though I really didn't have to. I knew his schedule by heart. He had an early morning flight, so a drink was out of the question.

"Sure," I said. "After work?"

"I'll meet you back here," he said.

"If you're back," I said.

He had a flight up to San Antonio to drop someone off with a quick turnaround. He or someone would go back in a couple of days to pick up the client.

"I'll be back," he said.

And I had no doubt that he would be.

46

KADE

I made a seamless takeoff.

And damn if I didn't wonder if Madison had been watching.

As my grandmother would say, I had it bad.

It had taken all my willpower to stay away from her apartment last night.

But I'd left her alone.

I knew that I'd see her today. And I didn't want to send her the other way.

I remembered how long it had taken me just to get her to go out with me that first time back in college.

We'd been inseparable after that, but it had been a lot of work to convince her that I wasn't a serial killer or worse.

Oddly enough, it was flying that brought us together back then. And it was flying that had brought us back into the same orbit.

I would take my time with her.

There was no need to rush.

I wanted her for the long-term. Not a short-term hook up.

I went into my office, took off my cap, and tossed it onto the desk.

I didn't mind wearing it.

It made me feel debonair. Like a man of the early 1900s.

A gentleman.

I opened up the computer and logged into the website.

It was time I spent some serious time on getting the learning curve out of the way.

It wasn't like me at all, to put off learning something like this.

I surely wasn't about to admit to Madison that I didn't have it figured out.

Rolling up my sleeves, I went to work the best way I knew how.

I made up a trip for myself and went through the process of setting it up.

Sure, that part belonged to Madison, but I liked to know how things worked from the ground up.

Knowledge was power and I like to have it.

Besides, I could delete the whole thing and no one had to know.

I invented a trip to Denver.

I figured I'd be flying to Denver a lot in the near future, so that was as good a place as any to start.

I put in one passenger. I even gave her a name. Doc.

After checking my schedule, I saw that I had no flights scheduled after Wednesday until Monday. So I put in a trip for Thursday through Sunday evening.

Went through the process of locking in the schedule.

I leaned back in my chair, my hands laced behind my head and admired my work.

I had conquered the system. At least this part of it.

There would be more to learn over time, but now I could control my own schedule if I wanted to.

My cell phone rang, jarring me out of my thoughts.

It was Quinn.

"Hey," he said. "Can you come into my office for a minute?"

"Sure."

I'd just seen Quinn walk past my own office. He could have stopped in.

Maybe it was just his managerial style.

I slipped my phone into my pocket, put my hat back on my head—just in case there were clients—and walked to the office next door.

"Come in," Quinn said, ushering me over to the little table on one side of his office.

So this wasn't a formal meeting. That was a relief. I didn't feel up to getting into trouble so soon after starting work here.

"What's up?" I asked, trying to keep my tone light.

I didn't want Quinn to know that he had the power to make me nervous.

I'd worked in the corporate world far too long. I knew how to do this.

"Can I get you some coffee?"

"Sure." I sat down and waited.

Why didn't Quinn just get this over with? Surely whatever it was, it couldn't be that important.

Quinn poured coffee into a mug, remembering that I liked it black.

Then he sat across from me. Adjusted his tie.

My thoughts went into self-preservation mode. I'd given up my corporate job for this one. If Quinn decided he didn't need me, I go out on my own. It would be more work, but I could do it. I had contacts.

"Look," Quinn said. "I know we had an agreement from the outset." He held up a hand. "And I know that these things always happen. You start out with one agreement and then the work just keeps piling up."

I was still wary, but I relaxed enough to get my heart rate under control. Quinn was talking about more work, not less.

I could deal with whatever he threw at me.

"I know we agreed that you'd have weekends off. That family is your first priority."

I knew what was coming. Quinn was right. This always happened. There was always more commitment required in a job than anyone was promised at the beginning.

"Right," I said. "What's going on?"

I hadn't gotten where I was by being difficult. I was a team player.

Now that I was older, I had good boundaries, but I was also a team player.

"Noah has a flight booked for this weekend. And one of the other guys had already scheduled vacation." Quinn took a deep breath. "Is there any way you can take a flight this weekend?"

I hesitated. Only because I genuinely had to think about what I had scheduled.

Quinn took my hesitation as a no.

"Look, man," Quinn said. "I really apologize for springing this request on you. It isn't how we normally operate. An agreement is an agreement. But I can pay you double for a flight that leaves on Thursday and returns on Sunday."

By the time Quinn had finished out his request, I had mentally gone over my calendar.

"I can do it," I said. And it wasn't about the money.

If I allowed myself to drill down deep enough I would find that I was doing it for Madison.

But that was only if I allowed myself to drill deep.

Either way, I found myself whistling to myself as I left Quinn's office.

47

———

MADISON

*T*hursday morning dawned as a beautiful day. It wasn't hot yet.

But even more important, there wasn't a cloud in the sky.

I'd gotten here early and held a large cup of Starbuck's coffee in one hand.

I parked my Jaguar sedan in the long-term parking and leaned against the door.

I wore a long flowing skirt. Different from my work attire. More what Kade would call breezy.

I wore white canvas sneakers. Very casual in spite of their red bottoms.

My cropped black sweater was layered over a longer t-shirt that I'd tucked into the skirt.

After straightening it with the flat iron, I'd left my hair flowing freely around my shoulders.

I should be excited. I'd secured my apartment online and this was my first time seeing it in person.

I was going to be meeting with my new supervisor. And I was looking forward to working with him.

We'd talked during the interview and seemed to be in sync about our teaching philosophies.

Yet as I stared out over the tarmac, I was… troubled. Maybe saddened was a better word for it.

I'd been looking forward to my first full-time teaching position since my first undergraduate psychology class.

I was the only one in my doctorate class who had such a clear picture of where I wanted my career to go.

I just hadn't thought it would take me so far away from home.

I sipped the hot coffee, a smooth latte, and allowed my mind to go blank.

It was just a weekend trip. And my father would be going along. I always had a good time with Daddy.

He was open to pretty much anything and he was an excellent listener.

Anytime I'd ever had a problem—with school or boys or whatever—Daddy and Momma were both there.

Unfortunately, I didn't have a good enough handle on what was troubling me to even think about trying to talk about it to Daddy.

So I'd put a smile on my face and enjoy this time with my father. With Daddy having six children, one-on-one time didn't happen very often.

Most people would say I thought too much.

And I didn't disagree.

But I couldn't help wishing that a certain pilot was going along with us.

A pilot who had been part of a large chunk of my life.

There was a time when I thought we'd get married.

But we'd both let our careers take precedence.

But that was then and this was now.

I'd learned, in my training as a psychologist, how important it was to focus on the moment.

Though it was something I'd worked with clients on, I knew first hand just how hard it really was to do.

My phone chimed, indicating a text message.

I pulled my phone out of my pocket and unlocked it.

MOMMA: *Hi Madison.*

She always started off with a greeting. Like a text was an email or a phone conversation. And it always made me smile.

ME: *Hi Momma.*

My fingers hovered over the keys. Normally I would have asked her what was happening, but something about it being early on a Thursday morning. And the fact that I was waiting here at the airport for Daddy, sent my stomach into knots.

MOMMA: *Daddy can't make it today.*

My knotted stomach clenched. Something was wrong. I knew it.

ME: *What's wrong?*

Daddy was never sick. And he was very careful not to disappoint anyone in his family.

I went into high alert. I even opened my door, prepared to jump into the car and race to their house about twenty minutes from here.

MOMMA: *Nothing for you to worry about. I'm taking him in to get checked out. I just don't think he should fly today.*

Momma was minimizing. I could tell when she did it. It even came through her text messages.

ME: *I'm on my way.*

MOMMA: *No. No. Please don't. We've already arranged things around to get you to*

Denver.

ME: *You don't understand. I can go to Denver another time. When Daddy's feeling better.*

MOMMA: *Daddy's right here. And he worked hard to set up someone else to take you. Don't disappointment him Madison.*

I flinched. Momma knew how to push my buttons. I

worked hard to never disappoint anyone, much less Momma or Daddy.

ME: *Ok. But you have to tell me what's wrong.*

I knew something was wrong. Not even Momma with her smooth skills couldn't pull this one over on me.

MOMMA: *I'll let him tell you when you get back. Just go. Enjoy your trip. Come by the house when you get back.*

I stared at my phone.

There was no way I was going to enjoy a trip anywhere while I was worried about Daddy.

Besides, it was hard to enjoy a trip when no one was here.

ME: *Momma. There's no one here. I'm just going to try again another day. I'll come by the house this morning and see how Daddy's doing.*

MOMMA: *He's just running a little late. It was a last minute switch, so you have to have some compassion.*

I was staring at the phone again.

Compassion, my ass.

Skye Travels pilots were on time and ready for anything.

ME: *Who is it?*

As soon as I hit send, I saw a car pull into the parking lot. And I knew who the pilot was.

My heart did a summersault.

It was Kade.

48

KADE

It was barely eight o'clock in the morning, and my day had already been rife with chaos.

Noah Worthington himself had called me just as I'd stepped out of the shower. Before I'd even had my first cup of coffee.

The bright spot was that it was a beautiful day. Blue skies. Not a cloud in sight.

A perfect day for a flight.

I'd known that Noah had been planning a trip to Denver with Madison today.

For some reason, something personal came up last minute with him and he couldn't go.

He didn't go into it with me, obviously, since it was personal.

All I knew was that the flight I was scheduled to take later in the morning had been given to someone else and I was assigned to take Madison to Denver.

I saw her standing next to her car as I pulled up.

She didn't look happy.

My best guess, based on her holding her phone, was that she'd just found out that Noah wasn't coming.

She sent off a quick text and slid her phone into her pocket.

"Good morning," I said.

Despite the chaotic way this flight had come about, I was quite happy about it.

I got to take Madison to Denver. Four days and three nights.

Nope. I was not unhappy. Not in the least.

Quinn was paying me double, but I would have done it for nothing. It was odd that he'd asked me to fly this weekend even before this came up.

"Hi," she said. "How did you get so lucky?"

"I don't know," I said with a smile. She meant it to be a snarky comment, but I seriously thought I'd gotten lucky to be the one taking her to Denver.

"Can I get your bags?" I nodded toward her trunk.

She didn't move away from her car door.

"We should just cancel the flight. Reschedule when Daddy can go."

"Your mom said he's going to be okay. She just didn't want him flying today." I stood behind her trunk. Waiting for her to open it.

"Daddy's never sick," she said. I heard the concern written all over her face.

"We could run over there. Then if you still want to, we can fly out later in the morning."

I would do just about anything to smooth out the concern she wore.

It didn't suit her.

The Madison I knew was confident and sure.

But this was her daddy we were talking about. Madison had always been a daddy's girl. That was never going to change.

Without commenting, she popped the trunk, but she still didn't move.

I waited.

She'd figure out what she wanted to do.

I just had to wait it out.

That's how it was with Madison.

She'd figure it out.

49

MADISON

Don't disappoint your daddy.

Momma's words struck a chord with me.

I squared my shoulders. Daddy wasn't getting any younger, but he was a strong man. He would be okay. He had to be.

Momma would take care of him.

They didn't need me hovering in the way.

Besides, if they needed me, I was just a short flight away.

Not much different than being across town at my sister's apartment.

Besides, I was going to have to get used to this.

I was *moving* to Denver, for God's sake.

I wasn't going to be around at every drop of a hat.

It wasn't lost on me that Kade had moved to Houston to be close to his mother to take care of her while I was leaving the state. Moving further away from my family.

It was supposed to help that there were five kids. Six if we counted Danielle, our half-sister.

Anyone who thought I was a daddy's girl hadn't met Danielle.

If she knew Daddy was sick, she'd have her husband flying her from LA to Houston in a heartbeat.

I decided right then that I was going to go.

Maybe it was the way Kade waited patiently for me to make up my mind. He didn't try to sway me one way or the other.

I appreciated that. Especially since I knew that Kade was a persuasive kind of guy.

He was the one person who could get me to do just about anything.

"All right," I said. "Let's go."

"Okay then," he said, pulling my bags from my trunk and carrying them to the plane.

My bags were not light, by any means, but Kade didn't seem to have any trouble with them. I wondered how he felt about having to handle people's luggage. Not something he had to do with the commercial job.

But as a pilot with Skye Travels, it came with the territory.

With everything packed, there was nothing to do except to get going.

I locked the car and followed Kade to the plane.

He helped me inside, just like he'd done a hundred other times.

This time felt different though.

This time we were actually going on a trip, not just a day flight.

It felt different.

I was still disappointed that Daddy couldn't come and if there was something seriously wrong with him, I was going to give mother an earful.

But on the other hand, it was Kade.

That part was unexpected. But I didn't mind.

In truth, I rather liked it.

I didn't know how Daddy had managed to rearrange this

weekend's complicated schedule. Or why he'd chosen Kade to be my pilot.

Though if I had to guess, I'd say Momma had something to do with that part.

Daddy trusted all his pilots.

But it was thoughtful of them to take my relationship with Kade into consideration.

I smiled at him as he buckled me into the four-point harness.

He went around to his side of the plane and climbed in. Clicked on the computer.

"Do you have any luggage?" I asked.

He looked at me blankly for a moment.

"I'm about to grab it now," he said.

Despite his smooth answer, I knew that Kade Johnson had just forgotten his own luggage.

That had to be a first.

It was a good thing the two of us made a good team.

The weekend had held promise from the beginning, but with Kade coming along, things had just gotten interesting.

50

KADE

I pulled my luggage from the trunk of my car and hauled it over to the plane.

I had actually gotten into the cockpit and was preparing to start a flight.

Without my luggage.

Madison Worthington had that effect on me.

After all these years, she could still distract the hell out of me.

I wouldn't tell her though. I would not tell her that I had gotten so distracted by her that I'd forgotten to load my own luggage.

I wouldn't tell her that she smelled like a field of daisies in a summer field. Like sunshine.

Leaning close enough to buckle her in had sent every nerve in my body on edge.

I didn't know how I'd ended up going on this trip with her. It had happened so fast it made my head spin.

But flying was flying.

And Madison was Madison.

Put the two together and I was in heaven.

I got back into the cockpit and ignored her smug expression.

She found amusement in my uncharacteristic absentmindedness.

She could be amused if she wanted to, but it was her fault for looking all sexy.

After I got myself buckled in, I winked at her.

She looked away and I smiled to myself at the light blush that spread over her cheeks.

I spoke to the air traffic controller and went through my checklist.

This was going to be fun.

And I could barely wait for takeoff.

As I finished up, and we began to taxi out to the runway, she texted on her phone.

"Ready?" I asked.

She smiled at me.

I stopped at the edge of the runway and without even saying a word, I cupped her chin with one hand and lightly stroked her cheek with the other.

Her lips parted and her eyes drifted closed.

A weekend with Madison in Denver. Alone. No family on either side to interrupt us.

With that thought I pressed my lips against hers.

She responded to my kiss and our tongues brushed.

Ignoring the controller's voice in my ear, giving us permission to take off, I deepened the kiss.

Something about kissing Madison was an exhilarating combination of familiar and new.

I had a feeling I was going to quickly earn a reputation for delayed takeoffs.

Madison put a hand on my arm.

"I think we're supposed to be in the air," she said. Her lips were already swelling.

I was thinking about turning the plane around and going back to the office. As much as I loved flying, there were other things that I'd rather be doing right about now.

"Last call," the controller said in my ear.

"All right," I said. "I get it" and assured the controller that I was ready for takeoff.

"Hold on," I said with a sideways glance at Madison.

And both of us knew perfectly well that I wasn't talking about the flight.

51

MADISON

*I*t was too noisy in this particular small jet to hold much of a conversation in the cockpit.

Since I didn't have cell phone service in this plane, I set my phone aside and opened my iPad to the book I'd been reading.

It was a good book and I was enjoying it quite well enough.

But I kept reading the same sentence over. And over.

It was impossible to concentrate with Kade sitting next to me—being the sexy pilot that he was.

I found it utterly charming that he'd forgotten his luggage.

It actually made me feel like maybe he had enough interest in me to be distracted.

And then there was that kiss.

That kiss left absolutely no doubt that our connection was still there and was still strong.

That kiss had been an intoxicating mixture of firm and gentle.

A combination that had me thinking about all sorts of possibilities for this weekend.

I felt a little guilty about being glad that Kade was here.

Especially since it meant that there was something going on with my father that had kept him from coming with me.

Daddy had been looking forward to this trip.

And if it was just a scheduling problem, he would have just told me.

Instead, Momma had told me. And she'd admitted that he wasn't feeling well and she was going to take him to the doctor.

I tapped my fingers against my iPad. Then I turned to Kade.

"Who called you about the schedule change?" she asked.

"Noah," he said.

"How did he sound?"

At first I didn't think he'd heard me.

"He sounded okay to me. He said he had a lot of phone calls to make this morning."

That was something, at least. It explained why Momma had sent me the text and not Daddy.

Daddy was a busy man.

He'd taken the time to call Kade. To make sure I was taken care of, then he'd gotten back to his business calls.

That little bit of information sent a surge of relief through me.

So much so, that I stopped trying to pretend to read and closed my iPad. I leaned back against the headrest and closed my eyes.

Practiced some of the relaxation techniques I'd taught my clients.

Sometimes they actually worked. Like right about now.

If anything had been serious with Daddy, they wouldn't have suggested a rescheduled trip. They wouldn't have sent Kade to take me off to Denver, knowing that we could turn it into a fun trip.

Momma wouldn't do that to me.

So since I couldn't do anything about it, I needed to focus on the moment.

To be in the moment and keep myself relaxed.

"He sounded okay to me," Kade said. "Really." He put a hand over mine in reassurance.

"Thank you," I said.

He kept his hand on mine, adding his touch to my own calming chain of thoughts.

This was going to be okay.

This trip was going to be fun.

It was what I told myself and what I needed to believe.

Now that my nerves were calming, I became aware of Kade's hand on mine.

It felt so right I barely noticed it at first, but now I couldn't think about anything else.

Between his hand on mine and the lingering sensation of his lips on mine, I could barely think about anything other than Kade.

This trip had been a bad idea.

A very bad idea.

Bad idea because I still liked him very much.

52

KADE

We had a smooth flight to Denver.

I'd had to be on top of my game because I didn't usually fly west.

And the weather around the mountains had a tendency to be more erratic than in the south.

But it had gone without incident. And the clear skies held all the way.

The landing went smoothly, then we taxied over to the gate.

Madison already had her phone out, scrolling through her messages.

"That was a smooth landing," she said, taking the time to glance over at me.

I grinned at her. Those simple words struck me all the way to the core.

I was inordinately pleased that she'd noticed.

Madison had been with me from the beginning. When I was first leaning to fly.

I liked it that she could see how far I'd come.

"Do we need to take a taxi to the hotel?" I asked.

She shook her head. "There should be a car waiting."

Of course. Sometimes I saw her just as Madison and forgot that she was the daughter of a man with an aviation empire.

"Right," I said. "Didn't know what you'd worked out."

After the plane was secure, we stepped out onto the tarmac. Just as we did, a car pulled up for us.

The wind was strong here. And dry.

The driver moved our luggage from the plane to the car.

Madison waited, nervously biting her lip.

"Are you okay?" I asked her.

"Sure." She smiled. "Momma said Daddy's home. Resting."

"Resting?"

"I know," she said. "Doesn't sound like Daddy."

"You should call him," he said.

"I would, but Momma said he'd call me when he wakes up."

I didn't know what to tell her. What to say to make her feel better. All I knew was that I wanted to make her worry go away.

And only a little bit of it was selfish on my part.

I wanted us to have a good time together.

But I genuinely wanted her to not be worried.

I wanted her to be happy.

We sat together in the back of the car as we rode to the hotel.

Though it took an hour, it didn't seem like it took any time at all.

Just being with Madison made time seem to fly past.

There was a barrier between us and the driver, so we had complete privacy.

Though we'd been alone most of the day, it seemed intimate to be sitting together in the back seat of the car. With nothing to do but just be with each other.

"Want to make out?" I asked.

She looked at me with such surprise that I laughed out loud.

"Kade Johnson," she said. "You are incorrigible."

"I know," I said, leaning back against the seat.

We rode about a mile. I laced my hands behind my head.

"We can though," I said. "if you want to."

She turned away, but not before I saw the smile on her lips.

That was a step in the right direction.

When her phone rang, she answered it almost before it even registered with me.

It was her daddy.

53

MADISON

I was still on the phone with Daddy when we reached the hotel.

Kade handled the driver and the luggage and pretty much everything.

He even checked us into our rooms.

It took a little work, but I finally learned that Daddy had been having some tests run.

He still didn't know the results yet, but he didn't seem to be worried.

The problem was that even if he was worried, he'd never let anyone know.

Except maybe Momma.

I'd never known Daddy to be sick.

He'd always been the strong one.

We stayed on the phone until he got another call. He said it was a business call.

It was comforting to know that he was still doing business. As long as he was doing business, he was okay.

At least that's what I told myself.

Just as I disconnected, Kade came over with the key cards.

"We got rooms next to each other," he said. "How's Noah?"

"It's hard to know," I said as we walked together to the elevator.

It was the same hotel I'd stayed at when I'd come out here to interview.

A huge lobby with a water fountain right in the middle.

"What floor are we on?" I asked, mostly in an attempt to distract myself.

"Thirty-first," he said.

"Good," I said, "Should have a nice view."

We stepped off the elevator and walked together down the hallway, looking for our room numbers.

"This is yours," Kade said, slipping the first key into the lock and pushing the door open.

"Where's yours?" I asked.

He glanced up. "I'm right here," he said.

"Good," I said. "I'll see you soon then."

As I stepped through the door, Kade handed me my key.

He tipped his hat before he closed the door.

As the door closed between us, I felt a sense of loss.

We'd been together all day, and it had been so easy to fall back into the companionship we'd had when we were younger.

My luggage was already in my room. I didn't even question how that had happened.

I'd probably been on the phone longer than I'd thought.

I dropped my handbag on the table just inside the door and walked around the room.

Just as I thought, there was a great view of the city and the Rocky Mountains.

There was nothing more majestic than the snow-capped Rocky Mountains.

I wandered back around the room and stopped in front of another closed door on the other side of the television cabinet.

When Kade had said our rooms were next to each other, he hadn't mentioned that they were adjoining.

I stared at the closed door.

Kade was on the other side of that door. Doing whatever it was he did.

Did he even know that we had adjoining rooms?

Putting my fingers against my lips, I replayed what I called our takeoff kiss.

Not matter what I'd told myself about those kisses the other night when we'd flown to Lafayette, today's kiss was just about as real as a kiss could get.

I didn't know what that meant yet, but it definitely meant something.

54

KADE

As I unbuttoned my shirt, I stood in front of the wooden door that separated my room from Madison's.

I'd known the rooms were adjoining. The girl who'd checked me in had made sure to point that out to me as though it was a nice prize.

It was a nice prize. Except that Madison and I were adults and if she wanted to come to my room, she could come through the main door and I could do the same if I wanted to go to her room.

Still. There was something tantalizing about sharing adjoining rooms.

I pulled a polo shirt on over my head and straightened my collar.

If I knocked on that door, would she open it?

The rooms were so big, if we opened the door, the two rooms together were bigger than most people's apartments.

It would sort of be like sharing a room.

And that was what made the whole adjoining rooms things so different.

Maybe the girl at the front desk was right. Maybe it was a prize.

I didn't even know what Madison's agenda for the next couple of days was.

Since I hadn't known I was coming, we hadn't talked about it.

And after finding out that her father was sick, she'd been preoccupied.

I knew Madison well enough to know that if she was worried or working something out in her head, she wouldn't feel like talking.

It was a good thing to know about someone.

It had kind of gotten me in trouble, though, in other relationships.

After getting used to Madison's way of dealing with anxiety in college, I'd automatically given other women space when they were worried about something.

Turns out it wasn't what most women needed. Most wanted to talk. Or at least to be distracted.

I never had really adapted to that.

I liked that Madison needed her space at times.

I was the same way.

Just another way that we were good together.

It was close to time for an early dinner.

And maybe a drink. I didn't have to fly for a few days, so I didn't have the no alcohol rule going on.

I was here in Denver, alone with Madison, and I planned to spend time with her.

ME: *Want to go upstairs? Check out the bar? See if they have anything good for dinner?*

I hit send before I had time to change my mind.

If she already had plans, she'd tell me.

If she didn't then it seemed like the gentlemanly thing to do.

MADISON: *Sounds good. Meet me outside our door in fifteen?*

I smiled.

The weekend was off to a good start.

55

MADISON

I'd been holding my phone when I got the text from Kade.

I'd been trying to decide if I should ask if he wanted to have dinner together.

I wanted to, but I wanted it to be his idea.

I'd brought jeans and t-shirts for hanging out with my dad and I'd brought a couple of cocktail dresses in case Daddy wanted to go somewhere nice. Since he always did, it was a safe bet.

I learned a long time ago that pilots knew the best places to eat.

Other than traveling a lot, they were given a lot of recommendations by others, especially locals.

But Kade wanted to go upstairs to the bar. And maybe the restaurant.

Either he didn't want to venture out too far or he didn't know the area.

After running a brush through my hair, and freshening up, I decided to change into one of my cocktail dresses.

I'd never worn the one I picked out and it still had the tags on it.

It was a sleeveless red dress that hugged all my curves and had a neckline that scooped down, stopping just soon enough to be tasteful.

Fifteen minutes flew by and, with shaky fingers, I opened the door and stepped into the hallway.

Just as I pulled my door closed, Kade stepped out of his.

"Wow," he said. "You look amazing."

I smiled. This was the reason I'd worn this dress. I loved that he noticed.

Leaning over, he kissed my cheek.

"You know," he said. "We could have made it a lot easier."

He took my hand as we walked down the hallway. I wrote it off as habit from our college days.

"How's that?"

"We could open the adjoining door."

I rolled my eyes at him.

"If we were going to do that, we could have just shared a room."

"And where is the romance in doing that, Madison Worthington?" he asked, pulling my hand up and kissing the backs of my fingers.

Kade had learned some new moves. I couldn't remember him ever doing that before.

"You're probably right," I said. "But I'm not sure it's a good idea to open that door."

"it's been open before," he said. And I instantly knew we were no longer talking about the hotel door.

We reached the elevator and he punched the up button.

"That was a long time ago," I said. "A lot of water under the bridge."

He just smiled. "Maybe so. But it's the same river. And last time I checked, rivers don't change."

I liked his analogy, but I didn't tell him.

The elevator door opened and we stepped inside with a young man wearing shorts and a t-shirt.

We rode up in silence. The man got off on the next floor and we continued up to the top.

"Do you think we're overdressed?" I asked.

"Not at all," Kade said. "But he might have been a bit underdressed."

The elevator door opened again and we stepped into the crowded hotel bar and restaurant.

We found an empty small table off to the side, near the window.

The view from here was even better than the one from my room.

"Drink?" Kade asked.

"Dirty martini. Extra olives."

I watched as he navigated his way to the bar.

Being here. With Kade. Was both familiar and new at the same time.

I needed to keep my eyes wide open.

And my heart guarded.

Here. Denver. Was about to be my home.

And Kade's home was in Houston.

The two of us didn't have a great track record with a long-distance relationship.

56

KADE

A dirty martini. Extra olives.

Another sign that the Madison I'd known in college had changed.

That and the red dress that hugged her lithe body like a glove.

The old Madison that I knew would have ordered a glass of pinot noir.

I had liked Madison before and I liked the grown-up version, too. Maybe even more.

I was older, too, and I was able to appreciate her more now than when I was younger.

Finally, the bartender handed me our drinks—two martinis—and I made my way back over to our table.

Madison stood out from all the other women here. By far the most beautiful. But it was more than that.

She held herself with confidence. Always had. But maybe even more now that she was a psychologist.

She'd had an innate sense about people that now seemed refined and honed.

And the truth was simple, really.

I was smitten.

She was staring out the window, but when I reached our table, she turned and smiled.

The years simply dropped away and we were a couple again.

It might take some work to get her there, but I saw possibilities.

Lots of possibilities.

I sat across from her and held up my glass.

"To possibilities," I said.

Our glasses clicked and we both sipped our smooth martinis.

"What kind of possibilities?" she asked.

I stretched my legs. "That's the great thing about possibilities," I said. "They're undefined by nature."

"Maybe," she said, running a finger along the edge of her glass. "But they usually fall into some kind of direction."

I nodded toward the direction of the majestic Rocky Mountains. "Right now I see endless possibilities for you here."

I saw the brief flash of disappointment that crossed her features.

I knew I was going in a different direction than either of us wanted. I couldn't quite pinpoint why. Maybe I just wanted to test the waters. To see just how committed she was to this move in her life.

She nodded and stared out the window again.

"What's bothering you Madison?" I asked. Maybe I shouldn't have gone in this direction.

I needed to dial it back.

"But as far as you're concerned, I don't see any limits on anything you might want to do."

She turned her gaze back to me and locked those mesmerizing green eyes of hers on mine.

"Thank you," she said.

I put a hand over hers and squeezed.

"It's good to see you again," she said.

I grinned. That was the first time she'd acknowledged that she was happy to see me.

As small an acknowledgement as it was, it was all the encouragement I needed at least for now.

"Well," he said. "I'm happy. I'm sitting in a fancy restaurant. With a beautiful, intelligent woman." I glanced quickly around. "The most beautiful woman in all of this fancy restaurant. What more could a man ask for?"

She laughed, then slid one of the olives off the toothpick with her teeth. She looked up at me with a little smile on her lips.

I swallowed hard. And all the blood rushed to my privates.

She knew exactly what she was doing.

Dr. Madison Worthington was no innocent college student. I knew for a fact that she wasn't as innocent as she looked.

I knew because I'd taught her a thing or two.

I ran a finger beneath the collar of my polo.

We'd just gotten here but all I could think about right now was getting her out of here and back to those adjoining rooms.

But she seemed to have other ideas.

"Tell me what you've been doing for the past eight years," she said. "the personal stuff. Not the work stuff." She waved a hand. "I've seen your resume."

She'd cut right to the chase.

She wanted to know about my personal life.

If I could get some blood flowing back to my brain, I could see that this was a good thing.

On the other hand, it was a little disconcerting to having Madison's undivided attention.

57

MADISON

I didn't know what Kade was up to.

It felt like he was playing some kind of game. Or maybe testing me in some way.

But I really did want to know what he'd been doing.

And even more than that, I wanted to know what his current relationship status was.

If I was going to open that door, both literally and metaphorically, I wanted to know what I was dealing with.

Part of the whole eyes wide open thing.

I hadn't decided how I wanted to ask him. And since he wasn't a patient, I didn't really have to.

I could just fly by the seat of my pants.

But I wanted to make sure the conversation headed in the right direction.

"You never married?" I asked.

"No," he answered quickly.

I would have liked to explore that quick answer a little more, but instead of trying to find out why he'd answered so quickly, I asked what a normal person would ask. "Why not?"

He was looking a bit uncomfortable.

"It was never right."

"I understand that."

"What about you?"

"No," I shook my head, but I wasn't ready to let him steer the conversation back to me.

"But you've had serious relationships?" I asked.

He shrugged. "I guess."

I swirled the olives in my glass with the toothpick. I'd barely touched the drink. I wanted to have a clear head about me while I was getting reacquainted with Kade.

"So not really?"

"No," he admitted. "Not really."

I couldn't tell if he was telling the truth or not.

But I let it go. It wasn't my job to seek out the truth.

Taking a deep breath, I jumped in there and asked what I really wanted to know.

"What about now?"

He shook his head. "I just moved to a new city with a new job. I didn't bring any baggage with me. If that's what you're asking."

It was what I was asking. Sort of.

But it wasn't enough.

I wanted to know if he was open to a serious relationship or if he'd joined the culture that so many pilots I knew seemed to be a part of.

The ones who seemed to be unable to resist hooking up.

So many women were attracted to the pilots in uniform. I personally knew one pilot who used to fly for Daddy who had a different girl in five different cities.

Five.

It had eventually blown up in his face and Daddy had to let him go.

But it had left a bad taste in my mouth.

The pilot had seemed like a genuinely nice guy.

Kade seemed to sense what I wanted to know.

"I don't even have a friends with benefits person."

I nodded with a little smile. "Okay. Good to know."

He looked out the window. "I don't think this view would ever get old."

"Even when you're used to seeing things from up high?" I asked.

"Not even."

I tapped the edge of my glass. There was still something that was bothering me. I just needed to ask it. I'd asked patients this question before. Surely I could ask Kade.

"What about booty calls?"

He looked at me as though I asked if he washed his hair in gasoline.

"You know," I said, leaning forward, though no one could hear us. "A fuck buddy."

"No," he said. "I do not have a fuck buddy. Why would you even ask me that?"

Shit. I shouldn't have gone down this road. This was not a good road. I needed to back track. But I couldn't stop myself.

"The night we flew to Lafayette. You had a date after we got back."

There. Now he knew where I was coming from.

After looking at me with a blank expression, he laughed.

"What's funny?" I asked. I didn't see anything funny about the whole thing.

He was talking about leaving the door between our rooms open. If he was one of those guys, I needed to know. I needed to know so I could make an informed decision about sleeping with him.

"Madison," he said. "How long have you known me?"

"Since college," I said. I didn't see how that had anything to do with this. "So?"

"You know I'm not that kind of guy."

I shrugged. "People change."

"I don't."

I felt like I'd offended him in some way.

He leaned forward and looked into my eyes.

"It was my mother," he said, his expression flat.

"Oh." Of course it was. It all made sense.

Now I felt like an absolute heel.

"I'm sorry," I said, taking my turn to stare out the window.

"Don't worry so much," he said. He put a hand on mine. "Madison."

I turned to look at him.

"I know you spend a lot of time around pilots. And I know that a lot of them aren't all that admirable in their relationships. But I'm not like that."

I nodded. "I know," I said softly.

"You have to trust me."

I looked away. He was right.

"Can you do that?"

I smiled.

My level of persistence didn't hold a candle to his.

I turned back to look into his deep blue eyes.

"Yes. I think I can do that."

Then he leaned over and pressed his lips against mine.

58

KADE

This conversation with Madison was a stark reminder.

A reminder that I had to handle her carefully.

I wanted to protect her.

And protecting her might just mean protecting her from everyone, including myself.

Before I acted on my baser impulses, I needed to make sure I was damn well ready to commit to her.

No matter what anyone said, I knew I'd hurt her eight years ago.

It was easy to say that the distance that had happened between us was mutual.

But I knew better. I was the man. And at the end of the day, it was the man who was responsible for staying in touch.

I'd seen it happen the other way around to know that it never worked when girls made the move.

Maybe only on the rare occasion when the girl had tried to push a guy away and he changed his mind.

But in everyday run-of-the-mill relationships, the man was the one who had to do the pursuing.

It was a man's nature to be the hunter and as much as I wanted to be unique, I was just a man.

"I'm sorry," I said.

"Sorry for what?" she asked, turning those big green eyes on me.

Her eyes were moist and I hated that.

I hated that she tried to force a smile when I knew that I had somehow said something that had hurt her.

"I'm sorry I didn't call."

"What are you talking about?"

"Eight years ago. I didn't call."

"Neither of us called," she said.

I shook my head. "It was my place to call you."

"Kade," she said. "You can't put all the blame on yourself."

Even Madison didn't blame me.

I wasn't sure I deserved her.

No one I cared about had ever loved me like she did.

Sure there had been women. And a number of them had loved me.

But I hadn't loved them.

What Madison and I had was rare. A gift, my grandmother would have called it.

Well, I couldn't go back in time and do it all over again.

So all I could do was to take it forward from here and try to get it right this time around.

The music changed to an old song that I remembered from our college days.

"Remember this song?" I asked.

"Of course."

At least some of the sadness was fading from her eyes.

I stood up and held out a hand.

"Dance with me," I said.

"Kade," she said, shaking her head. "No one is dancing."

"So what?" I kept my hand out. "We're not other people."

"You're insane." She narrowed her eyes at me and for a moment I thought she was going to refuse me.

Then she put her hand in mine and allowed me to pull her to her feet.

I pulled her close, wrapping one arm around her waist and taking her hand with the other. She put an arm around my neck and together we swayed to the music.

After a moment, she relaxed her cheek against my chest and I tucked my chin over the top of her head.

The other people in the restaurant faded into the background along with the rest of the world.

Nothing mattered but us. In this moment.

Our hips automatically began to move together. I pressed my hand against the small of her back, bringing her even closer.

She felt so good. So soft and she smelled like sex on a stick.

My body perked up.

How was I supposed to protect her from myself when I couldn't keep my hands off her?

When I wanted to slide that red dress up over her hips and gobble her up.

59

MADISON

Kade Johnson had done it again.

He'd gotten me to do something I wouldn't normally do.

And now that I was here, pressed against him, the music of one of my favorite songs from college spilling over us, I didn't want the moment to ever end.

And besides that, I'd accused him of being the kind of person he'd never been.

Kade had always been an honorable and trustworthy man.

He'd never, not once when we'd been dating in college, given me a reason to doubt him.

The only thing I'd had to compete with was his love for aviation and I knew at the outset to not even worry about that.

Growing up with a pilot as a father, it was something I was so used to, I didn't even question it.

But this... being with Kade like this, I could never get used to.

And, I realized, I had missed him more than I'd allowed myself to admit.

I'd missed how his arms felt around mine. The way he

smelled. He must have showered during the time it took me to change into this dress and brush my hair.

He smelled clean, without a trace of engine fuel scent. Not that I would have minded.

The music changed to a faster beat and he shifted back, then lifted our hands and twirled me around.

He pulled me close again and whispered against my ear.

"You're beautiful tonight."

I closed my eyes and fisted my hands in his shirt.

After a quick hug, he led me back to my chair and held it as I sat down.

He sat across from me and, taking both my hands in his, he leaned forward and gazed into my eyes.

That was how Kade functioned. When he was flying, he was completely focused on that, but when he turned that attention onto me, it was so intense, it was almost overwhelming.

"Do you want a fresh drink?" he asked.

I shook my head. "I'm good."

Who needed alcohol when they had the intoxication of Kade's attention turned on them?

And we had three more days ahead of us.

I had a meeting with my department chair.

And I wanted to check out my apartment, but Kade could go there with me.

Other than that, I had no commitments.

Kade and I could do whatever we wanted to do.

And if he didn't stop looking at me like that, we might not ever leave the room.

Kade had done it again.

He'd gone and made me fall in love with him all over again.

60

KADE

*A*fter a candlelight dinner in the hotel restaurant, we got on the elevator and started back downstairs.

Our fingers were lightly linked.

We'd talked about everything and nothing over dinner. Light, easy conversation with a view overlooking the city of Denver with the moonlit mountains in the distance.

I was a little bit jealous that she was going to be living here, but mostly I was disturbed that she was going to be living here without me.

The more I thought about it, the less I liked it, but there was nothing I could do about it.

It was just one of those things.

And it was another reason I needed to keep our relationship easy.

We rode down the elevator in silence and got off on the thirty-first floor.

Reaching our doors, I stopped and, taking both her hands, turned her toward me.

As I swept a finger across her cheek, her eyes fluttered closed.

But instead of kissing her, I swept a strand of hair behind her ear and kissed her lightly on the forehead.

"Good night, my princess," I said.

Her eyes blinked open and she looked at me with a questioning expression.

I held out my hand for her key card, swiped it, and opened her door.

She stepped inside and turned back to see if I followed.

I didn't.

"I'll see you in the morning," I said.

"Of course," she said, with a little smile before she closed the door.

She didn't know what to make of me.

Hell, I didn't know what to make of me.

I was here in Denver, alone with the love of my life, and I wasn't going to touch her.

Going to my own adjacent door, I swiped my key card and let myself in.

I walked to the window and looked out at the moonlit night.

At the headlights traveling up and down the highways and byways.

Denver was much like Houston in that way. But instead of the nearby ocean, there were mountains.

Maybe we'd have time to ride up to Estes Park. Take a look around.

Walk the streets as tourists or take a mountain hike.

Whichever she liked.

If I had to guess, I'd say maybe a little of both.

There were so many things I needed to learn about her.

So many things I knew and so many things I didn't know.

In a way, though, that was what made our relationship all the better.

Our relationship.

I smiled at the direction of my thoughts.

If I was honest with myself, I knew I'd never let go of the possibility that Madison and I would someday end up together.

Even if we didn't get together in time to have kids and all that, I knew in my heart of hearts that someday, in the end, we'd be together.

Maybe even in a retirement community.

But my life would never feel complete until it had Madison in it.

Too bad it had taken me so long to realize this.

It had been a huge risk, letting her go and not following up with her all these years.

She could easily have gotten married.

Wouldn't have changed the way I felt about her.

Nothing ever would.

Well, maybe if she shaved her head and covered herself with tattoos.

Maybe.

All bets were off when it came to Madison.

Something like her getting married would have only delayed us getting together. It wouldn't have stopped it.

I didn't know how I was so sure of that.

I just was.

Walking back toward the bed, I stopped at the door separating our rooms and scowled at it.

It didn't need to be there.

I didn't like having that barrier there between us.

I quietly unlocked the door and opened it wide.

Now. There was only one door between us.

And Madison controlled that one.

Wasn't perfect, but it was better.

Now I could sleep.

61

———

MADISON

K ade had been a perfect gentleman.

I stepped out of my shoes and peeled myself out of my red dress.

I thought about taking a shower, but decided to wait until morning. I was exhausted.

After putting on my pajamas—long cotton pants and a button-down shirt. I hung my dress in the closet. I could wear it again if I needed to, but I didn't really want to. I only had one other cocktail dress and two nights. We will see.

Walking past the door that separated our rooms, I went to the window and studied the view.

I couldn't help comparing Denver to Houston.

I'd always wondered why anyone would settle anyplace other than Houston.

There really was no other city that felt like home. And I'd never seen myself living outside of Texas for any length of time.

For college, sure, but not as an adult.

But there were no teaching positions available in Houston. I'd taken the best one I could find.

It couldn't possibly be a good sign that I was already wondering just how long I'd stay here before moving back to Houston.

I hadn't really had those thoughts until Kade had shown up.

Him showing up had changed everything.

I never expected us to just pick up where we left off after all these years. I'd expected there to be awkwardness. But it wasn't there. Being with him was the most natural thing.

Familiar and new all at once.

More familiar than new. Or more new than familiar? I hadn't decided yet.

I just knew that I had to tread carefully.

Only three months and counting before we would once again be separated by distance.

I dropped into the chair in front of the window and leaned my elbows on the chair arm.

So many cars traveling here and there. I always wondered where people were going.

How could there possibly be that many places for people to travel to and from?

I'd be one of them soon.

Probably traveling to night classes. Meetings. Early morning classes. Who knew?

It would be an adventure.

I had to think of it like that in order to get through it.

A teaching position was something I'd always wanted. Just like Kade to come along and make me question everything.

I thought too much.

All that thinking had served me well through graduate school, but now, maybe, not so much.

I'd be better after I met with the department chair and found out which courses I'd be teaching in the fall.

Fall was my favorite time of year.

It signified new beginnings. New possibilities.

Right now my head was too full of Kade to think straight.

It would work itself out though.

We'd have a good weekend. We always enjoyed spending time together.

It was hard not to fall back into the physical relationship.

That was his fault, too. He couldn't kiss me like he had and not expect me to think about falling back into where we'd left off.

But if he could do it, I could do it, too.

I was nothing if not competitive.

I walked back toward the bed, past the close door that separated us, and pulled out my iPad.

I was much too keyed up to be sleeping anytime soon, so I opened up an app and picked up where I'd left off in a novel I was reading.

It was a bit strange to actually have time to read for pleasure.

Hadn't been much of that in graduate school.

I climbed into bed and stared at the offending door.

Wondered what Kade was doing.

I was so in trouble.

62

———

KADE

Since I'd gone to sleep early last night, I was up early this morning.

During a quick exploration of the hotel, I'd found a Starbucks, just one block over.

I bought two big lattes and a couple of breakfast sandwiches and carried them back up to the thirty-first floor.

Most of the business people were already up and out while the vacationers were still in their rooms, so I was the only one on the elevator.

I stood outside Madison's door and sent her a text.

ME: *You awake?*

I leaned against her door and waited. Obviously she wasn't up yet. And I didn't expect her to be.

But a couple of minutes later, she answered.

MADISON: *No.*

I laughed.

ME: *How about some coffee?*

MADISON: *Sounds good. Room service any good?*

Somehow she thought I'd know the answer to that. And I probably would before the trip was over.

ME: *Pretty good.*

I waited a beat.

ME: *Especially considering it's waiting at your door.*

The seconds ticked past into minutes as I waited patiently, leaning against the wall and sipping my own coffee.

She opened the door wearing black button-down pajamas. Her long hair was in disarray around her shoulders.

Her eyes looked sleepy, like she'd just woken up. Her features were soft and her face slightly flushed.

"Good morning," I said, holding out her cup of coffee.

"Thank you."

Our fingers brushed as she took the cup from my hand.

And just that little brush of contact set my nerves on fire.

"I brought food, too," I said, holding up the Starbucks bag.

She turned around and left the door open, assuming I'd follow.

Which I did, of course.

She sat at the little table in front of the window and sipped her coffee.

"Perfect," she said, closing her eyes.

I sat across from her.

"Do you want gouda and bacon?" I held up one wrapped sandwich. "Or gouda and bacon?"

"I'll take gouda and bacon," she said.

"Good choice." I handed one of the sandwiches to her.

She looked at me from beneath hooded eyes.

"You don't look like you got much sleep," I said.

"Gee, thanks," she said.

I just grinned. I knew I was right.

And I had a feeling I knew why.

As I bit into my sandwich, my gaze swept to the closed door between our rooms.

She looked at me questioningly.

I winked at her.

This was going to be a fun weekend.

63

MADISON — BEFORE

The words on the page of my English lit textbook blurred. I'd read the same paragraph three times.

Leaving my arm inside as a bookmark, I closed the book. I had so much to read before Tuesday, I wasn't sure it was physically possible to get it all done in the amount of time left.

Pausing the music blaring in my ears, I pulled the ear phones out of my ears and listened to the comforting roar of the plane's engine.

We flew through a patch of white puffy clouds and came out on the other side to a beautiful view of Toledo Bend Lake below us.

The sun glinted off the water, people looking like ants, skiing and having fun.

I wasn't much of a water person. Like my father, I preferred the sky.

The mountains were nice, too. Momma and Daddy had a house in the Colorado Rocky Mountains. The view from there was nice, too.

Daddy said everything was always about the view. Whether

from an airplane or the top of a mountain or a penthouse over Houston.

But none of these thoughts were keeping me from reading boring literature.

It was the guy named Kade Johnson sitting two seats behind me.

He sat quietly, not making a sound, but I could *feel* him sitting back there.

He said he had a family emergency to tend to in Houston.

I hadn't asked what, of course. That was none of my business. A man was allowed his privacy.

I was curious though. While he'd helped get through my math problems—after being the one to distract me—I hadn't known he was from the same city I was from.

What were the odds that he was from Houston, too?

Most of the Louisiana Tech students came from Ruston and the surrounding areas.

Unless they played sports or something like that. Me. I just wanted to go someplace different. To get away from my three sisters and my brother long enough to figure out who I really was and what I wanted out of life.

With so much family around, all of them with their own opinions, it was hard to have my own thoughts.

So here I was going to school in small-town USA. Most weekends I went home to help out at Skye Travels, my family's business.

Someone would come and pick me up. Either Daddy or one of his pilots. Today Samuel had picked me up. Samuel was my step-sister's husband.

He was a good pilot. All of Daddy's pilots were good. He'd only ever lost one plane over the years and even then, no one had been hurt.

He had an excellent track record.

I was careful about telling people who I was. Especially

other pilots. Once they found out I was the boss's daughter…
well… there was one guy who had tried to suck up to me to get
a job with Daddy.

It hadn't worked.

Kade had found out who I was by accident.

And I'd been the one who'd invited him along.

He'd seemed so… lost. Coming to the airport, knowing he
was probably going to have to drive all the way to Houston
when he didn't really have the time.

With a sigh, I closed my book and set it aside.

Then I unhooked my seat belt and stood up.

I went to sit next to Kade. He wiped at his eyes before he
turned to look at me.

"Hi," I said.

I couldn't let him just sit here without making sure he was
okay.

"Hi," he said.

His eyes were red. Whatever family emergency he had, it
must be serious.

"Is there anything I can do?" I asked.

"I don't think there's much more you could do," he said.
"You've already let me stowaway."

"Don't worry," I said. "You're logged and accounted for. One
of three souls on board."

"Your Daddy is Noah Worthington," he said.

"What gave me away?" I asked, knowing full well that it
wasn't every college student who flew on a private jet with *Skye
Travels* emblazoned across the side of the plane.

He held up his cell. "I looked you up."

"Oh," I said. "Well, you could have just asked."

He ran a hand through his hair. "It didn't seem polite."

I didn't say anything. I was trying to figure out how asking
wasn't polite, but looking me up on the Internet was.

I was a first year psychology student and I didn't even

pretend to know how to figure people out yet. I had years of training ahead of me.

"When you land," I said. "where are you headed?"

He looked back to the window again, dropping his head.

"You don't have to tell me," I said. "I respect privacy."

"I'm sorry I looked you up," he said, turning back to meet my gaze. "It was wrong."

His eyes were as blue as the sky outside the window.

"I don't blame you," I said. "I'm sure I would have done the same."

"You didn't look me up," he said, a little smile playing about his lips.

"That would be a little bit harder to do," I said.

"Yeah," he said. "My family isn't all over the Internet." He looked away again.

I might not be a trained psychologist yet, but I would have bet money that someone in his family was sick. Or hurt.

"I'll be back in a few minutes," I said.

He glanced back and nodded.

He might not know it, but there might be a way that I could help him after all.

64

MADISON

e took a taxi over to the university to meet my department chair.

I could hardly leave Kade at the hotel. Besides, it was nice to have the company.

The traffic was awful. Worse than Houston on any day.

But my apartment was close to the university, so I should be able to manage it.

Kade was in an exceptionally good mood today.

He'd made himself scarce while I showered and got ready for my meeting.

"I found a couple of good places where we can have lunch," he said.

"We just had breakfast," I said, laughing at him.

He shrugged. "I didn't have much else to do. Besides, you need to know some good places to eat before you move here."

Kade's logic was sometimes interesting and it always made sense in some way or another.

"And which places to avoid, I guess," I said.

I didn't like talking about me moving here.

Kade kept bringing it up, though. It was like he couldn't stop himself.

Personally, I was dealing with it by trying not to think about it.

A little hard to do considering that we were on our way to meet with my department chair to go over my courses for the fall. The fall semester that was approaching much too quickly.

Although he kept bringing it up, it didn't seem to bother him.

"Hey," he said. "A penny for your thoughts."

I laughed. "A penny, huh? I'm not sure how much that'll get you these days."

He reached over and took my hand.

"It's ok," he said. "I understand."

I looked at him out of the corner of my eyes.

He probably really did understand. Maybe more than he should.

The taxi dropped us off at the psychology building.

"I can just take a walk," Kade said.

And that was what he probably should have done. But I wanted him to come with me.

"Want to come?" I asked. "See where I'm going to work?"

"Sure," he said.

Together we went inside the building.

It was a fairly new building, but it smelled like all the other academic buildings I'd been in. A mixture of clean and old. Clean from the cleanser and old from papers and computers and white board markers.

I felt a mixture of excitement and nervousness as we walked down the hallway toward the main office.

"His name is Dr. Bertrand," I said. "And his assistant's name is Mary."

Mary looked up and smiled as we stepped inside.

"Dr. Worthington," she said. "It's good to see you again."

"You, too, Mary." Mary was efficient and friendly. A combination not always seen in university offices.

"I'll let Dr. Bertrand know you're here."

She picked up the phone. "Dr. Worthington and her husband are here," she said.

I started to say something. To clarify that Kade wasn't my husband, but Kade nudged me in the elbow.

I looked at him out of the corner of my eyes. He shook his head just enough to make sure I didn't say anything to correct her.

"You can go right on in," Mary said.

We stepped into what looked like a quintessential professor's office. It didn't look like a department chair's office at all.

Dr. Bertrand was a working department chair. He even continued to teach classes, even though he didn't want to.

He'd told me during the interview that his first love was teaching. He was just filling in until they found someone else. So far, he'd been filling in for five years.

He pulled a stack of new textbooks from one of the chairs and moved them to the floor.

"Sorry for the mess," he said. "I was going through some textbooks for a new industrial organizational elective."

"That's always fun," I said.

He laughed. "Don't say that too much. I might just put you to work."

He went back around and sat at his desk, piled high with stacks of papers.

Kade and I sat in the chairs in front of his desk.

"Good to see you again," he said. "I always get a little nervous when people move across the country. Wondering if they're really going to show up in the Fall. But I feel better now that you've brought your husband."

He leaned across the desk to shake Kade's hand.

"What do you do?" Dr. Bertrand asked him.

"I'm a pilot."

"Is that so?" Dr. Bertrand's face lit up. "I've been taking a few lessons myself." He glanced at me. "Just a little hobby. Something I've always wanted to do."

"Good for you," Kade said. "There's nothing like it."

"I have to agree." He looked over at me. "Of course, teaching is my first love."

"It's good to have something different to do now and again," Kade said.

"We'll talk later," Dr. Bertrand said.

I could tell he really wanted to talk to Kade now about flying, but he shifted back to me, the task at hand.

"I made a list," he said. "and left you some options. Feel free to ask for something, but I thought I'd narrow it down for you. Make your life a little easier."

He handed me folder with a list of textbooks. "There's a schedule in there, too. Again, more options. Take a look and email me which ones you want."

"That's very generous and accommodating," I said.

"You're the first new faculty member we've had in three years. Everyone's very excited to have you join us."

He'd told me that last time. And I still wasn't sure if it was a good thing or a bad thing.

It was always hard to know how an established group would react to having someone new coming in. Especially a young profession, just out of school.

"Everything else, we can take care of when you get here in August." He looked from me to Kade. "You said you have a place to live already?"

"That's all taken care of," I said. "No problem."

And thirty minutes later, we were headed out the door, Kade's arms loaded down with textbooks.

I'm not sure what I'd expected, but this was not it. It seemed like a long way to come to get paperwork that could have been emails and textbooks that could have been mailed.

But that's how academia worked.

And I needed to talk to Kade.

He'd actually posed as my husband.

And I wasn't sure how I felt about that.

65

MADISON

"What do you think?" I asked as we walked out of Dr. Bertrand's office.

"I've always found college professors to be a bit… different," Kade said.

Coming out of Dr. Bertrand's office, we held the rest of that conversation until later.

"You should walk around the campus a bit," Mary said. "I can hold onto this stack of books until later." She lowered her voice. "I can mail these to you if you like. I know how hard it is to carry a bunch of heavy books on a plane."

I smiled and didn't say a word about how flying was no problem at all for me. I could take whatever I wanted on the plane.

"Actually, that would be wonderful," I said.

Mary seem pleased to help out. "Just write your address on here and I'll have them overnighted. They'll be at your house by early next week."

"You're very kind," I said.

Kade and I left the building and headed toward a little

restaurant within walking distance that Mary assured us was the best around.

"What did you mean," I asked. "About professors being different?"

He shrugged "They seem a tad bit disconnected from the rest of the world at times, but at the core, they're just like every other business."

"I see. So what was that about?" I asked. "Mr. Dr. Worthington?"

"If there's one thing I've learned over the years," he said. "Bosses like people in stable relationships. Changes their whole perception." He looked at her. "But then, I'm sure you already knew that."

"Of course," I said. "But I never told him I was married."

"Then he got a nice surprise."

I wasn't completely sold on the idea.

"It might be hard to explain why you don't come with me."

He grinned. "You'll figure something out."

"Gee, thanks." I looked at him sideways.

He dipped his head. "Always a pleasure."

"I'm glad you find humor in my discomfort."

He took my hand. "You? Discomfort? I find that to be highly unlikely."

I stopped and searched his gaze. "Really? You don't think I have discomfort?"

"I'm sure you do." He looked away and ran a hand through his hair. "But honestly, you're the most well-adjusted person I know. You always seem to know how to make your way through any situation."

"Maybe," I said. *Except for you. I don't know how to get myself past you.*

"I think this is it," he said.

I stopped. "I didn't realize it was a pizzeria."

He studied the menu posted on the wall next to the door. "Looks like they have sandwiches, too."

I looked at Kade Johnson and just smiled to myself.

It was odd having someone who knew me so well to know that I loved pizza, but if a pizza place had sandwiches, I loved that even more.

It was such a little thing to remember, yet it was one of those details that most people wouldn't bother remembering.

"Guess we should go inside, then," I said.

Kade ordered a small pizza and I ordered a cheese sandwich with black olives and tomatoes.

It wasn't very crowded. With it being summer and all, there weren't very many students about. I imagined that it would be quite different once the Fall semester started up.

We found a table off by itself and waited for our food to come out.

"It seems nice here," Kade said. "The university has a good atmosphere."

"Agreed," I said, toying with the straw in my soda.

I rarely drank soda, but the occasion seemed to call for it.

I was trying to be celebratory. To feel excited about being here. My first full-time teaching position was supposed to be exciting. An end goal for me.

But I couldn't stop thinking about how now that I'd reconnected with Kade, we were about to be separated again.

Granted, things were different now.

He flew for my father, so he could visit whenever he wanted to.

But would he want to? I knew firsthand how life got busy. And the day-to-day things took precedence. And he probably didn't even realize it, but taking on the care of his mother was going to consume more and more of his life.

He wasn't going to have time for a long-distance relationship.

And I wasn't sure I was going to either.

I was going to not only be teaching classes, but prep time, committee meetings, department meetings. I needed to do some research. To keep up with the whole "publish or perish mentality."

Anybody who thought being a college professor was a walk in the park, had a lot to learn. And I'd been no different when I was a bright-eyed and bushy tailed young college student thinking about how I wanted my life to go.

I had a vision of what being a professor was like.

Unlike Kade, I didn't realize how just how much of a business it really was.

But it was what I'd set out to accomplish. I had no choice but to go through with it.

Everyone who knew me, knew that I was going to be a professor someday and someday was here.

"Why the long face?" Kade asked.

"I was just thinking." I forced a smile on my face.

"Thinking about what?"

The server brought out our pizza and sandwiches.

"This looks great," I said, taking a bite out of my sandwich. "It is great."

I put half my sandwich on Kade's plate.

"Hey," he said. "I can't eat my food and your food."

I shrugged. "Okay." I grabbed a slice of his pizza, "I'll try yours, too."

"Any good?" he asked.

"Wonderful," I said. "Are you going to eat?"

66

———

KADE

I'd somehow forgotten just how much fun Madison could be.

Sure I remembered that we always had fun when we were together, but I'd forgotten the level of day-to-day fun.

No one else I'd ever dated had ever amused me like she did.

She was thin as a rail and in perfect shape, yet she'd managed to mix up our plates and try both her sandwich and my pizza before I even got around to taking a bit of anything.

And she did it with such ease and charm that it took me a minute to realize that what she'd really done was to avoid answering my question about what was bothering her.

I knew sad Madison when I saw her and for just a minute, she'd been sad Madison.

It was probably something I'd done or said.

It usually was.

If I had to guess, I'd say it was talking about her life here.

I'd been doing that a lot. And on purpose.

But I wanted her to know that I was okay with it.

That she should be okay with it.

Hell, even when we were young college students, she'd known what she wanted to be when she grew up.

And this was it.

I was determined to be encouraging. Even if it killed me. And it just might.

The thought of her living here. Being here without me was depressing as hell.

I didn't like it one little bit.

She was setting out on an adventure of a lifetime.

Granted, it was going to be hard work, but it was going to be an adventure, too.

And I certainly didn't want to rain on that parade.

Maybe that was why I'd never called her back all those years ago.

Maybe I'd been unconsciously letting her find her own wings. Setting her free so she could fly on her own without me holding her back.

Not that I would have on purpose. But I was busy finding my wings. Literally. And I guess I knew that we'd influence each other. Maybe too much. Maybe not.

But that was then. And this was now.

I hoped she was going to be good with a long-distance relationship because that was what I had in mind for us.

We'd each found our own way in the world. And now that the universe had so kindly brought us back together, I didn't plan on squandering it.

I just had to get her on board.

Without pushing her.

Pushing Madison Worthington never got anyone anywhere except going backwards.

"Maybe I should go order something for myself," I said.

She looked at me blankly, then smiled and put a slice of pizza on my plate next to her sandwich.

"It's really good," she said. "You should try it."

Amused, I tried the pizza and her sandwich.

"I'm not sure which is better," I said.

"Me either."

Then in the typical Madison fashion that I remembered, she stopped after eating only one slice of pizza and half of her half of the sandwich.

"Mary was right," she said. "This was a good choice."

Determined not to let worrying about the future take away from our time together, I pulled out my phone. Checked something.

"I have an idea," I said.

MADISON

"I know why you picked this," I said, leaning against the putter and watching as Kade hit his golf ball through a tunnel, bringing it out on the other side in just the right place to set him up for his next shot.

"Why is that?" he asked, looking up at me innocently.

It was at least ten degrees cooler here in Estes Park than it was down in Denver.

There was a group of preteens playing ahead of us, laughing and squealing as they played.

And behind us was a family of four. A mother, father, and two children, probably somewhere around eight and ten years old. They were quieter, but still seemed to be having a good time.

I tried not to think too hard about the fact that the parents were about the same age as Kade and I were. Maybe even a bit younger.

They were about where Kade and I would have been if we'd started a family right after college.

"Because you're good at it."

"I don't think anybody's really good at mini-golf," he said.

"Right," I said sarcastically as my ball hit the edge of the tunnel and came right back toward me.

"But," he said. "Some people are especially *not* good at it."

I pointed my putter at him. "It's not nice to gloat."

He easily putted his ball into the hole. "Who's gloating?" he asked.

I rolled my eyes. "Any sane person."

He laughed and stuffed the score card into his pocket. "We're not keeping score anyway."

"That's not fair. We have to keep score."

I hit my ball again and this time it went through the tunnel and went downhill on the other side.

"Besides, once I start winning, you'll want to know."

He leaned against his putter and looked at me sideways. "Did anyone ever tell you that you have messed up logic?"

I walked to the other side of the set and stood poised to hit my ball uphill.

"All the time," I said, watching my ball miss the hole and come right back down the hill. "Like I said, you only picked this game because you're good at it."

"Okay," he said. "Then you get to pick our next activity."

We waited for the kids in front of us to move on.

"So I get to pick something?" I said.

He grinned at me. "Bring it on," he said.

"Ah. Be careful when you make a challenge like that."

"I'm pretty good at most things you might want to do," he said.

I laughed. "Yes, you are." And I knew by the way he was looking at me that he wasn't talking about mini-golf or fly fishing. Which, by the way, I'd never even tried and hoped he didn't decide we needed to try.

Standing in an ice cold river trying to lure a fish onto a bait did not sound like a good way to spend an afternoon.

While he made his next shot, badly I might add, I checked something on my phone.

"Okay," I said. "Prepare for vindication."

I lined up my ball and aimed. It somehow bounced off the little windmill and went down the wrong direction.

He looked at me. "I don't feel vindicated."

I bit my lip to keep from laughing. "Just wait," I said. "You can't be good at *everything*."

And even though I told him that, I didn't believe it.

Kade Johnson was good at everything.

I had one secret skill up my sleeve, though, that just might turn the tables in my favor.

68

KADE

After sorely kicking Madison's butt at minigolf, I followed her directions back downtown to the heart of Estes Park.

Tourists walked up and down the street and we had to park a ways away from the address she was looking for.

She still hadn't told me where exactly we were going or what we were going to do.

I didn't mind. I was with her and I didn't care what we did.

I took her hand as we walked along the street lined with tourist shops.

"Hey," I said, tugged her to a stop. "I need to go in here."

We stepped inside what could only be called a tourist trap. It had a little bit of everything. T-shirts. Pine-scented incense. Jewelry. Glass-blown hummingbirds, Chocolate-covered apples.

Madison stopped at the jewelry counter while I went to the back where the children's t-shirts were. It didn't take but a minute to pick out the perfect shirt for my niece.

Anything pink and she would love it.

I paid at the back counter and, taking my bag with me, went

back to the front where Madison was engaged in a lively conversation with the sales clerk about the different stones in the showcase jewelry.

It was funny watching the girl who could walk into Tiffany's and buy anything she wanted without even having to consider the price tag looking at what looked to me like handmade American Indian jewelry.

"See something you like?" I asked, as the sales clerk went to ring up another customer.

"See that pink stone?" she asked, pointing to a collection of astorite gems. "Pretty huh?"

"I think you have something in common with my niece."

"Yeah?" she asked. "What's that?"

"An affinity for anything pink."

The girl behind the counter, most likely a college student working a summer job, didn't seem to care if Madison bought anything or not.

"Let me know if you want to try anything on," she said.

"The bracelet," Madison said.

The girl unlocked the counter and handed the bracelet over to Madison.

"What do you think?" she asked after she slid it onto her wrist.

"I think pink is a good color for you," I said. It was a pretty color and a pretty bracelet, but anything would have looked good on Madison.

"I'll take it," she said, pulling out her credit card.

While the girl finalized the sale, Madison turned her attention on me.

"What did you get?" she asked, eying my bag.

"Just a t-shirt for my niece," I said. "Pink."

"Can I see?"

"Of course." I pulled out the little t-shirt and held it up for her inspection.

"How cute," she said. "I love it. I might come back and get one for myself."

"We have adult sizes, too," the college girl said, handing me my own bag.

Madison thanked her and we walked out. The sidewalk was more crowded than it had been a few minutes ago.

It was Friday night in Estes Park.

"Are we there yet?" I asked.

Madison held her bracelet up to the sunlight, then after looking at me with a smile, looked down at the GPS I didn't know she was using.

A girl after my own heart.

She pointed to the street corner.

"It's right there," she said.

69

MADISON

Graduate school had been a lot different than undergrad.

In undergrad, we went to our classes, then went home and studied. Some people went out and partied and some, like me, worked in their free time.

I studied all week, then flew to Houston to work the weekends. A bit unconventional only in that my commute involved flying instead of driving.

After Kade and I started to date, spending time with him had been woven into my life and became a part of it.

A lot of it involved more flying.

I'd logged a lot of flying miles. Sometimes I thought it would have been interesting to have kept up with it, like pilots kept up with their flight times, but geez, I would have had to start keeping logs before I could manipulate a pencil.

Then Kade had gone in one direction and I'd gone in another. Grad school.

Grad school was much, much more social.

There were six of us in the class. And I just so happened to have been the only girl.

Three of us became fast friends.

One of those friends, a guy named Scott was local and his dad owned a pool hall.

So we spent a lot of time studying together. But we also spent a lot of time blowing off steam in Scott's pool hall. Though it was his dad's at the time, it belonged to Scott now. He'd finished his coursework, but instead of going on internship, he'd cashed in his studies to run the family business after his father passed a couple of years ago.

At any rate, I'd learned quite a bit from Scott.

It wasn't the least bit crowded in this particular bar with a pool table in downtown Estes Park. There was music playing in the background and a few clumps of people sitting here and there.

"You can't beat me at drinking," Kade said.

I laughed. "Not my plan. But a beer would be nice."

Kade looked at me as though I'd suddenly sprouted another head.

"Are you serious?" he asked.

"Why wouldn't I be?" I took a seat at one of the barstools.

"Then that's what I'll buy you," he said.

"Make it a light beer," I said as he walked toward the bar.

He waved a hand behind him and I laughed.

There was one pool table. Currently unoccupied.

A couple of minutes later, Kade came back with two bottles of beer.

"Thank you," I said, holding up my beer. "To vindication."

He laughed.

"You have me in suspense, my dear," he said.

After a quick sip, I hopped off the bar stool and started toward the pool table.

"Come on," I said. "Double or nothing."

"Pool?" he asked as I chose a pool cue.

I grinned over my shoulder.

He put his hands on his hips and studied me.

"Dr. Madison Worthington. Pool and beer. I never would have guessed. Not in a hundred years."

"Problem?"

"No. But please don't tell me you have a tattoo."

"Nope. No tattoo. So we're all set."

"Except for one thing." He chose a pool cue of his own as I racked up the balls.

"What's that?" I asked, lining the balls up just right.

"I don't think double or nothing is pool terminology."

70

KADE

$\mathcal{I}$f someone—anyone—had walked up to me eight years and told me that I'd find Madison in a pool hall playing pool and drinking beer, I would have laughed in their face.

But there she was. Wearing a black business skirt and jacket with a silky green camisole thing beneath the jacket. High heels. Her hair loose around her shoulders. A mysterious smile on her face.

And holding a pool cue.

I'd never seen anything so damn sexy in my entire life.

Maybe we could forget the pool game and go find a bathroom. I could hike up that dress and...

"You want to break?" she asked.

"Sure," I said, reeling my thoughts back to the problem at hand.

The problem being that I had a sneaky feeling that Madison was about to kick my ass in pool.

Well, I'd asked for it.

I was really good at minigolf. And not so bad at regular golf either.

And I had been the one to challenge her to find something she could beat me at.

From the look on her face, that thing must be pool.

I'd played a little. But pool wasn't the usual hangout for pilots. Not like the golf course.

Before breaking the balls, I walked to stand in front of her.

"A kiss for luck?" I asked.

A flash of surprise crossed her features.

She blinked, her lashes smudging the pale skin beneath her eyes.

"Luck for you or luck for me?" she asked softly, but her lips softened and her chin tilted up.

I put a finger beneath her chin and tilted her face up to mine.

"Seems to me like we would both win." I pressed my lips against hers. "Don't you think?'"

"Yes," she said on a breath. "I think so."

I grinned and turned to the pool table. With one hit, the balls went everywhere. I got lucky. One solid went in. Then a striped ball went in.

"I'll take solids," I said.

If I'd been smart, I would have taken stripes. There wasn't a solid ball on the table that I could get in a pocket.

But I wasn't there for the game.

I wanted Madison to win.

When it was her turn, she put in two striped balls in a row. Then a third.

Okay, I had to admit, she was good.

She missed the next shot.

"You're good," I said.

"Of course, I am," she said.

I lined up my next shot. "You know," I said. "I never would have taken you for a pool shark."

She grinned. "Learned a lot in graduate school."

And I missed a perfectly easy shot.

Thinking about her and all the possible things she could have learned in graduate school threw me off my shot.

"You did that on purpose," I said.

"What?" she asked, innocently and put three more balls in the pockets.

"Now I know what the Ph.D. behind your name really stands for."

"Yeah? What's that?"

I walked over and kissed her again.

This could become a habit in just about no time.

"Pool Hall Diva."

She grabbed my shirt and pulled me close.

And the kiss that followed was just about enough to send me over the edge.

71

MADISON

e'd only had one beer each, but it was late by the time we moved aside so another group could use the pool table.

"It's too late to drive back," Kade said.

"I can drive," I said.

He shook his head. "It's not the beer. It's the mountains. It's late and neither one of us has enough experience on these roads to be driving at night. While we're tired."

"You're probably right."

But I was wishing I'd worn jeans and a t-shirt today.

The thought of having to put this same skirt back on in the morning wasn't my idea of fun.

"If we can find rooms," I added.

Kade held up his phone. "Reservation already made and secured."

"Where are we staying?" I asked. I hadn't even seen him doing that. But he was right. It was too late to be driving.

"The Stanley Hotel."

"Great," I said, sitting back.

"What's wrong with it?"

I cut my eyes at him. "They say it's haunted."

"Aw," he said. "*They* say a lot of things. Doesn't mean they're true."

I shrugged. "It should be okay."

"Don't worry," he said. "I'll keep you safe."

"How—?"

I didn't get to ask him how he was going to keep me safe when he was in another room.

"Madison? Is that you?"

I looked up to see a dear old friend standing in front of me.

"Andrew," I said, standing up to give him a hug. "How are you?"

"I'm good," he said.

I stepped back toward Kade.

"This is Kade," I said.

"Actually," Andrew said. "Kade and I go way back."

The two men shook hands.

"You know each other?"

"It's a small world," Kade said. "Have a seat, Andrew. I'll buy you a beer."

Andrew held up a hand. "I don't want to intrude."

Kade looked at me.

I shrugged.

"It's no intrusion," Kade said.

Kade left me there with Andrew while he went to get our drinks.

"How are you?" he asked.

Andrew was a few years younger than my father. He'd actually spent some time at our home before I left for college. I hadn't heard Daddy mention him lately, so I didn't know if they'd stayed in touch.

"I'm good," I said. "I'm going to be living in Denver starting this fall. I got a teaching job at the university."

"Really? Your dad didn't say anything about that to me."

"You still talk?"

"Sometimes."

Kade came back and passed the bottles out. Then he sat and put a hand possessively on the back of my chair.

I would have to think about that later.

"To old friends." Andrew lifted his bottle, then he looked at me. "I'm really surprised he didn't tell me."

I glanced at Kade. "I haven't known that long," I said.

Andrew scratched his chin. "I thought he'd want to keep all of his kids close to home, you know?"

An alarm went off in my gut. But I put it aside. Andrew was just making conversation.

"He's used to us all doing our own thing."

Andrew nodded. "I know. But in a time like this, it just seems like it'd be important." He tipped back his bottle and seemed completely unaware that he'd just tipped my world sideways.

My hand found Kade's and I held onto it.

"A time like what?" I asked.

Andrew looked at me then. "Oh crap. You don't know."

72

———

KADE

*M*adison and I stood outside the pool hall.

After listening to Andrew spill just enough of her father's secret, she'd dashed outside to get some air. To get away from Andrew, no doubt.

"I have to call him," she said, pulling out her phone.

"Madison," I said, putting a hand over hers to stop her. "It's late."

"I don't care," she said.

"You can talk to him tomorrow," I said. "Your father needs his rest."

That seemed to stop her from dialing Noah's cell phone at what would be nearly Midnight his time.

She paced to the street corner and back.

"Why didn't he tell me?"

I ran a hand through my hair. Tried to imagine why a man might not tell his daughter that he might have prostate cancer.

"Maybe he didn't want to worry you."

She stood right in front of me, her eyes welling with tears.

"I get that," she said. "I do." Her chin trembled. "But he told…" she pointed vaguely toward the pool hall. "That man."

I pulled her toward me and she fell against me like a rag doll.

I wrapped my arms around her and she sobbed against my shoulder.

She had a valid question.

And she'd had a valid concern yesterday when her father hadn't shown up to go with her on this trip.

I'd convinced her that she should come.

I'd been selfish.

It was my fault.

"You know what?" I said softly. "That old man may not even know what he's talking about. You know as well as anyone how easily things get twisted around.

She nodded. But the tears didn't stop.

I just held her and gently rubbed her back.

A couple of people left the pool hall and looked at us questioningly.

"Let's get out of here," I said. I couldn't bear the thought of anyone seeing Madison like this.

She deserved her privacy.

She nodded and allowed me to lead her to the curb where an Uber waited. I'd called them a few minutes ago.

We slid inside the back seat of an old beat up car—there weren't a lot of options, especially this late at night.

I held her all the way to the Stanley Hotel and by the time we got there, the worst of her tears had stopped.

I kissed the top of her head. "We're here, my love."

We made our way up the stairs, across the wide porch, and went inside.

Any other time, we both would have taken the time to admire the grand old hotel.

But right now, she just needed to get a bed and sleep.

"Wait here," I said, nudging her into a chair. "I'll check us in."

I came back a moment later with a box of tissues. She tried valiantly to smile at me as she took the box. "Thank you."

"I'll be right back," I said, kissing her softly on the lips.

At the front desk, the clerk confirmed what they'd told me over the phone.

They only had one room available.

73

MADISON

I reached deep and pulled out the necessary tools to keep myself from crumbling.

The old saying *Physician heal thyself* kept rumbling through my head.

I needed to help myself through this. No one else could.

At least not right now.

My thoughts raced. I could call Emily. Or any one of my sisters. Though I knew that this was not the right time to call anyone.

I didn't know anything for certain.

Kade was right. Andrew may not have all the information.

It wasn't like they talked every day.

And Momma would make sure Daddy told us when it was the right time.

When he had enough information.

I took a deep shuddering breath.

That was probably it.

Momma had said Daddy was having some tests run.

So they didn't really know anything yet.

Just because Andrew said that something might be going on, didn't mean that it was necessarily true.

At any rate, I would be flying home first thing in the morning.

It took everything I had to keep from asking Kade to fly me home tonight.

But we'd been drinking.

And there was no way he would risk either his license or our lives by getting into a cockpit in this condition. I'd be doing good to get him to fly us in the morning.

Twelve hours bottle to throttle.

And Daddy insisted on twenty-four hours.

I blew out a breath.

That meant we'd have to get someone else to fly us.

I'd call in the morning and get someone here to pick me up.

Kade could stay with the plane and take it home on Sunday.

Concentrating on details helped to calm me enough to pull myself together.

I'd fallen apart in front of Kade. I wouldn't let that happen again. At least not if I could help it.

He had such a strong shoulder.

And instead of judging, he seemed to truly understand.

I lifted my chin when I saw him walking back toward me.

He held out a hand and pulled me to my feet.

"You okay?" he asked.

I nodded, still not trusting myself to speak, despite my resolve at staying strong.

"We're on the second floor," he said. "We can go up these stairs."

I followed him, feeling completely drained and worn out.

When we got to our room, he opened the door, then followed me inside.

I was too drained to worry about it, much less even ask him about it.

I went to the bed and fell into it.

Kade chuckled and sat down next to me.

He pulled off my shoes and tucked me under the covers.

I closed my eyes before I even knew whether he stayed or left.

Right now it didn't matter.

I would sleep. And deal with everything tomorrow.

74

KADE

After tucking Madison into bed, I went into the bathroom and stared at myself in the mirror.

Lucky for me, I carried an extra t-shirt and pajama bottoms in my leather computer bag. Since my iPad was small, I had plenty of room in there. Madison wasn't so fortunate. She had to sleep in her clothes.

I had to get her home.

There was absolutely no way she was going to be able to stand being here when there was even a remote possibility that her father might be dealing with a life threatening illness.

Twenty-four hours bottle to throttle.

I would have to find a way to get her home that did not involve me flying.

Damn it.

I knew better than to have a drink when I was with Madison.

I was supposed to be the one taking care of her.

Yet, here I was. I was going to have to call her brother tomorrow and have someone else, another pilot, come and pick her up while I waited for the alcohol to leave my system.

I'd wanted to impress Madison. To take care of her.

But I'd failed miserably.

She needed me and I couldn't help her.

Turning the faucet handle, I splashed water across my face and dried it with a clean towel.

I'd go downtown in the morning. Get coffee. And buy Madison a t-shirt so she would at least have something comfortable and fresh to wear on the flight home tomorrow.

In the meantime, we had no choice but to sleep in our clothes.

I tiptoed back into the bedroom, so as not to wake Madison and, sitting on the couch, removed my shoes. The only light came from the window where the shades were up.

Moonlight spilled into the room, breaking the darkness.

I found an extra blanket in the little closet and went over to the bed to steal one of her extra pillows.

"Are you coming to bed?" Madison asked.

I froze. Stolen pillow in hand.

Maybe she was dreaming.

I wasn't sure whether I should answer or not.

I'm just going to sleep on the couch," I said, erring on the side of caution that she might really be awake.

"Nonsense." She patted the empty side of the bed. "This is a huge bed. There's plenty of room for both of us."

The thought of getting Madison into bed had been at the forefront of my mind since I'd stepped off that elevator the first day at Skye Travels.

But not now. She was distraught about her father.

And I needed to make sure I gave her enough space.

Clutching the pillow to me, I took a step away from the bed.

"I'd like the company," she said softly.

"Right." Of course she would.

Madison was an extravert. She needed human contact.

Unlike me. I could spend hours alone in the cockpit of an

airplane with nothing other than my thoughts to occupy myself.

I found the time to be relaxing and blissful.

But not Madison.

She needed someone to talk to. Or at least to be with.

"All right." I relented. But I promised myself that it went against my better judgement.

She was right though. The bed was huge and I was pretty sure we wouldn't even know the other was there.

I replaced the pillow and climbed into my side of the bed.

Careful to stay as close to the edge as I could, I closed my eyes and pretended to sleep.

I would have gotten a whole lot better sleep on the couch.

But what did it matter? I wasn't flying tomorrow anyway.

75

MADISON – BEFORE

Tonight was the night.

I wore what my sister would call a slinky red dress.

It hugged my curves like a glove and dipped down just enough to remind anyone who bothered to look—and who could resist looking at this gorgeous red dress—that I had perfectly formed boobs beneath this dress. According to my psychology professor, men were drawn to bright colors. They couldn't help it.

Kade had a tendency to focus on everything airplanes. But this red dress might just be enough to snag his attention.

Beside, I'd gotten to know him well enough to know that all I had to do was to get his attention and his focus would be completely on me.

Momma said Daddy was the same way when they'd dated.

He'd gotten better, though. Momma had been training him for years.

He would never ever live down the time he disappeared on her for fifteen years.

It had definitely put them late at starting a family. But once they'd started, they'd done it up right.

Five children. All in the span of ten years.

Momma was nothing if not a trooper. And she'd continued to grow her career as a psychologist at the same time.

I was in awe of her.

So tonight I wore the red dress so that I could have Kade's full attention.

He'd mostly seen me only in blue jeans and t-shirts.

Except for the few times he'd traveled on Skye Travels planes. On those flights, I always wore business attire since I was, after all, going straight to work.

A unique commute, for sure.

But one that worked for me and my family. When a girl's father owned an empire of airplanes, anything was possible.

I was the oldest and I'd spent the most time at Skye Travels learning everything.

Everything except flying.

I left that to my little sister.

I much preferred to analyze people as they came and went through the airport.

Kade and I were meeting in an upscale bar in the River Oaks area of Houston. Since we were both here in Houston, it seemed like a good time for us to step out of character. Just a little.

Stepping into the bar, I immediately spotted Kade.

It was hard to miss the most handsome man in the room. And sometimes it still felt surreal that he was with me.

He saw me, too, and stood up.

The expression on his face told me I'd gotten the reaction I'd hoped for.

He reached my side in seconds and, taking both my hands in his, kissed me on the cheek.

"You look beautiful," he whispered to me, over the loud music playing in the background.

The feel of his breath against my ear sent all sorts of tremors through me.

Kade was an enigma I had yet to figure out.

He was persistent in pursuing me, yet he kept me at a safe distance.

Nothing more than kissing. Not that I was complaining.

The boy could kiss.

In fact, we'd sometimes spend hours doing nothing but kissing.

And I wouldn't trade that for anything.

But something seemed to be missing from our relationship.

And I wanted to subtly let him know that being a perfect gentleman all the time wasn't completely necessary.

It was endearing, but I wanted to up our level of commitment.

We were spending a lot of time together and maybe this was my way of testing our future.

To get a feel for where we were going.

Besides, I wanted to see him in my world for a change.

"What would you like to drink?" he asked.

"A martini. Dry. Extra olives."

He smiled and repeated my order to the formally dressed bartender. Then ordered one of the same for himself.

"What are we celebrating?" he asked, sliding onto a barstool.

He held the barstool next to it as I sat down.

"Who says we have to be celebrating?"

"Let's see…" he said with one finger on his cheek. "We've been dating… how long?"

I smiled. "Long enough."

"And this is the first time we've done…" he waved a hand around the bar. "this."

The bartender carefully set a martini in front of me and one in front of Kade.

I took a sip and looked into his beautiful blue eyes.

"Well, Ruston does not exactly have that many places like this."

He laughed. "Yeah. There is that little bar downtown."

"They do have really good shrimp po'boys." I bit an olive off my toothpick and grinned at him."

"So what's good here?"

I just raised an eyebrow. He assumed I'd been here before. He was right. I had been here before.

But not on a date. I'd been here with my younger sister. This was, in fact, her favorite place to go out. And her dress.

If I had to blame someone for getting me out of my comfort zone, I would have to blame her.

This was her idea. At least the dress and the venue. Even though at eighteen, Brianna shouldn't even have a favorite venue,

When I'd told her what I was thinking, she'd jumped on board and decided I needed to do more than slip on a pair of jeans and go to a bar.

Brianna was the fashionista in the family. She'd taken after Momma in that way.

There were so many facets to Momma and we each seemed to have taken after her in our own ways.

No one could be everything Momma was.

"The martinis are good," I said.

"The martinis are excellent," he said. "But we should order something to eat."

He was doing that thing again. That think where he took care of me.

He wasn't about to let me just drink on any empty stomach.

"Everything's good," said. "You pick."

He eyed me for a moment as though he couldn't decide whether or not he should argue the point.

Then he motioned for the bartender. "Can I get a menu?"

The bartender pulled two menus from the beneath the counter.

"Just one," Kade said. "we're together."

Without so much as a blink, the bartender put the other menu back and left us.

"I know you like po'boys and hamburgers," he said. "But they don't have either of those here."

I smiled. Brianna said men liked a girl who was mysterious. "Just pick something."

"Alright."

I watched him as he ordered. I liked the way he adapted to this new dynamic. Usually, I was quite opinionated and always told him what I wanted.

Tonight, I wanted him to be in charge.

I sipped my martini, then slid it slightly away. The drinks here were far too smooth.

And already, my lips were starting to tinkle a bit from the alcohol.

The bar was getting crowded, pushing us together in our own little bubble. I liked it that way.

The noisier and more crowded it was, the better I liked it.

Kade had to lean closer to hear me. I definitely liked that.

"You don't have to fly tomorrow, do you?" I asked.

I knew perfectly well that he didn't. Just like me, he was here for the Thanksgiving holiday.

And as a student, he wouldn't have the opportunity to fly.

"Not that I know of."

"Good," I said.

I was just making conversation, but he was looking at me as though he was trying to figure out what I was up to.

I liked it.

It was time Kade Johnson had his world turned upside down.

76

KADE — BEFORE

*M*adison was up to something.

And if she wasn't wearing that red dress that showed off every one of her curves, I might have been able to think clearly enough to figure out what exactly it was.

But as it stood, I just gave up and went along for the ride.

Spending time with Madison was right up there with spending time flying.

And that was saying a lot.

I'd ordered some crab cakes for us to snack on.

If she was still hungry, I'd order something else, but Madison didn't eat much and I had a feeling she wouldn't be wanting anything else to eat.

I leaned closer to ask her something, but a whiff of her perfume sent my thoughts scattering. She smelled like vanilla and honeysuckle with an undertone of jasmine.

She leaned in, too.

When I didn't say anything, she smiled. "What?"

"It's a bit loud in here," I said. I wasn't about to tell her that her perfume had just made my mind go blank.

A woman didn't need to know that she had that much power over a man.

She shrugged and took a tiny sip of her drink.

I knew for a fact that she wouldn't drink more than a few sips.

"I like it," she said.

I nodded. "Somehow I thought you would."

"Why do you say that?"

"Madison," I said. "You like people. You like being around them."

"I like being around you," she said.

I slid her drink over. Sniffed it. It didn't seem to be too strong.

She watched me with a raised eyebrow.

"Something wrong?"

"Not a thing," I said, tipping back my own drink. "Nothing wrong at all."

She pulled another olive off the toothpick with her teeth.

But if she didn't stop doing that, we were going to have to do something besides sit crammed into this tiny little space in this fancy bar.

Fortunately the server brought the crab cakes. One plate with two forks. The bartender had obviously misunderstood me.

But, unfazed, Madison was already breaking off a bite with her fork.

She held up the fork for me to take a bite.

She held the fork steady as I slid the bite of crab cake from her fork.

"How is it?" she asked.

"Good," I said. "Hot."

"As it should be," she said, taking a bite herself.

Those lips captured my attention and wouldn't let go.

This was the first time she and I had been out together. I didn't count the campus cafeteria.

We'd spent some time in her apartment kissing.

But like most college freshmen, she had a roommate. I figured that was good thing. It kept me honest.

I considered myself a gentleman, to begin with. And second of all, I had to tread carefully with Noah Worthington's daughter.

My aspirations were with the larger, more mainstream airlines, but still, aviation was a small, close-knit industry.

Right now, Madison seemed to be enjoying teasing me.

I didn't mind.

And I didn't plan on going all the way with her.

She was too young. Too innocent.

And I liked her too much.

Liking a girl too much was as good a reason as any to keep it in the pants.

77

MADISON

While Kade had been in the bathroom, I'd taken some time to settle myself. Used some of those relaxation techniques I'd peddled onto my patients.

That stuff actually worked. Who would have thought?

I didn't mind that the Stanley Hotel only had one room or that maybe he'd only booked one room.

This might be our last night together.

It wasn't every day that we got thrown into a trip like this.

My father was going to be okay. He had to be.

At least that's what I told myself. He had the best doctors in Houston and they would take care of him.

In the meantime, I had Kade here.

Kade had always been able to resist me. At least to an extent.

I'd driven him crazy in college. And I believed to this day that was the reason he'd stayed with me as long as he did.

I also believed that it was also the reason he left and didn't bother to stay in touch.

Our relationship had limited intimacy.

We'd been kids. I gave him that. And he was a little bit older than I was.

So I never held it against him.

It was just… I wasn't sure that letting him go again without exploring what could be was a good idea.

We had an undeniable attraction.

And we weren't kids anymore.

I needed to… no… I wanted to… make love with him.

I didn't want to go through life not knowing Kade that way.

Besides, maybe it would get him out of my system and I could move on with my life.

As a psychology trainee, I'd had the opportunity to think some about my own issues. And Kade was one of them.

I'd decided that he was blocking me from emotionally bonding with anyone else.

I'd tried, of course. But it was never Kade.

Nonetheless, something told me the time wasn't right. Not quite. Not yet.

He needed to make the first move.

And he had to some extent. He'd kissed me.

But there could be so much more.

I closed my eyes. Right now I was emotionally drained. Not a good time to think about having sex with my ex-boyfriend.

Even if said ex-boyfriend was right here in the bed with me.

There was no way I was going to be able to sleep.

But I closed my eyes and forced myself to relax anyway.

Kade was being perfectly quiet.

He wasn't asleep either.

I sighed and let my mind go blank.

I needed to give the guy a break.

This was no time to impose my issues onto him.

We had a lot to do tomorrow. A lot to figure out.

It was regrettable that we had to cut our trip short.

But it couldn't be helped.

I needed to see my father.

I needed to see for myself that he was going to be okay.

78

KADE

I put my hands behind my head and smiled to myself. Madison was sound asleep.

I could tell by her steady breathing and what could almost be called a snore.

Probably a result of her being so upset.

But with her being asleep, it took some of the pressure off of me.

I didn't know what to do.

The thing with her father threw a wrench into everything.

I wasn't sure whether to coddle her or to give her space.

I certainly didn't think trying to make out with her was appropriate considering the circumstances.

She needed time to process everything. To come with her own way of coping with the infinite possibilities she was being confronted with.

My own father had died of prostate cancer when I was in college.

He'd lived two days after my mother had called me home. That was the day I discovered who Madison was. Sometimes when I was feeling low and missing my dad, I imagined that he had brought us together.

There was a strong possibility that if he hadn't gotten sick when he did, I might never have seen Madison again.

Not that I would have given up on trying to find. And, besides, she had my phone number.

But still. The possibility brought me comfort.

So since my mother hadn't wanted to bother me with news of my father's illness until it was too late, I empathized with Madison.

Why parents did that sort of thing was a mystery. It was as though keeping things from us was somehow beneficial.

We were going to find out sooner or later. And the sooner we knew what was going on, the sooner we could start dealing with it ourselves.

I started to drift off to sleep.

It had been a long day. A long, stressful day.

I had barely closed my eyes when I started dreaming about Madison.

I jarred myself awake and went back into the bathroom. Splashed cold water onto my face.

Why was it that just so much as being in her proximity gave a me hard on.

I thought about rubbing one out, but it didn't seem right with her on the other side of the door.

So I went and climbed back onto my side of the bed.

While I was gone, Madison had rolled over in her sleep and was sleeping crossways in the bed.

That was just like her.

Taking up all the room.

I was hanging on the side of the bed trying not to touch her.

I wasn't sure what would happen if I did. Things might explode.

79

MADISON

I was having a most delicious dream.

In my dream, I was in bed with Kade.

It wasn't a memory because I'd never been in bed with Kade.

At least not like that.

Sure, he'd slept over a few times, but we'd just kissed a while, then cuddled, and fell asleep.

It was all very innocent.

And it wasn't like we had that many options. My roommate was a recluse. I hardly ever had more than a few minutes in our apartment to myself. The girl was so bad, she even took mostly online classes.

Except for that night when I'd worn the red dress.

Things had gone a little bit differently that night.

We'd actually gotten a room.

It had only happened one time, but it had given my imagination a lot to work with over the years.

What my boyfriends didn't know, wouldn't hurt them, right?

But right now, in my delicious dream, Kade was wrapped

around me. First, his legs tangled with mine.

Then he put his arms around me and pulled me close.

He smelled so good. Like pure masculine sex on a stick.

I turned into him and pressed my body against his. Wrapped my arms around his neck and tangled my fingers in his soft perfectly cut hair.

Ah. My breasts pressed against his chest, bringing my nipples to a peak.

I tried to get closer to him, but we were pressed together.

His lips found mine and he over hovered me, kissing me in that way that made me forget my own name.

Our tongues stroked each other and I surrendered completely to him.

He was rock hard against me.

And I would have put my hands on him except that he was holding my hands above my head.

Then his lips trailed kisses of fire across my cheek until he reached my ear. He moved so slow... dreamlike... like he had all the time in the world. Like there was no where else he wanted to be.

I moved against him. I was so hot for him.

This was better than my other dreams.

Then his lips were back on mouth.

This was the best dream I'd ever had.

And that was saying a lot.

Kade Johnson was the kind of man who gave a girl everything she could ever want and left her wanting more.

It felt so right.

And I'd never forgotten the way he felt against me.

He pulled me over on top of him and I opened my eyes, but it was too dark to see him.

We were in total darkness.

But it didn't matter. I knew.

I wasn't dreaming.

80

KADE

I'd quickly gotten past my qualm about taking advantage of Madison in her moment of distress.

She didn't seem so very distressed right now.

In fact, she seemed to be the antithesis of distressed.

She was soft and pliable. And… oh… so… sexy.

I think maybe she'd thought she was dreaming at first.

But she was awake now. Either that or she was an incredibly active dreamer.

She laid on top of me, rubbing herself against me.

We needed more than this.

I turned her over again on her back and ducked beneath the covers.

I ran my tongue over her panties. Panties so wet I could barely stand it.

I dipped my tongue beneath the lacy panties. It was like discovering a buried treasure. And I had to treat it very gently.

Because I remembered. I remembered from that one night so very long ago that Madison liked to be touched gently.

But this Madison grabbed hold of my hair.

I stopped for second, but she wasn't pushing me away. She was pushing me down against her.

And her legs were spread wide.

I groaned.

I needed to get in there.

I pulled the offending panties aside and thought seriously about ripping them. But before I could, she reached down and pulled them off before spreading her legs again.

My God, I loved this girl.

While she was at it, she pulled her shirt over her head, but her arms got tangled, so she just left them there, giving me full access to her beautiful, hot body.

I kissed the inside of her thighs first.

Then slowly worked my way up.

If I went in there, I could come in about two seconds.

But prolonging the experience was exquisite torture. One I never wanted to end.

She tilted her hips up and I took that as my signal to continue.

My tongue pressed against her, then I slowly started to lick.

She tasted so good. Like fresh cucumber water.

I licked slow, then fast, then slow again.

She was getting close.

Putting my tongue on the sweet spot, she groaned. "Don't," she said, barely able to speak. "stop." She took a breath and tried again. "Don't stop."

I didn't. I stayed right there on that spot and licked faster and harder until she cried out and pulled her legs together to savor those lingering waves of pleasure.

I didn't mind.

I knew what made my girl happy.

I wiped my mouth on the sheet and, after helping her untangle her hands from her shirt, pulled her close against me.

Her heart was pulsing too fast. She needed to settle.

As she came back down to earth, she laid her head on my chest and didn't move.

I wasn't sure if she was asleep yet.

If she wasn't, she was close.

I wondered if she would remember this as a dream when she woke up in the morning.

"I love you," I whispered against her ear.

I had to strain to hear, but I heard her response.

"I love you, too."

81

MADISON

When I woke the next morning, Kade was already up and gone.

I sat up and realized I wasn't wearing any clothes.

I found his t-shirt deep inside the sheets and pulled it on over my head. Kade had left a pair of pajama bottoms at the foot of the bed and, since they were the quickest thing I could find, I put them on, too.

Sitting up with my back against the headboard, I replayed my dream from last night.

My dream that wasn't a dream.

I smiled to myself.

This was so much better than that time Kade had peeled me out of that red dress.

He'd gained some experience.

Oddly enough, I didn't mind.

I liked it that he knew his way around a woman's body.

My body.

And I felt deliciously relaxed, my mind full of nothing other than Kade.

Then I saw the note on his pillow.

Went for coffee. Be right back.

Love, Kade.

Love Kade.

I read the little note over and over.

There was so much to it.

The obvious, of course, was his declaration of love.

He'd said it last night, too, when he'd thought I was asleep.

But he'd taken the time to write it on a sheet of hotel stationary.

Not a text message.

An actual note.

I held it to my chest and closed my eyes.

I was so in over my head.

Kade Johnson had always been able to talk me into anything.

And this time, I thought, with a flush of heat on my cheeks, he hadn't had to say a word.

Then my phone chimed with a message, pulling me out of my love hazed thoughts.

It was a message from Momma.

MOMMA: *Good morning.*

ME: *It's early.*

Momma had never learned that a text message was supposed to be quick and dirty.

ME: *What's wrong?*

MOMMA: *Nothing. Just wanted to make sure you're enjoying your trip.*

Well, there were some things Momma did not need to know.

ME: *It's going ok. Worried about Dad.*

MOMMA: *Daddy's good. Puttering in his shop.*

She still wasn't telling me anything. And she didn't know that I knew.

ME: *Can I call?*

MOMMA: *Your sister's calling. I'll have to get back with you. Go. Have fun.*

I stared at the phone. Momma would talk to my sister. But not me.

Well, Momma didn't have a favorite.

Maybe I should call Daddy. I was definitely Daddy's favorite.

I was about to dial his number when Kade came back into the room, laden with Starbucks coffee and bags.

"You're my hero," I said.

He glanced at my tousled hair and crumpled t-shirt.

"I know," he said. "Breakfast in bed?"

"Ok," I said. I was waiting for the morning awkwardness to hit. But it didn't.

Not until he stopped to pick up my panties and toss them toward me.

"Need these?" he asked.

I blew out a breath. He was enjoying this way too much.

82

KADE

*S*ometimes a man knew what he needed to do. And he would do it even if it went against every grain in his body.

I handed Madison her coffee and settled onto the bed next to her.

Her face was flushed and she was keeping her gaze down.

She definitely remembered last night.

I knew she would, of course. A night like that wasn't something anyone could forget. Especially since it was eight years overdue.

There had been that one night in Houston when she'd worn that red dress, but other than that, I'd managed to keep things from going too far.

I hadn't wanted to hurt her.

Of course, now, I knew that life's lanes didn't have to be exclusive.

Lanes could travel side by side, all running in the same direction.

"Everything ok?" I asked, noting that her phone was unlocked beside her.

She unwrapped her breakfast sandwich and looked at me.

"I don't know," she said.

"What happened?"

"Momma texted me. Acted like there was nothing wrong." She paused to sip from her coffee cup. "Said Daddy was outside puttering in his shop."

Madison's brow was furrowed with obvious concern.

"That's good, right?" I asked, biting into my own sandwich.

"I don't know," she said, tapping a finger against her cup. "I guess. But when I asked if I could call her, she had to go talk to my sister."

I laughed. "Sounds normal to me."

"Yeah," she said, trying to smile. "Weird though, don't you think?"

"Maybe," I said. "But maybe everything is alright."

"I'm thinking about calling Daddy."

"You should," I said. "Talk to him yourself."

I was being completely selfish and I knew it. I rarely ever did things out of selfishness, but this was a unique case.

If Noah could convince his daughter that he was well enough, maybe she'd stay another night as we'd planned. We could have another night together.

We could finish what we'd started.

"Yeah," she said. "That's what I'm going to do."

Taking her phone and her coffee, she climbed out of bed and walked to the balcony. She'd barely touched her sandwich, but I knew she was finished with it.

"Thanks for breakfast," she said over her shoulder as she opened the sliding door.

"Sure," I said, but she didn't hear me.

She was wearing my pajama bottoms.

It was such an incredibly intimate thing. The blood all rushed from my head.

I finished my breakfast, then as I watched her pace the few

feet of the balcony, her phone pressed to her ear, I finished off the rest of hers, trying to ignore my wayward erection.

Then I leaned back against the headboard and watched her while I sipped my cold brew.

Madison Worthington had turned my world upside down. Again.

And once again, I had to do what was best for her.

83

MADISON

"*I* love you, too, Daddy. Talk to you soon."

I hung up the phone and slipped it into Kade's pajama pocket.

I'd even asked him how his appointment went. He'd sidestepped it like a pro.

While we spoke, I heard him sanding a piece of wood in his shop. He really did sound like he was doing okay.

When I told him I was flying back today, he'd stopped sanding and made me promise not to cut my trip short.

"Enjoy it," he'd said. "When you go back up there, you'll be going to work. It'll be different and you won't have time to enjoy yourself."

I leaned against the railing and looked across the city of Denver. Soon to be my home.

Daddy was right, of course.

But I'd feel so much better if I was there. So I could look him in the eye and make him tell me that he was going to be ok. That Momma had overreacted and his friend, Andrew, was mistaken. And an idiot to boot for scaring me.

Not that I could do anything. Especially since this was the weekend.

If he went to the doctor next week, I could go with him and speak directly to the doctor. Find out what was going on.

But not today.

I blew out a breath and realized that I was cold.

I hadn't even noticed until now.

In Houston right now, it would already be too hot to be outside. This cold weather, even in early summer, was going to take some getting used to.

Sliding the door open, I went back inside, closing it behind me.

Shivering, I ran to the bed and climbed in, wrapping a blanket around me.

"It's freezing out there," I said.

Kade smiled. "I know. You had me thinking you were tough."

I pulled the blanket closer. "I'm not tough," I said.

"No," he said, tucking a strand of hair behind my ear. "You're not tough, but you're beautiful."

I gazed into his blue eyes. And he was handsome. So handsome it made my heart hurt.

And somewhere deep inside, I was grateful to my father for twisting my arm into spending another night.

I wondered if he knew what he was doing. If he knew he was keeping me and Kade together another night.

Kade had mentioned that Daddy had called himself to ask him to do this trip last minute.

I watched Kade sipping his on-purpose cold coffee.

I'd finished mine while I was outside.

Daddy was a smart man.

He knew exactly what he was doing.

He'd set this whole thing up.

I'd heard rumors about a legend surrounding Skye Travels. A legend that said people who worked there often fell in love.

I ignored it. People fell in love all sorts of places. Not just Skye Travels.

Besides, even if it was true, I'd been falling in love with Kade Johnson since that day we'd spent the afternoon doing math problems in the computer lab.

84

KADE

"You talked to your Dad," I said.

She fisted her hands together and shivered.

"I did."

"How did he sound?" I tucked the blanket closer about her shoulders.

She looked up at me from beneath her lashes.

"He actually sounded good."

"Did he say anything about… you know?"

She shook her head. "No. And I even asked him how he felt. He said he was fine."

"You believe him?"

"I don't know." She stared toward the window. "It's hard to tell."

I hated seeing her sad like this.

Pulling her close, I tucked her head beneath my chin and gently rubbed her back.

I needed to change the subject.

"He made me promise," she said, her voice soft against my shirt.

"What kind of promise?" I kissed the top of her head.

"That I would stay until tomorrow."

I pulled back and searched her features. "For serious?"

She nodded.

I grinned and pulled her close again. "I love your dad."

She laughed softly. "I guess he likes you, too."

"Why do you say that?"

She sighed. And didn't answer at first.

Maybe it was just a stray comment.

"I think he arranged this whole trip," she said. "with you."

"What makes you think that? Surely your dad isn't that devious."

"Oh. He finds a way to get what he wants."

I pushed her back and looked into her eyes.

"You think he backed out on purpose?"

"I don't know about that. But I do think he intentionally chose you to bring me out here."

"I always did like him."

I pulled her hair around to one side.

"You know," I said. "I don't think we should disappoint him."

She laughed softly again.

"You're a funny man."

"Sometimes," I said. "But this time I'm serious."

I put one finger beneath her chin and tilted her face up. Her eyes drifted closed and her lips parted.

I pressed my lips against hers.

I'd wanted to make love to this woman since the day I'd first seen her.

But I'd always waited.

I waited because I didn't want it to be the wrong time.

I didn't want to hurt her.

And now it was about to happen all over again.

Would the time ever be right for us?

Maybe the right time was when it happened.

Maybe the right time was right here. Right now.

I pulled her into my lap and leaned her back, my lips never leaving hers.

Somehow I got her unwrapped from the blanket.

"Do you know how sexy you are wearing my pajamas?" I asked.

She smiled against my lips. "Maybe."

"You do, don't you?"

"Maybe," she said. "you should show me."

85

MADISON

I didn't want Kade to stop this time.

I didn't want him to ever stop.

We'd always only gone so far. But he always stopped before we went all the way.

I'd tried asking him about it once, but he'd only said something vague about it not being the right time.

I admired his self-control.

I'd even tried to get past it. Especially the night I'd worn the red dress. I'd really wanted him to love me that night.

I wanted to know that he loved me *that way*.

Sometimes he was distant and I wasn't so very sure. But then he'd do something charming and reaffirm what I knew in my heart.

He was hard for me right now. His hardness pressed against the inside of my thigh.

I wanted him inside me.

I couldn't think of a single reason why he shouldn't. And I hoped he couldn't either.

He pulled my t-shirt—his t-shirt—over my head and

marked a trail of hot kisses down my chin, my throat, and stopped right there at the base of my neck.

Every nerve in my body was coming alive.

I tangled my fingers in his hair.

His fingers slowly traveled over my breasts before he swept a thumb over one nipple. Then did the same to the other.

"Kade," I breathed.

"I know, my love," he whispered.

The things he was doing to my body combined with his words and I nearly came undone.

We shifted at the same time. I spread my legs and he moved to rub himself over me.

I lifted my knees to give him free access.

He ducked his head to suckle one nipple, then the other.

His mouth on me this way was almost more than I could bear.

Last night had only been a preview of what was to come.

He brought his lips back to mine while he slid a hand to my center.

"You're so wet," he said, one finger dipping inside me.

I moaned and tilted my hips toward him.

I couldn't bear it much longer.

He did things with his palm and his finger that had me unraveling.

"Oh." I tilted my head back. I was going to come. Just like this, I was going to come for him.

He breathed against my ear and it was my undoing.

Just as I cried out, he put his lips on mine and kept them there while I orgasmed in his hand.

"Now," I said. I needed to feel him inside me. I wanted him to know the same pleasure I was feeling.

To my complete and utter surprise, he did.

Reaching down, he cupped his penis and pressed against my soft opening.

"Are you sure?" he asked.

"Please," I said. "Yes."

He slowly and gently slid inside me.

It was exquisite torture.

Finally. After all these years.

He was so gentle. So careful with me.

Too gentle. Too careful.

I wrapped my hands around his back and scraped my nails along his back.

It seemed to be all he needed.

He began to move with urgency now.

Back and forth. Deeper and deeper.

I held on to him.

He shifted again and put a hand between us.

Pressing a finger against that sensitive spot.

The one he knew where to find.

I came against his hand. Again. Hard.

86

KADE

I held Madison close as she shuddered against me.

I removed my hand from between us and, wrapping my hands in her hair, let myself revel in the feel of being inside her.

So tight.

So soft.

So exquisite.

Why hadn't we done this years ago?

If we'd done this years ago, things might have been completely different.

We might be married with two kids by now.

But I wasn't one to dwell on regrets or missed chances.

Life only moved forward.

Besides, we wouldn't be who we were today, if we hadn't gone our separate ways.

I captured her lips with mine as I moved inside her.

She moved with me and I knew she was going to come again.

With our tongues together, our bodies together, all my thoughts blurred.

All I could focus on was Madison.

She wrapped her arms around me and scraped her nails on my back.

It was enough to increase the heat in my body.

I never wanted this moment to end.

I held onto my release until I felt the sweetness of her pulsing around me as she came.

Then I let go and released inside her.

I rolled to the side, bringing her against me.

We were both gasping.

"Madison," I said, cradling her against me. "My love."

She was quiet. So quiet.

I shifted to look into her eyes. They were red-rimmed, glistening with unshed tears.

"Oh, Madison, did I hurt you?"

"No." She shook her head, forcing a smile.

"I did, didn't I?"

I kissed her lips. Her eyelids. Her cheeks.

"I'm not hurt," she said. "I'm just… overwhelmed."

"I'm overwhelmed, too," I said, cradling her against me again. "But you're so perfect. We're so perfect."

"I know," she said.

"I love you," I said. I couldn't bear to have her think otherwise.

I couldn't bear to have her think that this had just been a one-time thing. A fling.

She was so much more to me. She was everything.

There had never been another woman for me. I'd always known that. I'd just run away from it.

But was all so clear now.

"Kade?"

"What is it, my love?"

"Nothing."

87

MADISON

Fifteen minutes later, I stood in the shower, letting the hot water pound over my head.

I had told Kade that I was overwhelmed.

And that was true.

But there was so much more that I didn't tell him.

I wasn't sure I could do this with him.

Kade had a propensity to consume me.

I had things I needed to focus on. There was my father. I didn't even know for sure what was wrong with him, but if his friend was right, it could be serious.

Then there was my job here in Denver.

In about two months, I'd be moving here to Colorado, leaving Skye Travels, my family, Houston, and Kade all behind.

Kade and I didn't do long-distance.

He'd broken my heart eight years ago.

I never told anyone that. I'd barely even admitted it to myself.

I'd poured myself into graduate work and that had dulled the ache from missing him.

And now he shows up and rocks my world again.

With not only kindness and attention, but mind-blowing sex.

I couldn't do two months of this, then just leave it behind.

Maybe it was best to just nip it in the bud now. Before it went any further.

It was probably too late, but better late than never.

Looking ahead, I saw nothing but heartbreak.

I just couldn't do it.

I don't know how long I stood there, letting the hot water run over my head.

Long enough to know that I was in serious trouble.

Kade had said he loved me.

And I didn't doubt that.

I couldn't bear to hurt him.

But if we stayed together, it would only get deeper and hurt worse when I had to leave.

The truth was, I didn't know what to do.

In an ideal world, I would keep him close to my heart and never let him go.

But we didn't live in an ideal world.

I turned off the water and grabbed a towel for my hair.

I did know one thing.

I didn't have a crystal ball.

That meant I didn't have to decide anything right now.

Kade and I could spend the rest of the day together doing something. Something outside of this room would probably be a good idea.

Then tomorrow we'd fly back to Houston and we'd both go back to work.

With work came natural distance.

He'd be spending his time in the air.

And I'd be on the ground, doing the schedule. I needed to start interviewing for my replacement.

I'd been putting it off, but I'd only been avoiding the inevitable.

It would give me something to take my mind off Kade.

A way to start preparing myself mentally for moving away.

There.

I'd decided not to decide anything.

It was something of a relief.

It meant I was free to enjoy being with Kade for as long as we had, knowing that things were free to change at any moment.

I slipped into my clothes and opened the bathroom door.

Kade was standing on the balcony, the phone pressed to his ear.

He was pacing. Much as I had done earlier.

He looked concerned. Very concerned.

I straightened up the room while I watched him.

I'd been in the shower thinking about our relationship while Kade was dealing with what looked like something very serious.

With everything done, I sat on the edge of the bed and waited.

Finally, he hung up the phone, but instead of coming back inside, he made another call.

This one was quicker.

Then he stood looking out over the city for a few minutes.

I thought about going to him.

But I didn't know if I should.

I wouldn't have hesitated before the mind-blowing sex.

But now everything was confusing and different.

I didn't know what to do.

So I sat on the bed and waited.

He'd come inside when he was ready.

A couple of minutes later, he came back inside, closing the door behind him.

"Hey," he said.

"Hey. Everything ok?"

He shook his head. "No."

"What is it?"

He ran a hand through his hair and looked up at the ceiling. "She 'um… they…"

I did go to him then. I put my hands on his arms and led him back to the bed.

"Tell me what's happened," I said, taking his hand.

"They're taking my mom in for surgery."

"Surgery? For what? Her leg?"

"Not her leg," he said. "It's her heart."

"What? What's wrong with her heart?"

Kade seemed to be having trouble concentrating, much less figuring out what he needed to say.

"I have to go," he said. "I have to be there."

"Ok," I said. This was what I knew how to fix.

With my psychology skills and my connection to Skye Travels, I could get Kade home in no time.

And although he was perfectly fine to fly in my opinion even after last night's drinks, he was in no place emotionally to fly.

"Take a minute," I said, pulling out my phone. "You can tell me anything, but I need a minute to arrange a flight back for us."

"You can stay here," he said.

"Don't even think about it," I said. He was not going there. He was not going to push me away.

I was in this now. I'd been in it all along, but I was really in this now.

Turning away, I spoke to Quinn.

Normally, I would have called my father, but he had enough to deal with. He needed a stress-free day to just enjoy himself in his wood shop.

This was what Quinn got paid to do.

"Quinn," I said when he picked up. "I need a flight. Now."

88

KADE

I watched as Madison paced the room, her phone to her ear.

She was beautiful. Even without makeup and her hair still damp from the shower, she was the most beautiful girl in the world.

That was about as far as my brain could go before it circled back around to my mother.

They said there was blockage and if they didn't do something immediately, she could have a heart attack and die.

Since I was her power of attorney, they needed my permission to do the surgery.

It was scheduled in the morning. Coronary artery bypass.

She had a broken leg and dementia. She wasn't supposed to have to have major heart surgery.

There were risks with surgery. Too many to think about.

But they said the risks of not doing it far outweighed the risks of doing it.

There were top-notch doctors in Houston. They knew what they were doing.

I just needed to be there. Right now.

I needed to be with her.

She would be alone and scared.

I took a deep breath. Not alone. Her caregiver Susan was there.

And apparently Mom didn't have a very clear idea of what was going on.

In this case, that was actually probably a good thing.

"Alright," Madison said, hanging up her phone and coming to sit next to me. "We need to check out and get to the local airport. Someone will be picking us up in an hour."

"That fast?"

She smiled. "We make things happen."

"What about the airplane in Denver?"

"Don't worry. Everything will be taken care of. We'll have you home in no time."

She stood up. "Come on," she said. "we should head out."

I nodded and stood up.

It was a relief I couldn't describe to let her handle the details.

Madison was capable and I trusted her.

As we checked out of the elegant Stanley Hotel, I regretting that we hadn't had time to look around. Maybe another day.

As we drove to the airport, Madison let me sit in silence. She had no idea how much of a gift that was.

I had things to process before I could talk about any of it.

We got to the little local airport just as the small jet landed and taxied toward us.

A pilot I'd never seen before was in the cockpit.

"Hey Paul," she said. "Thank you so much for doing this."

"I'm happy to help out," he said. "Luggage?"

"No," Madison said. "It's in Denver. We'll get it later."

In minutes, we were buckled up and taking off.

Madison, sitting right next to me took my hand.

"Kade," she said. "don't keep all this inside. Please. Tell me what you know."

"There's blockage," he said. "They thought she had an infection, a UTI, but they ran some tests and found out that her heart was shutting down."

I closed my eyes. This was the most painful thing I'd had to face since my father...

"But they're doing surgery," she said, pulling me back from the memories.

"Yes," I said, focusing on what they'd told me. "They can fix it. The surgery is first thing in the morning."

Madison nodded. "That's good, right?"

I nodded. "I just never thought... This wasn't supposed to happen."

"They'll take good care of her," she said and I knew that Madison believed that with all her heart.

It was ironic. Just an hour ago, she was struggling with her own father's health issue and I'd been the one reassuring her.

Now the roles had flipped.

But the truth was, I was terrified.

Good doctors or not, there were a million things that could go wrong.

I'd moved back here to be closer to her, but maybe I'd waited too long.

I'd waited until everything started falling apart.

"You'll be there for her," Madison said, seeming to read my mind.

She reached over and kissed me on the cheek.

I forced myself to breathe.

Mother would be ok.

She had to be.

I hadn't given up my job and moved all the way back home to Houston just to have her die on me.

89

MADISON

As we landed at the airport in Houston, my heart was heavy.

It had been a life altering weekend for me.

Yet Kade had barely said anything on the flight home.

I know he was worried about his mother, but even though I'd been worried about my father, I'd still focused on Kade.

Kade and I had made love for the first time. For me, that meant a lot.

I tried to be understanding and as a psychologist, it was easy to do.

But as a woman who'd just put herself out there, I was struggling.

"Thank you," Kade said, reaching over to squeeze my hand.

"For what?"

"Thank you for getting me here in time to see my mother before she goes into surgery in the morning."

"You don't have to thank me." In fact, I felt a bit selfish now. Bypass surgery was serious and I'd been thinking about myself.

As the plane came to a stop, he leaned over and, putting a hand under my chin, pressed his lips against mine in a kiss.

I closed my eyes and leaned in, savoring the feel of his lips on mine.

"I'll call you later," he said, pulling back.

"Ok." I nodded.

When the doors opened, Kade stood up and exited the plane.

I watched him get into the car I'd ordered for him and drive off.

Then I exited the plane and got into my own car.

I would have gone with him to the hospital.

But he hadn't shown any sign that he might want me to go with him.

So as I drove out of the parking lot, I sent Daddy a text.

ME: *Can I come by?*

DADDY: *Of course. But I'm not home. I took a last minute flight. Won't be home until late. Everything ok?"*

No. Everything was not alright.

ME: *Everything is good. Just landed in Houston.*

DADDY: *Thought you were staying til tomorrow.*

ME: *Kade had a family emergency.*

I leaned back and blew out a breath. Putting it into words helped me put what had happened in perspective. Kade hadn't just run off after our trip. He'd had an emergency.

It was just bad timing.

I had no choice but to forgive him. It was Kade after all.

Not ready to go home yet, I sent Emily a text.

ME: *Are you busy?*

EMILY: *Not really. What's up?*

ME: *Just landed. Want to meet at the Skyhouse?*

EMILY: *Be there in 15*

I smiled. I could always count on Emily.

By the time my car pulled up to the door of the Skyhouse, Emily was pulling into the parking lot.

I stood and waited for her.

"How did you get here so fast?"

She looked a little guilty, which made no sense at all. "I was in the neighborhood."

She quickly diverted the attention away from herself.

"You look rode hard and put up wet."

I laughed. "I guess you could say that."

There was no one in the bar this time of day except for the bartender. It was too late for lunch and too early for an after work cocktail.

"I thought you were coming back tomorrow."

"There was a change of plans."

We took a seat in one of the booths that were hardly ever available.

"How's your dad?" Emily asked.

I knew I was about to open a door that Emily would pounce on, but I did it anyway.

"Daddy was sick and couldn't go."

"Oh. Is he ok?"

"I think so. He's on a flight right now, so he must be."

The server brought our martinis.

He was a thirty-something guy who was always business and always remembered our drink order. "Anything to eat?" he asked.

"Not right now," I said. The thought of food right now made my stomach queasy. There was far too much going on.

Emily was looking at me over her cocktail glass.

"You went by yourself?" she asked. "Who was your pilot?"

She knew me far too well.

"Kade," I said, then quickly sipped my own drink.

"Ah ha," she said.

"What is that supposed to mean?"

"I knew you two were going to get back together."

"We're not back together," I said, but my words carried no conviction.

Emily tapped her drink with a perfectly manicured fingernail.

"There's something…"

"There's nothing," I said. "Except his mother is having heart surgery in the morning."

"Why aren't you with him?"

"He didn't ask," I said.

She just raised her eyebrows.

"What?" I said. "It's complicated."

"You had sex," Emily said.

I just looked at her. "Why would you say that?"

"It's really the only complicating thing that could happen between you two."

I didn't deny it. I didn't confirm, but I didn't deny it either.

Emily was right. Emily was always right.

Sometimes I think she knew me better than I knew myself.

"It was just bad timing," I said.

"When's the surgery?" she asked.

"First thing in the morning."

"You have to go," she said.

I was already shaking my head. "I can't intrude on his privacy."

"He doesn't need privacy. He needs support. You have to be there for him."

I sat back. "I don't know. It feels weird."

"It only feels weird because you've been in love with him since day one. If you want to be part of his life, then be part of his life. Part of the important parts. And he's like you when it comes to family."

And she was right again.

Family was very important to me. Always had been. How could I fault a guy for putting his own family first when I'd do the same?

And if I were in his shoes, wouldn't I want him to be there for me?

The bartender stopped by again. "Another round?" he asked.

We both said no.

"But in the meantime," Emily said. "You need to get your butt home and get some sleep. You definitely don't need to show up there. Or anywhere. Looking like this."

"Who needs enemies?" I said under my breath.

"You know I'm right," Emily said. "Go home. Go sleep."

And once again, Emily was right.

Besides, I'd feel better after a good night's sleep.

Maybe I could find a few minutes tomorrow to talk to Daddy, too.

Looked like Kade and I were going to being needing each other a lot.

90

KADE

*I*t was only eleven in the morning, but it had already been an interminably long day.

Since it was Sunday, I was the only person sitting in the hospital waiting room. It was quiet here, isolated from the rest of the hospital. No announcements. Not even any piped in music. I didn't know if it was because it was Sunday or because this was such a specialized area.

The nurses and orderlies had been there at five o'clock to roll Mother out of the ICU up to surgery. They expected the surgery to last twelve hours, depending on how she did.

Unfortunately, they'd given her a sleeping pill last night that had only kept her awake and hallucinating.

My older sister, Noelle, was in Europe, so she couldn't have gotten here in time even if she'd tried. I didn't even bother to think about it. I just dutifully kept her updated via text.

I sat at a little table, a cold cup of black coffee sitting in front of me, and waited for the social worker to come out with an update. She'd been out twice already. Said everything was going smoothly.

Instead I saw Madison coming around the corner. My heart skipped a beat.

Thinking about her had been the one thing that had kept me sane over the last twenty-four hours.

I was still wearing the same clothes I'd worn two days ago. I hadn't shaved or showered.

Madison looked rested and fresh. An absolute balm on my tired eyes.

She was wearing a white flowy dress with a blue jean jacket over it and navy canvas sneakers. She was carrying a paper bag with handles.

She smiled when she saw me and I gave her what had to be a tired, weary smile in return.

She slid into the chair next to mine and hugged me quickly before pulling back.

"How are you holding up?"

I blew out a breath. Seeing someone I knew, seeing her, was an overwhelming relief.

"I've been better," I said.

"How's your mother?"

I glanced at my watch. The social worker was overdue to come out for her every two hour or so report.

"I haven't heard anything in a couple of hours."

"How often—"

The door to the surgical area opened and the social worker stepped out. Wearing scrubs, she tugged her cap off and looked around for me.

I'd moved from across the room since she was out here last time. She looked tired.

I grabbed Madison's hand and held on.

My thoughts swirled with possibilities, none of them good.

"Hi," she said to Madison.

"I'm Madison."

"It's good that someone is here with Kade.

Oh shit. Something must have gone wrong.

I forgot to breathe as the social worker turned to me.

"She's doing well. The doctor has cleared the blockage."

The social worker kept talking, but I didn't hear another word she said.

All I heard was *she's doing well* and my mind was flooded with relief that blocked everything else out.

As the social worker walked away, Madison nudged me with her arm.

"Hey? Are you okay?"

"As good as I can be," I said.

She squeezed my hand before using both hands to open the bag she'd brought.

"I brought you lunch," she said.

I bent over and kissed her on the cheek.

As I unwrapped the taco she handed me, my hands trembled.

Madison was an angel.

91

MADISON

*K*ade wasn't doing so well. I should have come earlier, but I'd listened to Emily who insisted I needed to be rested.

I knew that Kade would be alone. His sister lived in Europe and he had no other family that I knew of. I just hadn't realized what the implications of that would be.

He was literally sitting here alone. Waiting for a social worker who looked as tired and worn out as he did to come out with periodic reports.

This should not have been allowed to happen.

As Kade unwrapped his taco with shaky hands, I was determined to try to make his day a little bit better.

I slid a bottle of water in his direction.

"At least it's quiet in here," I said.

"True." He bit into his taco. "All I need is the roar of an airplane motor in the background to feel at home."

I smiled. At least he hadn't completely lost his sense of humor.

"That is true. Spoken like a true pilot."

He looked at me then as though his brain had suddenly cleared. "Have you talked to your dad yet?"

"Not yet." I didn't tell him that I'd slept far too late.

"You look rested," he said. "Good."

"Thanks," I said. "You don't look so good."

He almost laughed. "Probably not as bad as I feel."

"I'm so sorry Kade," I said. "I should have come earlier."

"No," he said. "I'd much, much rather see you here like this." He squeezed my hand again. "Looking rested and beautiful."

His phone chimed. "My sister."

"It must be hard on her not being here."

"I don't know," Kade said. "I think she got the better end of the deal."

I agreed with him, but I didn't tell him so.

Actually, it was hard for me to imagine being in Kade's shoes.

With five siblings in our family, there was always plenty of support. Always a roomful of people when anything happened.

Kade must have been starving. He ate three tacos. I'd brought up two each, but I didn't have the heart to tell him. I couldn't have eaten but one anyway.

"You don't have to stay," he said after we finished our lunch.

"I'm not leaving you," I said, gathering up the trash, including a coffee cup with stale coffee.

I saw the twitch of a smile at the corner of his lips. "Good," he said. "You have no idea how good it is to see you."

As I walked the bag of trash across the empty waiting room, I couldn't help but wonder if he was glad to see me or just glad to see anybody.

It didn't matter though.

I was here now.

92

KADE

I got into the office early the next Tuesday.

I had a short flight later this morning, but I had some paperwork to catch up on.

Madison wasn't in yet and without her, the building was not only dark, but seemed lifeless.

Since I didn't know how to turn on the lights in the lobby, I went straight back to my office and turned on the computer.

Madison had stayed with me all day Sunday. She'd waited until my mother had successfully come out of surgery before she'd left.

I hadn't seen her all day yesterday, but I hadn't expected to.

She'd called and offered me the rest of the week off, but I needed a break. I needed to get out of the hospital and have something of a normal day.

An hour later, Quinn stopped as he walked by.

"Hey," he said. "what are you doing here?"

I took off my computer glasses and glanced at my watch. "I have a flight."

Quinn came in and, sitting down across from me, stretched

out his legs. "Madison was supposed to keep your schedule clear for the week."

"I asked for a flight. I needed to start getting back to normal."

"I understand," Quinn said. "I heard everything went well."

"As well as can be expected." I shrugged. "Major heart surgery and all."

"I can't even imagine. But I'm glad it all went well and that you're back." Quinn stood up and tapped his hand on my desk. "Take care of yourself."

"Will do." I closed my computer. It was time to start getting ready for my flight.

The lobby was lit up now and the morning sun was coming through the windows.

Madison had her eyes on her computer and was talking into her headset, but she saw me immediately.

Seeing her was like a punch in the gut. It took the air out of my lungs.

And when she smiled, for just a minute, if pressed, I would have had trouble remembering my name.

This was what I'd needed. I'd needed to see Madison. The flight was just an excuse to see her if only for a minute.

I went up to the reception counter and leaned against the desk, watching her as she finished up her call.

It wouldn't be long before she wouldn't be doing this anymore. She'd be seeing patients and helping them with their problems.

She was going to be good at it.

She used her skills every day just answering this phone.

But right now her skills were unappreciated. At least working as a psychologist, she'd be recognized for what she was doing.

"Hi," she said, after she ended the call. "How do you feel?"

"A little off-kilter."

She nodded. "I know the feeling."

I wasn't sure if I felt off-kilter from being out of the office for almost a week or from seeing Madison.

I thought about her all the time.

Our timing had not been the best.

We'd gone from having an intimate weekend together to me rushing back home for a family emergency.

I felt like something was unfinished. I'd like to start over.

The phone rang again and she held up her hands with a shrug.

As she listened and tapped on the computer keys, I reached over and picked up a pack of yellow post-it notes and a pen.

I wrote a note, pulled it off, and pressed it on the desk in front of her.

Without looking at it, she placed a hand over it and waved to me as I walked off.

I wanted to get my flight over with.

It was going to be a long week.

93

MADISON

After scheduling a flight for Friday to Florida for a customer, I clicked off the phone.

I'd really wanted to talk to Kade, but he'd already left for his flight.

He'd looked tired, but that was to be expected. I felt for him. His sister had really thrown him under the bus.

Kade needed her there. Taking care of his mother by himself was more than any child should have to shoulder alone.

But she was in Europe doing whatever she wanted to do.

Needless to say, I was not a fan of his sister at the moment.

I picked up the post-it note and my heart skipped a little at Kade's familiar handwriting.

He'd simply written three words.

Date Friday night?

But those three words put a smile on my face and turned my whole day around.

In four days I had a date with Kade.

Though Friday seemed like a long time away, it was also soon. I needed to go shopping.

I sent him a text.

ME: *Yes*

He sent back a smiley face emoji.

It was good enough for me.

I stood up, stretched, and walked over to the window overlooking the tarmac.

Kade was there, clipboard in hand, talking with one of the mechanics.

Kade was taller than the other man. And leaner.

Tall, dark, and handsome.

He had my heart. He always had.

I just had to be careful. I didn't know which way the winds were going to blow.

The passenger's car arrived right on time and Kade greeted the man, Mr. Williams with a handshake before walking with him to the boarding stairs.

Kade was a perfect fit for Skye Travels. A competent pilot. Friendly personality.

People liked him.

He was going to be good for business.

I'd already had two people ask for him specifically. That was a good sign. People didn't always care who their pilot was, especially with Skye Travels. Skye Travels had a reputation for always having the best.

So he already had repeat customers.

That was fast.

But that's what happened when you hired good people.

After Mr. Williams boarded, Kade spoke to the mechanic again, then clapped him on the shoulder.

I watched as Kade walked over to the boarding stairs.

He put one hand on the railing, then turned back and looked toward the window where I was standing.

He saw me and smiled.

Then raised one hand in a little wave.

I waved back.
Then he turned and hurried up the stairs.
I pressed my palm against the cool glass of the window.
My heart was so in trouble.

94

—

KADE

*I*t was a perfect day for flying and I was glad I'd taken this one. I'd been right. It had been good for me to get away.

And the fact that Madison hadn't fought me on it just confirmed my instincts.

Mr. Williams seemed like a genuinely nice man. He was probably early forties. Still in good shape. He'd called his wife before we took off and again right after we landed.

After we landed at the little airport in Ruston, Louisiana, Mr. Williams announced that his client had a family emergency and wouldn't be making their meeting.

He didn't even bother to hide his disappointment.

"I hate I had you me fly all the way up here for nothing," Mr. Williams said.

"Are you kidding?" I asked, sitting down next to him and adjusting my tie. "I went to college here."

"No kidding?"

"Yeah," I said. "I learned to fly right here at this airport."

Mr. Williams laughed. "Well, I'll be. Isn't that something?"

"In fact…" I glanced at my watch. "Do you like po'boys?"

"Are you kidding?" Mr. Williams said. "I grew up in Lafayette. I love good seafood."

"There's a place I used to go. On Main Street." I pulled out my phone. Did a quick search. "And it's still there. You want to grab some lunch before we head back?"

"That's the best idea I've heard all day," Mr. Williams said. "But if we're going to lunch, you've got to call me John."

"All right, John," I said. "Let me secure the plane and we'll be on our way."

It was good to be back on my old stomping grounds. I had a lot of good memories here from my years at Tech.

And every one of them I could think of right now had Madison involved in some way.

I thought about texting her. To tell her that we were going to have lunch in one of our old favorite places, but I decided to wait.

If it was still good, maybe I'd surprise her with a trip up here one day.

In no time, we'd grabbed an airport loaner car and headed off toward downtown.

A few things had changed. There had never been much out by the airport other than the hospital which had doubled in size. There was a new apartment complex near the airport. That would have been a convenient place to live.

I pointed things out to John as I drove.

When Wiley Tower come into view a knot formed in the pit of my stomach.

That's was where I'd met Madison.

And we'd spent countless hours there studying.

Hell. We studied everywhere. My place. Her place. The library. The airport.

We'd been good for each other. Kept each other on task.

Probably contributed a lot to how successful we both were as adults.

As always, Main Street was crowded, so we had to park a ways over and walk.

The restaurant looked the same. But the servers looked like children.

Either they were hiring them younger or I was definitely getting older.

While we waited to be seated, I saw someone waving to me.

At first I thought maybe they were waving at John.

I didn't know anyone here anymore.

But then I realized I did.

Damn.

It was Mike. Mike Phillips.

Mike spoke to his server.

The girl, had to be a college freshman, looked over at us.

"Sir?" she said coming over to me. "That man over there would like to invite both of you to sit with him."

"It's my old college mentor," I said to John. "Do you mind?"

"Not at all," John said. "But I don't want to intrude."

"Nonsense," I said. "Mike's a great guy. You'll like him."

Mike and I greeted like the old friends that we were. And I introduced him to John.

Mike had gotten older. Reminded me of Noah Worthington. But still looked like he took good care of himself.

We settled into the booth and ordered our po'boys.

I realized I was still wearing my captain's cap and pulled it off.

"Let me guess," Mike said. "You're working for Noah Worthington."

I was dressed in standard pilot uniform, but nothing identifying me with Skye Travels.

"How did you know?" I asked. This truly was a small world.

Mike grinned. "The cap. It's Noah's thing."

"Right." I set my cap down next to me and laughed. "I've been there nearly a month."

"Good career move," Mike said. "Noah has built himself an empire and made a good place to work at the same time."

"I agree," I said. "It made the decision to move back to Houston a whole lot easier."

The young girl came back a few minutes later and dropped off our food.

"Can I get y'all anything else?" she asked.

I smiled to myself. Madison and I sometimes tried out the southern accent on each other and I remembered clearly just how sexy I found it when she talked to me with that southern drawl that I swear came second nature to her.

"So," Mike said, almost seeming to read my mind. "How is Madison?"

Of course he would remember her. Not just for her, but because she was Noah's daughter. Madison Worthington had a last name that opened doors whether she wanted it to or not. Especially in the world of aviation.

Sometimes I forgot about that. Sometimes I just saw her as Madison.

"She's great," I said. "She a licensed psychologist taking her first job as a college professor."

"Good for her," Mike said. "I always knew she'd be successful." He bit into his sandwich. "Good as always."

It was as good as always. I was definitely bringing Madison here.

Mike looked at me. "How many kids do you two have?"

95

MADISON

I finally got some time with Daddy scheduled for that afternoon.

He'd been at the Dallas/Fort Worth office and had just gotten back from a flight.

I sent the phone calls to the answering service and met Daddy over at the Skyhouse.

He looked good. Daddy was a strikingly handsome man. He had salt and pepper hair. The streaks of gray only added to his distinguished appearance that turned heads anytime he walked into a room.

The bar was starting to fill up with the after-work crowd, but we found a quiet table in the back. The bartender brought a martini for me and a crown on the rocks for Daddy.

"So…" Daddy said. "Momma said your trip to Denver went well. Other than having to come back early."

I felt a blush across my cheeks. I didn't want to think about what had made my trip so special. The night spent with Kade. That wasn't something I wanted to even think about in front of my father.

"It was good," I said. "It was nice to spend some time getting reacquainted with Kade."

Daddy smiled. "I thought you might enjoy that."

"You set that up on purpose, didn't you?" I asked.

"What?" Daddy asked innocently. "Your mother and I just thought that you'd like some time with Kade."

"Daddy," I said, sliding my drink aside and leaning forward. "Momma said you had a doctor's appointment."

Nodding, he tapping the ice in his drink. He always did that when he was giving himself time to thing.

"I did have a doctor's appointment," he said.

"And?"

"Everything was okay."

"Daddy," I said. "While I was in Estes Park, I ran into Andrew."

Daddy turned pale. Even in the dim light of the bar, I could see it. "Andrew?"

"Yes," I said. "Your friend Andrew."

"I haven't seen him in awhile. How is he?"

"Good, I guess." I shook my head. "He said you two still keep in touch."

"I talked to him… maybe… a couple of weeks ago."

I pulled my drink forward and took a sip. Daddy wasn't telling me anything.

I'd given him every opportunity to come clean, but it looked like if I wanted to know something, I was going to have to be straightforward.

"He told me." I lowered my voice and swallowed hard. I couldn't bring myself to say the words. It was funny how it was so much easier being straightforward with a stranger than it was with someone I loved.

Daddy sat back, stretched out his legs.

I took a deep breath. I always told my patients to just say it out loud. *Saying something out loud takes away its power.*

Easier said than done.

"He said you have cancer," I blurted.

Daddy stared blankly at me.

Then he leaned forward and spoke softly.

"They did some tests," he said.

I waited. It was so hard to quietly let the seconds tick past as I waited for him to continue.

"They thought it was prostate cancer, but the latest test came back negative."

I blew out a breath and felt like I was going to collapse. "Thank God," I said.

He nodded. "The doctor suggested I start exercising and eating more live food."

"Sounds like he's been talking to Momma."

"I know," Daddy said. "Takes all the fun out, doesn't it?"

He held up his glass for a toast.

"To hamburgers and Crown Royal whisky."

I lifted my glass to his.

"To family," I said.

96

KADE

The flight home was the best kind. Uneventful.

John sat in the back of the plane, dozing and reading.

I couldn't turn my brain off long enough to relax and enjoy the flight.

Seeing Mike again had been completely unexpected and such a nice surprise.

Yet his words haunted me.

Mike had been one of my mentors in college, but we hadn't stayed in touch.

I'd heard his name tossed around a few times and he'd probably heard mine.

But we hadn't really kept up.

He'd mostly known me when I was with Madison.

In fact, he'd known me better than anyone else, including my own family. Outside of Madison, of course.

But he'd known *us*. He'd known me and Madison as a couple.

We'd had dinner with Mike and Mike's wife.

Those had been good times. I had some fond memories of those days.

But what troubled me was that Mike had assumed that Madison and I had gotten married.

That we had children.

Something in my gut told me that we should have.

That instead of letting us grow apart, I should have married her.

We should have children.

I'd avoided answering Mike. I must have looked like a deer in headlights because John had jumped in and changed the subject.

More support for my impression that John was a good man.

Right now I felt like such an idiot.

I'd screwed up with Madison.

It was a wonder she'd even spoken to me again, much less allowed me into her bed.

It was more than I deserved.

She deserved better.

I felt like such a cad. I'd done her wrong, then she'd forgiven me without so much as a hitch.

I kicked myself all the way back to Houston.

And somewhere during that flight, surrounded by white puffy clouds, I made myself a promise.

I promised myself that if I couldn't treat Madison the way she deserved to be treated, then I didn't deserve her.

Part of me wanted to kick myself to the curb for her.

But another part of me couldn't bear to be apart from her.

It was almost like the years had just folded away and we were back where we'd left off.

Only better.

I'd asked her out for Friday night.

She was giving me another chance, so I would only make things worse if I backed out on her now.

We'd moved too far forward for me to let her down again.

I would be a cad in the first degree if I slept with her then disappeared.

She certainly deserved better than that.

But I would be careful with her.

It was the least I could do for the woman I loved.

97

MADISON

I was nervous.

Kade would be here any minute to pick me up for our date.

It's just Kade, I told myself.

Kade. The man I'd known forever.

Kade. The man I was falling for all over again.

I ran my hands down my waist, smoothing the silk material of the little black dress I wore. It hugged all my curves in all the right places. After stepping into my red bottomed heels, I checked my lipstick in the mirror.

I wore my hair long and loose. I'd spent the afternoon with Momma, both of us being pampered. We'd gotten our nails done. Our hair styled.

We'd spent some time in Nordstrom's and I'd come out with this dress.

We hadn't talked about anything important. Momma knew I had a date with Kade. That was about it.

We hadn't even talked about Daddy. We'd just needed some stress-free quality mother-daughter time.

My sister was out. As usual, so I had the run of the house myself.

I wandered into the kitchen and drank half a bottle of cold water.

Then, right on time, Kade sent me a message. I keyed in the code for him to come up and went to wait for him at the elevator doors.

The doors opened and Kade stood there, handsome in a black tux.

He hadn't said where we were going. I just assumed dinner and had dressed accordingly. Apparently, we'd been on the same wave length.

He stepped out of the elevator, his hands behind his back.

"Hi," I said.

"Hi." He leaned over and kissed me lightly on the lips.

Then he stepped back and pulled an ivory rose from behind his back.

"For being my best friend," he said.

My hands shook as I took the flower from him.

Best friend. Not exactly the sentiment I was going for.

Before I had time to sort this out, he handed me a pink rose.

"For being the person I've always admired."

As I put the pink and ivory roses together, he brought out a lavender rose.

"Because you're my princess."

"Where did you find this?" I asked, knowing that lavender roses were hard to find.

Instead of answering, he handed me a green rose.

"For starting over," he said.

My eyes were misting over.

Then he handed me seven red roses.

"Because, quite simply," he said. "I love you. And seven is supposed to symbolize infatuation. One for every day of the week."

I held the bouquet of roses in my hands and bit my lip as I smiled at him. Then I stretched up and placed a kiss on his cheek.

"I'll put these in some water," I said.

Kade followed me to the kitchen and leaned against the counter, watching me.

My hands were still trembling as I grabbed a vase my sister kept on the counter, filled it with water, and carefully placed the flowers, one by one into the vase.

Eleven roses. Seven red, a pink, a white, a lavender, and a green.

They made a surprisingly beautiful bouquet.

"Thank you," I said, looking up at Kade.

He was so incredibly handsome. And the way he was looking at me did strange things to my heart.

Kade. The man I was in love with. Always had been.

98

KADE

*A*s Madison and I followed the hostess to our table at the back of the restaurant, we turned heads. Or rather, Madison turned heads.

She was absolutely stunning.

I could barely take my eyes off her.

I held her chair as she sat and placed her handbag on the table next to her.

I sat next to her. Across the table was too far away.

Once we were seated, I took her hand and kissed it as the hostess handed us our menus.

Madison laid hers aside without opening it so I did the same as I order a bottle of pinot noir.

"Kade," she said. "This is so… perfect."

"You deserve perfect," I said. "Every day."

She ran a finger along the stem of her wine glass.

"Madison," I said. "I need to tell you something."

I knew her well enough to know that she steeled herself.

"Please tell me it's something good," she said.

I smiled. "That's depends on how you look at it."

"Okay," she said. "What's on your mind?"

"I messed up. All those years ago. I should have stayed in touch with you."

"Kade, I didn't either—"

"No," I held up a hand. "I'm the one who should have made the effort. But I was young. And dumb."

She smiled. "We both were."

"We missed so much time together."

"But…" She squeezed my hand. "We have now. Right?"

Yes. We had now. But I wasn't sure that right now was enough for me.

I felt like I needed to make up for lost time.

Like I needed to spend every minute, every second possible with her just to make up for all those years I'd wasted.

I'd always known there was no one else for me.

Even when I'd dated. When I'd had girlfriends. I knew that they were just place holders.

Keeping my heart warm while I waited for Madison.

The tragedy of it, though, was that I hadn't understood it at the time.

I'd known something was missing. And I thought about Madison a lot.

But it was only now that I was putting it all together. And figuring out what it all meant.

"Yes," I said. "We have now."

He held up a glass. "To an endless supply of nows."

We drank to my toast.

"So," I said. "Do you already know what you want?"

"Pretty much," she said. "You've been here before, right?"

"No," I said.

And that's when a waiter dressed in formal black attire placed shrimp cocktails in front of us.

"Here's something to get you started," he said.

I looked over at Madison.

She just shrugged. "It's what they do."

99

———

KADE

I rarely gave much thought to the fact that Madison was a billionaire by birth.

I'd known her as a regular college student. We drank beer and pizza like all the other college students.

She lived in a college apartment with a roommate just like everyone else.

Sure, her part-time weekend job's commute involved an airplane, but since I stayed in the air as much as possible and aviation was my world, I didn't pay much heed to any of it.

Most students outside of aviation thought all pilots, even those still in school, were automatically wealthy.

The truth was my family came from a normal professional class world. Upper class, but not wealthy to that extent.

My mother didn't work and my father was an engineer.

After he passed, my mother was well taken care of. And I had a college fund to take care of all my tuition. Even the extra fees required for flying.

So for the most part we lived in the same world.

But tonight was one of those nights when I was reminded that there were parts of her world I didn't even know existed.

My mother lived in a nice house in a nice Houston neighborhood. Madison lived with her sister in a high rise condo with a private elevator.

My idea of a dinner date was an Italian restaurant and a bottle of wine.

I'd made reservations at this place through a recommendation by Quinn.

The servers wore tuxes. The tables were covered with white tablecloths and fresh flowers in the center of each.

Madison didn't need a menu because she already knew what she liked from here.

The servers were so good at what they did, that they brought appetizers without even asking.

By the time the customer was seated and had ordered their drinks they pretty much knew what the customers were going to like.

I wondered if the menus were merely window dressing. Something familiar to customers like me who were used to having to scour through descriptions on a menu to pick out something that I might like.

Most ordinary people—and I considered myself ordinary—didn't eat at places like this.

Maybe somewhere in the back of my mind, I'd stored information like this. The knowledge that my world and Madison's world didn't completely overlap.

There were fringes of the Venn diagram that were so far out on the edges, it was hard to imagine.

But when she looked at me like she was looking at me right now and smiled, I reminded myself that all couples were like this.

No two people ever completely shared the same experiences. It wasn't possible or even normal if it did happen.

But still... sometimes I wondered if it was a problem for her.

She certainly knew wealthy men.

Filthy rich men who could give her anything and everything.

But I knew that love was something that didn't come with dollar signs.

"What's troubling you?" she asked, putting a hand over mine.

And there was the disadvantage to dating a psychologist. There could be no secret insecurities. Everything had to be laid out and dealt with.

Unless, like me, a man was really good at keeping himself private.

"I'm just glad we're together tonight," I said.

She looked at me sideways.

"No…" she said. "that wasn't your happy to be here look. Something's troubling you."

I blew out a breath and took a long sip of wine.

Decided to go with the real issue at hand. Not my rambling thoughts that when it came right down to it had nothing to do with us.

"I just regret that we only have a few more weeks before things get more… complicated."

She smiled. "Kade. You know that things will work out."

I shook my head. "We've been down this road."

"Like you said, we were young."

"I don't like the fact that history repeats itself."

She looked at me with that look that said she was trying to look deeper into my psyche.

There really wasn't much to find if she did analyze me.

I loved airplanes. My family. Dogs. Hot dogs and apple pie.

And Madison Worthington.

100

MADISON

As the summer weeks clipped past, Kade and I settled into a routine.

We had dates on Friday and Saturday nights. Sometimes those dates involved fancy restaurants with white tablecloths. And sometimes they involved pizza delivery and binge watching Virgin River.

He started sleeping over two nights a week.

Sometimes we just held each other and slept. Other times he rocked my world.

In the process of having this time together, we learned that we had more common interests than we'd known.

At some point after our separation, we'd both taken up jogging. So on Saturday mornings, we'd load up and go jogging in Memorial Park.

We'd have lunch with his mother and dinner with my family or vice-versa.

We didn't talk about our relationship. We simply lived our relationship.

History did, indeed, repeat itself.

But I was constantly aware of the steady ticking of the clock counting down the days until I got on that plane and moved into my apartment in Denver.

I used the slow times at work to prepare lectures for my classes. Although it was a good use of time, it kept my impending move at the front of my mind.

I wished everyday for time to slow down.

But the more I wished it to slow down, the faster it seemed to move.

On this particular lazy Sunday morning, I woke and reached across the bed for Kade, but instead my fingers brushed a piece of paper.

He was so adorable. He still left me notes instead of simply sending a text.

Be right back. Don't get up.

I rolled onto my back and smiled up at the ceiling.

I couldn't remember ever being this happy before.

Kade made me happy.

Sometimes I'd wondered what it might be like if we ever got back together, but I never allowed myself to think that it might actually happen.

And now that we were, it was so much better than I imagined.

We didn't have the pressures of being students and having to study all the time.

We actually had days when we weren't required to do anything we didn't want to do.

And sometimes that involved absolutely nothing more than just lying in bed and talking.

I sat up when I heard the elevator open.

Kade stepped into the bedroom with coffee from Starbucks and a little bag. He always brought me something to eat as a surprise. It was as though he worried that I wouldn't get enough to eat.

He sat down, handed me my latte and set a newspaper down on the bed.

"What's this?" I asked.

"What? Don't you ever read the newspaper anymore?"

"Sure," I said, sipping my coffee. It was smooth as always. "Online."

He grabbed up the newspaper and spread it out on the bed.

"But it's so much more fun to read the comics together when we can hold the paper in our hands."

"The comics," I said, laughing. "Alright. Let's read the comics. And leave the news to the serious people."

He dug through the paper until he found the colorful comics. "Here we go."

"What did you bring me to eat?" I asked.

"What makes you think I brought you something to eat?" he asked, tousling my hair.

"Because," I said. "you wouldn't be you if you didn't."

He grinned and handed me the paper bag. "Take your pick."

I chose a blueberry muffin.

"Never would have thought you would have picked that," he said.

"Just shows," I said teasingly. "You don't know everything about me."

I peeled the paper off the muffin and took a bite.

"Mmm," I said. "that's good."

"Let me try a bite," he said.

I broke off a bit of muffin and placed it in his mouth.

"That's good," he said. "but I happen to know something better."

"What? Your egg and cheese biscuit thing?"

"Nope," he said, sliding over close to me.

He had that look in his eyes that told me exactly what he was hungry for.

Putting his hands on either side of me, he gave me a little kiss on the lips.

"I like yours better," he said, subtly pushing me back onto the bed.

I giggled and wrapped my fingers in his white t-shirt. "It's the same thing."

"I am afraid Dr. Worthington," he said, giving me more little teasing kisses. "you are sorely mistaken about that."

Pulling on his t-shirt, I pulled him closer and his kiss turned serious.

His tongue brushed the corner of my lips, sending a delicious shiver up my spine.

I was on my back now and he was pressed against me. I closed my eyes and let the muffin roll away, landing on the floor.

His tongue found mine and I gained a new appreciation for the taste of blueberry muffins.

His hardness pressed against my thigh and I shifted to position him between my thighs.

He continued to kiss me as he moved between my legs. The only thing between us was his jogging pants and my pajama shorts.

It was too much.

I slid a hand down to my waistband, but he grabbed my hand to stop me and lifting my hands above my head, he clasped my fingers with his.

He was moving his hips in little circles.

Oh my.

My senses were overwhelmed with his hand holding mine captive, his lips kissing me senseless, and his hardness rubbing against me.

I wrapped my legs around him and gave in to the overwhelming sensations.

He knew just the right spot to concentrate.

I didn't want him to stop, but I couldn't speak to tell him that.

There was no need, though. He didn't stop.

This man could make me come with our clothes on. And I was… so… close…so…close.

Then my body exploded and my limbs went limp.

He held me close, letting me ride the waves that shook me to the core.

"I love you," he whispered, his breath against my ear.

"I love you, too," I said.

If only we could stay this way forever.

101

KADE

From my office at Skye Travels, I had a view of the tarmac. Not a corner office by any means, but a view nonetheless.

I watched as one of Noah's planes landed. The bright red Skye Travels logo said so much.

Skye was Noah's wife's middle name. Savannah Skye Richards Worthington.

He'd named his legendary company after his wife, Savannah.

I loved Noah and Savannah's story. It was strangely similar to mine and Madison's, at least so far.

They'd been college sweethearts, then were separated for fifteen years.

Fifteen years. I'd been apart from Madison for eight years and that seemed like an eternity.

It was some kind of miracle that they'd had five children after they got back together.

Noah's romance, like his company, was the stuff legends were made of. In my mind, Noah embodied the American dream.

Besides a view of the tarmac, there was a calendar sitting on the desk. One of those little cardboard calendars with the monthly pages that tear off.

I reached over and ripped off the July page. Today was August 1st.

The month I'd been dreading all summer.

I didn't know what day in August Madison was planning on leaving. We didn't talk about it. But I knew it was August. I'd known that all along.

My life was draining away with the passing of time.

All things considered, I was doing a fine job of living in the moment.

But August was always there in the back of my mind.

I slammed the calendar face down.

Just because it was August, didn't mean I had to look at it.

My phone chimed. Thinking it might be a text from Madison, I picked it up. We were supposed to have lunch together today.

Just like we'd been doing every day I'd been in town. Just like in college, we were inseparable. The thought of her not being here made me sick to my stomach.

But the text wasn't from Madison. It was from Mike.

MIKE: *Are you flying today?*

ME: *No. In the office.*

As a matter of fact, I had no flights today. Skye Travels was obviously busy. I'd have to ask Madison why she hadn't scheduled anyone with me.

MIKE: *I'm headed your way. Lunch?*

ME: *Having lunch with Madison.*

MIKE: *This is kind of important.*

ME: *Mind if she comes along?*

I tapped my phone as I waited for him to answer. I hadn't talked to him since that day we'd had lunch in Ruston. He'd been my mentor, not my friend.

Was he trying to strike up a friendship now? That happened sometimes.

MIKE: *I really need to talk to just you. Alone.*

ME: *I'll see what I can do and let you know.*

MIKE: *I wouldn't mind her coming along, but it's personal. It's important.*

I stared at the phone as though it was going to give me answers.

If it had been anyone other than Mike, I would have pleaded off.

But I was curious what Mike could possibly have to discuss with me. With all that had been going on with my own mother and Noah, my thoughts jumped to the worst. That generation was getting older.

Leaving my office, I went to the lobby to let Madison know I'd be missing lunch with her today.

And I was already thinking about what I could do tonight to make up for it.

102

MADISON

Since Kade had bailed on me, I met Emily for lunch at the Skyhouse.

She waved from across the room as though I didn't know where to look for her.

Emily was dressed casually in jeans and long t-shirt with a leather jacket.

"I didn't think about it being your day off," I said, sliding into one of our favorite booths against the far wall.

"It's not," she said. "I'm working from home today."

"Oh. How are you doing that?"

Emily was a high school teacher.

She shrugged with a little smile. "Even high schoolers are learning online today."

Something was going on with Emily, but I was too bummed to delve into it right now.

In fact, I was trying hard to keep a smile on my face.

Since I made the schedule myself, I knew that Kade had no flights today. Yet, at the last minute, he'd canceled.

And he'd been vague about it. Some kind of meeting, he said.

Emily leaned forward.

"But enough about me," she said. "You've been keeping a low profile."

"Things have been crazy," I said, looking toward the door.

Emily tapped her fingers on her water glass as she studied me.

"How's Kade?" she asked.

My gaze snapped back to her. "Good."

"You two are back together, aren't you?"

"Stop smirking, Emily," I said.

She sat back and nodded. "I knew it was going to happen. I called it."

A server I didn't recognize came over with a basket of bread and we both ordered a salad.

"Stop it," I said, after the server left. "We've just been hanging out. It can't go anywhere."

"Never say never," Emily said, taking a slice of bread. She slapped butter on it and took a bite.

"What's up with you?" I asked.

"What?" Emily slid the bread in my direction.

I shook my head. "You never eat bread like that."

"You're trying to change the subject." Emily held up a finger. "Not working."

I took a piece of bread and broke off one of the edges.

"You do know I'm leaving soon, right?"

"How could I not?" Emily asked. "You remind me all the time."

I looked at her blankly. Then scrunched my face.

"I do, don't I? You must be sick of hearing about it."

Emily reached over and patted my hand.

"Not sick of it. Just worried about you. Worried that you're making the wrong decision."

I took a deep breath.

The server brought our salads and refilled our water glasses.

"Emily," I said after he left. "It's my dream job. You know that."

Emily shrugged. "I know. But as your best friend it's my job to tell you when you need to think something through. Right?"

"Of course," I said, staring at my plate and absently stirring my salad. Then I looked up at her.

"But weren't you supposed to tell me this three months ago?

"Maybe," Emily said. "But I didn't want to tell you wrong."

"So what makes you think you're right now?"

Emily smiled.

"I can see it in your face," she said.

"What are you seeing?" I asked, though I was afraid of the answer.

"I see a lot of things. But mostly I see doubt."

I wanted to tell her she was imagining things. Seeing what she wanted to see.

But I knew she was right.

My best friend was putting into words what I'd been feeling for some time.

103

KADE

I'd barely finished lunch with Mike when Noah sent me a text.

I was standing on the sidewalk outside of a little pizza place not too far from the airport. Mike had wanted someplace quiet and private. So the Skyhouse was out.

Since I'd driven, Mike stood next to me. Waiting.

At the Skyhouse, we were likely to run into anyone from the office, especially Noah or Quinn or even Madison.

The three people who would ask too many questions to keep Mike's meeting private.

NOAH: *I noticed your schedule is clear today and tomorrow. I need you to take a flight.*

"Hold on," I said. "I need to answer this."

"Take your time," Mike said. "I'm in no hurry."

ME: *Ok. When do I leave?*

NOAH: *ASAP. A client has a family emergency.*

Damn. No matter where it was, there was no way I was going to get back in time to take Madison to dinner.

"Come on," I said. "Might as well head back to the airport. I've got an unexpected flight."

"The name of the game," Mike said.

"Yeah." We got in the car and turned on the air conditioning.

I sent Noah another text before backing out.

ME: *Where to?*

NOAH: *Boston.*

My stomach clenched. Now I was certain. Not only was I not going to be home for dinner, this was going to be an overnight trip.

"Looks like I'm flying to Boston today," I said.

"I understand." Mike pulled out his own cell phone. Then glanced back over at me. "It's good to have options, isn't it?"

"Maybe." I pulled into traffic.

Everything was so easy for Mike.

"You sure Noah doesn't know you're talking to me?" I asked as the airport came into sight up ahead.

Sending me on a trip to Boston sure sounded like some kind of punishment.

"I'm positive," Mike said. "I just told him I had a couple of options and would get back to him before we made any decisions."

"Huh." I parked the car.

I had another message from Noah.

NOAH: *You could be there for several days.*

This week was definitely not turning out the way I'd planned.

Not even close.

NOAH: *I'm sorry. You're the only one who can do it. I'd go myself, but I have an appointment.*

An appointment. Madison had said that Noah's medical issue was resolved.

Maybe he hadn't told her everything.

No matter. I couldn't leave Noah in the lurch.

104

MADISON

I stayed longer at lunch with Emily than I probably should have. One of the perks of being the boss's daughter was having flexibility.

Emily and I had changed topics and talked some about her job and what was going on with her, but we'd steered away from any more serious topics.

I stepped off the elevator and walked around the corner to the lobby.

Daddy sat at the reception desk, doing something at the scheduling computer.

Kade stood at the counter with the leather satchel he used to carry his iPad and his travel bag sat at his feet.

My heart lodged in my throat.

Kade was taking a flight.

An overnight flight.

Every day that we were apart, my heart ached.

I knew that we only had a few more days to spend together before we would find ourselves separated by what may as well be thousands of miles.

Again.

Unable to look at Kade, I walked around him and stood in front of my father.

"Daddy?" I asked, forcing a little smile. "What's going on?"

The founder and CEO of Skye Travels was not supposed to be sitting at the reception desk taking calls and making schedules.

He glanced at me, then turned his attention back to the computer.

"The phone's still set to the answering service," he said. "So you'll need to check that. I cleared out Kade's schedule for the rest of the week and gave his flights to other pilots."

"Okay," I said, setting my purse on the counter. "What's happened?"

"Mr. Baker had a family emergency. I would have gone myself, but my schedule is already booked. So I gave the flight to Kade."

I put my hands on the back of the chair and looked over my father's head at Kade.

Our gazes locked.

"When does he come back?" I asked. It was hard to speak with my heart in my throat.

Kade's expression was blank.

"I don't know," Daddy said. "Mr. Baker needs him to stay until he's ready to come back."

Sometimes clients did that. Especially clients like Mr. Baker who had enough money that it didn't matter to them.

Did Daddy know what he'd done? I hadn't told him how I felt about Kade.

But wasn't he the one who'd sent us to Denver together?

"I'll get out of your hair," Daddy said, standing up. "You can make sure everything looks good."

I watched him walk around the counter. He really was clueless.

He stopped and turned around. "Oh. Before I forget. Quinn

is supposed to have someone coming this week for you to train. Not sure about the details."

I shifted my gaze away from Kade to Daddy. If I'd even remotely thought about going with Kade, Daddy just trampled all over that possibility.

I was the only one who could train someone to take my place.

Daddy looked from me to Kade and back again.

It occurred to me then that it wasn't Daddy who'd set up our trip to Denver together.

It was Momma.

"Kade," Daddy said. "Mr. Baker is waiting on the tarmac."

105

KADE

r. Baker sat quietly in the back of the plane. He hadn't asked for anything other than getting to Boston quickly.

No one had told me what kind of emergency he had and I hadn't asked. It wasn't my business.

As I took the airplane into the sky, I felt like my world had just caved in around me.

Somehow in the span of a handful of minutes, I'd gone from feeling like things were finally going to work out to feeling like everything had gone wrong.

The pain in Madison's eyes was more than I could bear.

I kicked myself for letting Noah usher me off like that.

But unfortunately, I was well schooled in keeping the client satisfied above all else.

There was something unique about being a pilot. There was plenty of time alone to think.

Nothing to do, in fact, but to think.

As I reached cruising altitude, I made myself a promise.

A pact with myself.

This was the last time I was going to put my job over my family.

And by my family, I meant Madison.

My conversation with Mike had given me options.

Options that I might not have considered if everything hadn't converged just the way it had.

I'd left my job with the commercial airline to be closer to family, specifically my mother.

But Mother could live anywhere, so I filed that aspect away to think about a bit later.

Now I had Madison again.

And Madison was relocating.

But I wasn't going to let it all happen again like it had eight years ago.

Mike had presented me with an option.

An option that I never would have considered until now.

I checked the computer monitors and sat back.

Things were going to work out this time.

It was just going to take some unanticipated maneuvering.

Some would call it a pivot.

So I was going to pivot.

After I landed, I would start making phone calls.

I had a lot to do.

I didn't consider myself to be impulsive. I was true and steady.

But this decision wasn't one born of impulse.

This was a decision that had been brewing for a long time.

A very long time.

Probably neigh onto ten years.

Since that day I'd met Madison.

Finally.

Everything was going to come together.

106

MADISON

After work, I went straight home, only to find my sister, Ainsley, sitting on the sofa.

She was wearing a pair of sweatpants and a t-shirt. No makeup. A full glass of red wine on the coffee table in front of her.

"You're home early," she said.

"Not really." I sat down across from her. Her eyes were red-rimmed.

Ainsley was one of the most put-together people I knew. She was level-headed and also opinionated.

Momma claimed that Ainsley, her oldest daughter, took after Daddy. Anytime any one of us did something Momma didn't like, she blamed it on Daddy.

And since Ainsley was a pilot like Daddy, she was automatically more like him than the rest of us.

Ainsley claimed that made her Daddy's favorite.

I, of course, knew that she was mistaken about that.

At the moment, though, something was definitely not right with my sister.

"What's happened?" I asked.

Ainsley shook her head. "I don't want to talk about it."

I waited, not saying anything.

"Men," Ainsley said.

"I figured. So what's happened?"

"It's nothing," she said. "Nothing that an indefinite moratorium won't fix."

I laughed. "A moratorium? That sounds serious."

I tried to remember the guy's name that she was currently dating.

Ainsley didn't date anyone steady.

I personally think it was because she worked with men. And pilots weren't known for their commitment.

If I hadn't known Kade while we were in college—before he became a pilot—I sometimes wondered if I would feel the same way.

But I trusted Kade.

He'd never given me a reason not to.

Ainsley just shrugged.

"So what are you doing here? Don't you have a date with Kade?"

"Why would you assume that?" I asked.

"You always have a date with Kade."

Always was close to right.

"Well," I said. "Not tonight. Daddy sent him on a trip to Boston."

Ainsley sat up.

"Overnight then." It was a statement not a question.

"Actually. It could be as long as a week."

"Why didn't he send me?"

I picked up her wine glass and tasted it. "Probably because you don't work for him."

"Right," she said. "Not enough experience."

It spoke to Daddy's commitment to his company that he wouldn't put his own daughter on the payroll until she had what he considered enough experience. And that could take years according to Noah Worthington's standards.

"You could have gone with him," Ainsley pointed out.

"Yes. I suppose I could have except that our dear brother Quinn has decided that this is the week I have to train my replacement."

"I say screw Quinn. He should have done that weeks ago."

"Agreed," I said, sitting back with her glass of wine. "You're not drinking this?"

"Already had one," she said. "Have you figured out what you're going to do?"

Ainsley always had been one to cut to the chase. In that way she was not like Daddy, but in my opinion was a lot more like Momma, though Momma denied that particular trait in herself.

I smiled just a little. "I'm getting there," I said. "I just have a few more things to work out. And it's fortuitous that you're here because I need to talk to you about something."

107

KADE

"I'm not sure I like surprises," Madison said as I went down the pre-take off checklist.

"I'm pretty sure you'll like this one," I said.

We were flying a sweet little Cessna today, one of Noah's private's jets with the bright red Skye Travels logo across the tail.

If I'd built a company like Skye Travels, I was pretty sure I'd plaster the logo all over everything.

Noah knew the purpose of this trip, but I'd sworn him to secrecy. I hadn't minded asking him either, since the way I figured it, it was all his fault anyway for sending me off like that to Boston.

Also, how could he possibly not have noticed that his daughter and I had picked up our relationship again?

It was the Saturday after I'd gotten back from my trip to Boston.

I'd called Madison every day of course and we'd texted at random throughout my trip, but there was something different about her.

She was being distant.

I know she understood that I'd had no choice but to take this flight. I hadn't told her that her father had a doctor's appointment. That didn't seem like my information to share.

I couldn't tell if she was cross with him about it or with me in general.

She also hadn't said a word about moving to Denver. The couple of times I'd brought it up, she'd quickly changed the subject.

So today was the day I made it all up to her.

She fiddled with her phone as we taxied across the tarmac.

Before long, we got the go ahead to take off.

"You ready?" I asked.

She nodded.

She obviously hadn't gotten over being cross with me.

I took her hand and pulled her to meet me halfway. I pressed my lips against hers.

It was the first kiss we'd shared since before I left for Boston.

It seemed like forever ago.

Her kiss was definitely not distant or reserved.

I entertained the thought of turning around. We could go on our trip later.

But the traffic controller came through my headset loud and clear.

"Hold that thought," I said, winking at her.

She smiled at me and turned her attention to the window.

Status quo. Maybe it was my imagination that she was being distant. Maybe, as she would suggest, I was projecting.

The wheels left the ground and the plane went into ground effect.

We made a slow circle and headed northeast.

Madison turned slowly and looked at me.

Her voice came through my headset loud and clear.

"Kade," she said. "You're taking me to Ruston, Louisiana?"

I shrugged. I knew she'd know as soon as our course was set.

She had made this particular flight probably a hundred times over the years.

I was pretty sure she could even have piloted the plane if she had been so inclined.

In between business calls and making arrangements online, I'd had a lot of time to think in Boston.

I'd decided that Ruston—the place where we'd started—was the best place for us to set our course for the future.

It was like making a full circle around and picking up the thread of where we'd gone wrong.

But this time, I was determined that we would get it right.

108

MADISON

*S*itting in a booth at the back of the seafood restaurant near Louisiana Tech where Kade and I had spent so many hours hanging out in college, was a blast from the past.

Except that the servers were all so impossibly young.

We had lunch along with the usual weekend crowd, but then we stayed as others cleared out. As the crowd cleared out, the noise level dropped and we could actually hear each other talk.

But this time, we didn't have books spread out across the table, getting ready to study our respective subjects.

Instead, I had something I needed to tell Kade.

Something that was making me so nervous I'd barely eaten a thing.

He seemed a little nervous, too, but I was pretty sure I was projecting my nervousness onto him.

"So I've been thinking," he said.

"So have I."

He grinned that lopsided grin that always did funny things to my heart. "We usually are on the same page, aren't we?"

"A lot of the time, yes," I said, clasping my hands together tightly beneath the table.

"And," he said. "since we started in Ruston, I thought maybe this was where we needed to pick this up."

My stomach plummeted. After all the plans I'd put into place, he was going to break up with me. To say that our relationship had run its course. That the summer had been nice. That—

"Madison," he said, interrupting my spiral of thoughts. "I didn't tell you, but I ran into Mike a few weeks ago."

"Mike Phillips? Really? Where?"

"Here, actually."

"Oh wow. How is he? Why didn't you tell me?"

"He'd doing great. And I didn't tell you because I wanted to bring you here. As a surprise. And I couldn't tell you about Mike and give you this as a surprise at the same time."

I rested my chin on my hands and smiled at him. Sometimes his logic was so funny it was adorable. "I see," I said.

"But that's not the point," he said. "The point is he offered me a job."

"But…" Mike was a professor. "Here? In Ruston?"

Oh no.

I could see Kade as a professor. He was at a good age to transition into teaching.

I tried to force a smile, but it fell flat.

No. This was not good.

This was bad. It was so bad that I thought I might be sick.

Kade would be moving to Ruston.

Just as I had figured out how to stay in Houston.

109

MADISON

"Are you okay?" Kade asked. "You don't look so good."

"I'm okay," I lied. I sat up straight and fanned my face. "It's just a little warm in here."

Kade looked at me sideways, then got up and came over to slide into my side of the booth.

"You didn't eat much," he said, putting the back of his hand on my forehead.

"Stop it," I said. "I'm fine." But he was making me laugh.

"Good," he said. "You didn't let me finish what I wanted to tell you."

I took a deep breath, clasped my hands in my lap, and looked into his bright blue eyes. Whatever it was, I'd congratulate him, then I'd hold myself together until I got home.

I could do it.

"What is it you want to tell me?"

"You know that your dad and Mike are good friends, right?"

I hadn't given it much thought lately. Daddy had lots of friends. But, yes, I knew.

"Since you're moving to Denver, your dad decided he needed a small office there. He asked Mike to manage it."

I nodded. That sounded like something Daddy would do.

"So Mike is going to be setting up and managing an office in Denver and you're going to take his teaching job. Here."

Kade looked at me blankly.

"No," he said with a little chuckle. "That's not how we're doing it."

"Then how?"

"Mike's close to retirement, so he turned it down. But he offered to take care of finding someone else. To manage the office in Denver."

He was looking at me with such happiness.

Then it all clicked.

"You're going to be in the Denver office?"

"Yes," he said, grinning. "Madison. I never want to lose you again."

I'd never had a panic attack before, but in this moment, I had a pretty good idea what it might feel like to have one.

"Kade," I said, squeezing his hands. "This is... so… good."

"But… you don't look happy about it."

"No," I said, swallowing the lump in my throat. "But…"

"Madison." He took my hands. Kissed my fingertips. "I love you. I never want to be apart from you again. I'll follow you to the ends of the earth if I have to."

"Kade," I said, barely able to speak. "I feel the same way."

"Then tell me why you look so sad."

He swept a finger over my cheek. Then over my lips.

I closed my eyes.

"Kade," I said. "I did a thing."

"What thing, my love?"

110

KADE — BEFORE

Today was a perfect day. The sky was blue. There were a few white puffy clouds and the air was the perfect temperature.

The wings of the little prop plane glinted in the sunlight.

It was Saturday, so there was no one else at the airport. It was just a quiet, clear day at the university airport.

I had my paperwork. My clipboard. Everything was cleared.

I'd flown solo before, but this was my first time taking a passenger up with me.

Two souls. That's what the paperwork said.

I opened the passenger door to the plane and Madison hopped in. She was wearing blue jeans and Tech t-shirt that matched her white baseball cap. Her long hair was pulled back in a high ponytail.

"Need some help?" I asked.

She turned and smiled at me. "I've got it." She deftly strapped herself into the four-point harness.

I closed her door and went around to the pilot's side.

I was so nervous my hands were trembling.

It was funny because Madison didn't seem the least bit nervous. She trusted me way more than I trusted me.

But at the same time, this was one of the most exciting moments of my life.

To be taking my girlfriend up in an airplane, meant that was officially a pilot.

I climbed inside, fastened my own belt, and went down the checklist on my clipboard.

"You ready?" I asked.

"Ready when you are," she said.

I remembered my flight. I'd been fifteen years old when my grandparents had flown me with them to Alaska. I was hooked.

After that, the only thing I talked about was airplanes. I researched them. Studied them.

I built a model airplane that I still had.

Then I started researching schools. I wanted to learn to fly. I wanted to be a pilot.

And here I was.

Today.

And I was sharing this special moment with the girl I was in love with.

We taxied down the runway to get into position for takeoff.

I looked at Madison.

She put her hand over mine and smiled brightly.

"You've got this," she said. "You're going to be great."

I nodded.

She instinctively knew I was nervous.

But I took a deep breath and smiled at her.

She was right. I knew what I was doing.

If I didn't, I would never have taking Madison in the air.

Madison and I had been inseparable for about two months now.

I'd been wanted to kiss her since the first day I'd seen her.

I thought I'd shown extraordinary gentlemanly restraint.

But right here. Right now. I decided it was time to change that.

I pulled gently on her hand, bringing her closer.

"A kiss for luck?"

She smiled and I leaned toward her, her eyes fluttered closed.

I slowly lowered my lips toward hers.

My heart was pounding dangerously in my chest.

It was a combination of my nervousness about flying and my nervousness about kissing Madison.

My lips hovered over hers for a moment. Then I pressed my lips against her.

And everything inside me shifted into perspective.

It was a simple kiss that changed my life.

I was no longer nervous.

I had everything I wanted in life right here in my hands at this very moment.

Madison Worthington and my hands on the yoke of an airplane.

I straightened and grinned at her.

As long as I had Madison next to me, I could do anything.

And together, I knew that whatever life threw at us, we could figure it out.

And I knew that I wanted to spend the rest of my life with her.

111

———

KADE

Madison didn't seem to understand how much I loved her. How I would do anything to be with her.

I wasn't going to let her slip out of my hands again.

Her eyes were moist.

The servers in the kitchen were talking to each other in the background.

Our server stopped by.

"Can I get you two anything?" she asked.

"No," I said, glancing at the young girl. "Thank you."

I turned back to Madison.

She took a deep ragged breath.

"I found a way to commute from Houston."

"Wait…" I stared at her. "Commute?"

A slow smile spread across her lips.

"Turns out some of the universities courses are being taught hybrid. Partly online and party face-to-face. So I can be there three days a week and in Houston for four day weekends."

Then we both broke out laughing.

I pulled her into a hug.

She smelled like honeysuckle and sunshine.

"I never doubted that we'd find a way to stay together," I said. "All we needed was half a chance."

She nodded. "Me too. So what are we going to do?"

I pulled back and looked into her eyes.

"The way I see it, this is the best possible problem to have."

"We'll figure it out won't we?" she asked.

I pulled her close again.

"I'm not letting you go this time."

"I'm not letting you go either, Kade Samuel Johnson," she said.

Our paths had once again intersected and this time we wouldn't stray.

Madison Worthington was my true north.

112

MADISON

My mind raced in a thousand different directions as we flew back toward Houston.

It was a route I knew by heart.

One that I would never forget no matter how far I strayed.

I spent an entire summer stressing over something that sorted itself out in the end.

As a psychologist, I learned from this. Things tend to sort themselves out.

As a woman, I also learned. I should always listen to my heart. Because the heart knows.

No matter what, the heart knows what it wants.

And when everything comes together, the heart settles into a special place of contentment and happiness like nothing else.

We flew through a white puffy cloud and I looked over at Kade. Clouds made some people nervous because you couldn't see anything. In a car, that would definitely be a problem, but not in a plane. I saw flying through white clouds as good luck.

Kade and I had spent three hours sitting in the restaurant talking about all our options.

It was ironic how we'd both been making changes to be with the other.

My sister Ainsley was letting me live in her apartment as long as I needed to. And she was okay with Kade moving in with me. She was rarely home anyway and she couldn't possibly use all the space in her condo.

So Kade and I could stay in Houston if we wanted to. Kade had been living in a hotel for three months. Almost like he knew better than to lock something down yet.

Or we could move to Denver. I could teach at the university and he could run the Denver office of Skye Travels. Running the office would keep him in town more and out of the air.

He could pick and choose when he wanted to fly.

That was a sacrifice for him, but he assured me he was willing to make it to keep us together.

The one loose end was his mother. If he moved to Denver, she'd have to move with him.

He'd already checked into assisted living homes and had found a place that he thought would be perfect for her. She'd have her own cottage, but she'd have other people her own age to socialize with and around the clock care. But Kade wouldn't have to be the one in charge of that care.

It sounded like a great option for her.

We would still have plenty of time to fly to Houston to see my family.

So after we'd talked through everything, it was sounding like Denver was the best option.

But we didn't have to decide right away.

We would have my sister's condo to live in and we'd have my apartment in Denver.

If Kade didn't like running the office, he could hire a new person to manage it and he could go back to flying for Daddy.

I had a feeling, though, that once he had a taste of being the one in charge, he'd like it.

It was hard to go back after being the one to make your own schedule.

He took my hand and grinned at me just as we came out of the clouds.

Like our lives, the world opened in front of us.

As long as we were together, anything was possible.

EPILOGUE
MADISON

I sat on the couch draped under a blanket while Kade carefully placed thick kindling in between thick logs in the fireplace. He'd been quiet today. Preoccupied even.

But at the moment, he was focused on getting this, our first real fire in our fireplace going. I wasn't sure he knew what he was doing, but his determination made up for any lack of experience.

I was impressed when the fire roared to life.

"There," he said, turning around and dusting his hands. He wore a proud grin. "That should keep us warm through the night."

I didn't bother to point out that we had electric heat in the apartment.

"Not bad for a southern boy from Houston," I said. "How did you learn to do that?"

"Google," he said, crawling over me and settling behind, pulling me into his arms.

"Google, huh?" I kissed his cheek. He smelled wonderfully masculine. Like pine and the minty scent of his toothpaste. "What else have you learned on Google lately?"

"Well…" He lifted my hair and kissed the back of my neck, sending delicious shivers down my spine.

"There was this one thing."

I grinned up at him.

"But first I have something for you."

"Yeah? What's that?" I had a feeling I knew exactly what he had for me. I could feel his erection pressing against my bottom.

He pulled a little square white box from somewhere… behind the sofa cushion, maybe, and placed it in my hands.

"What's this?" I asked. My heart rate went into an involuntary little race as I held the little square box that could be anything at all. A necklace. Some earrings. Whatever it was, it was some type of jewelry.

Kade mostly brought me flowers and little treats to eat. If he flew someplace he thought I'd like, he'd bring me something back. Usually something practical like a t-shirt or something romantic like a scented candle.

"Madison," he said, shifting me in his lap so he could look into my eyes. "I've had this for a while." He took a deep breath. "And I've been waiting for the right time to give it to you."

My hands shaking, I lifted the lid of the velvet box.

I blinked as I realized that this wasn't a necklace or earrings.

It was a diamond ring with a rose gold band and with little touches of pink astorite around the edges of the diamond. The little hint of pink matched the bracelet I'd bought in Estes Park. The evening before we first made love.

"Where did you get this?" I asked, looking up at him. Though the stone was similar, it was different from anything I'd ever seen.

"I had it made," he said. "If you don't like it…"

I put my fingers over his lips. "I love it," I said. "It's perfect."

"Wait," he said. "I think I was supposed to ask you first."

My lips curved into a smile. "Ask me what?"

"When do you want to get married?"

"Kade," I said. Had he suddenly lost all sense of romanticism?

First he hands me a box. Then he asks me when I want to get married?

He dumped me onto the seat next to him and got on one knee on the floor in front of me.

He took my hands and looked into my eyes. That's when I knew that he'd done this all backwards on purpose.

"I love you. I always have. I always will."

Those three simple statements nearly took my breath away in their simplicity.

He kissed the back of my fingers. "Dr. Madison Worthington. Will you marry me?"

I hadn't thought I could get any happier than I'd been these last three months spending all my free time with Kade. But my eyes were misting over out of sheer joy.

I was so overwhelmed and this was so unexpected, I could barely catch my breath.

"Yes," I managed, then threw my arms around him. "Kade."

He kissed me on the cheek, then his lips found mine.

His tongue slid against mine and I slid forward to sit on his lap.

With his lips still on mine, he picked me up and set me back on the sofa.

Tugging my shirt off over my head, he pressed me back against the soft cushion.

I wasn't wearing any underwear. None.

It wasn't something I normally did, but I'd been relaxed and ready for bed for Kade had come in carrying a cord of firewood.

He sat next to me, pulling me with him onto his lap. He'd changed into an old pair of soft sweatpants. And I knew from experience that Kade never wore underwear under his sweats.

His tongue touched the roof of my mouth as he shifted me so that I sat straddled over him.

He was hard beneath me and I moved against him.

His lips blazed a trail of heat down my chin… my neck… my collar bone… then his lips were on one nipple, then the other.

I leaned my head back and let the sensations flood my system.

Somehow he managed to pull my pajama pants down and his own sweatpants down at the same time.

My hands tangled in his soft short hair. He moved his lips back to mine and linked the fingers of one hand with mine. Using his other hand, he guided his hardness to press against me.

I shifted my hips up, wanting more. Wanting all of him.

I needed to spread my legs, but my pajama pants were holding me captive. The sensation of being unable to move was like sweet torture and I expected my pants to rip at any moment with the way I was pressing against them.

I slid down over him, pressing my core against his shaft.

Just as the pressure started to build, he shifted again, laying me flat against the sofa cushions. He pulled my pants off and slung them somewhere.

He seemed to notice for the first time that I wasn't wearing panties.

"Nice," he said, against my ear, as his fingers swept over my bare bottom.

I smiled against his lips, pleased that he approved.

He shifted himself over me and kissed me again.

"So…" he said.

Why was he talking?

"So… what?" I asked.

He nibbled my earlobe, his breath warm against my skin.

"After we're married, we can do this all the time."

"I thought we did," I said. He wanted more? We did it most every night.

"I can't get enough of you," he said as he deftly plunged inside me.

I gasped, like I always did at the way he filled me up and any other thoughts I might have had dissipated.

Holding my hands over my head with one hand, he slowly ran his fingertips across my body with the other. He slowly touched my stomach. My breasts. My lips.

All the while, he moved his hips in little circular motions.

I wrapped my legs around his back as he put a hand between us to rub that sweet spot that sent me into another world.

I moaned against his lips. "Don't… don't stop."

"Never," he murmured and he increased the speed until I toppled over the edge.

I gasped as my world exploded into a million pieces, leaving me feeling like my bones were made out of liquid. And that's when he let go, plunging deep as he took his own release.

We lay there, both riding the waves that shook our bodies inside and out.

He pulled out slowly, turned on his side, grabbed the blanket, and snuggled me back against him.

"What did I do to deserve you?" he asked.

My eyes were already starting to drift closed.

"You must have been very, very good," I said.

I felt his soft laughter against back.

I snuggled my butt against him.

"Watch it," he said.

"Ha. You don't frighten me."

With his arms wrapped tightly around me, I felt like I was in heaven.

"I love you," I whispered.

"I love you more," He whispered back.

I just smiled. I'd let him think that if he wanted to.

Either way, we were both winners.

Kade had been teaching me some of his aviation terminology.

And in my sleepy haze, I realized that Kade Johnson was my magnetic north.

Wherever he went, I would follow.

And I had a very good feeling that he felt the same way about me.

We had always been aligned with each other and we always would be.

Those eight years we'd spent apart were merely a blip on our life's radar.

**Keep reading for a preview of Ainsley and Wyatt's story,
Second Chance Secrets...**

SECOND CHANCE SECRETS PREVIEW

Chapter 1
Ainsley Worthington

I'd had better days.

I sat in a small private Cessna jet on the tarmac at a little airport just out from Aspen, Colorado.

The sun came through the windshield with a vengeance. It was hot for an October day.

A ridge of trees, flocked with shades of red, yellow, and gold started just off the edge of the runway and traveled up the mountainside until they gave way to bare rocks and finally snowcapped peaks.

A flock of birds left the trees and flew into the sky.

Yet I was left sitting here on the tarmac in this plane.

The tail of the plane wore bright red letters. Skye Travels.

One of Noah Worthington's planes.

Noah. My daddy.

Daddy was known to hire only the best pilots to fly for the company he'd built from the ground up.

It was an aviation empire now. One that rivaled some of the smaller commercial airlines.

Out of six children, I was the only one of his children who became a pilot.

Six. One brother. Three sisters. And one half-sister.

Both my half-sister and my older sister had married pilots, but that didn't count.

I had Daddy's blood running through my veins.

Yet he wouldn't hire me on until I had enough experience.

Frankly, I thought he was being harder on me than anyone else.

He'd let me haul cargo, but not people.

"Miss Worthington?" A mechanic climbed up on the wing and stuck his head through the open door of my plane.

"Did you find one?"

"I'm sorry," he said. "We have to order one from the factory. Won't be here for two days." He glanced upwards. "And with the weather they're predicting, all bets are off."

Damn.

"Is there another plane I can use?"

"You'll have to check inside. I don't have that information."

Of course he didn't.

I tossed my leather satchel over my shoulder, but left my pilot's cap on the passenger seat.

Daddy insisted that all his pilots wear a cap. He thought they added a level of distinctiveness to the pilots.

"Come on Beau," I said. "Let's get out of here."

I picked up the leash and, leaning back, hooked it on Beau's collar.

This was supposed to be a day trip. Fly up. Get the dog—a cute, friendly solid black lab—and fly back to Houston.

Simple.

But then the alternator had gone bad.

Apparently there was a shortage of alternators right now, at least for this particular plane.

And on top of that, there was a snow storm coming in.

I didn't do snow.

I was a Houston girl. Born and raised.

My older sister, Madison, lived in Denver with her fiancé. But that was about as close to snow as I got.

Though I was only picking up a dog, I was still flying a Skye Travels plane, so I was wearing part of my full uniform. White shirt. Low heels. Black jeans.

I used every opportunity to show Daddy that I was ready to fly passengers, but today seemed like a good day to bend the rules.

I had become adept at getting in and out of small planes, even wearing heels.

The big dog was a bit of a different story.

I barely had my feet on the ground before Beau jumped out, landing behind me.

He shook his whole body, fur flying, and looked at me expectantly.

I didn't know a whole lot about dogs, but I could tell Beau was still a puppy. A big gangly puppy.

Though the sun had been hot coming in through the windshield, there was a cold bite to the wind. I was wearing a little suit jacket. It wouldn't do much to keep me warm though.

"Let's go," I said, starting off across the tarmac toward the office where I'd left just an hour ago.

Beau practically pulled me along behind him.

He was being shipped from one family member to another. That's all I knew. I'm sure there was a story behind it all, but my job was just to get Beau from one airport to another.

My sister Madison would have known the whole story

before she even had the flight scheduled. But she was a psychologist.

Me. I was all about the flight.

But right now I was stuck in an airport in the Rocky Mountains with a dog named Beau.

I went inside the little office and walked up to the desk.

"Hi," I said to the young lady sitting behind the desk. Her name tag said her name was Claire. She was a tall, thin woman with short blonde hair. Her features were angular and sharp.

"Hi," Claire said with a bright smile, mostly for Beau.

"They had to order a part," I said. "for my plane."

"I know," Claire said. "I'm sorry."

"So… can you get me out of here?"

"Unfortunately we don't have any extra planes." She said it with a straight face.

"I didn't think you would," I said, plastering a smile on my face, refusing to get snippy. "Do you have access to other flights out of here?"

"I do," she said. "There's nothing. The storm."

"Right," I said. "The storm. But would you please check again?" Beau tugged at his leash and I had to catch myself to him from pulling me with him. "I have this dog I have to get to Houston."

Claire started to refuse, but I just raised an eyebrow and stood as though to say I was going to wait right here until she checked again.

Claire clicked keys on the keyboard.

Then looked back at me. "I'm sorry," she said. "There's nothing."

"Alright," I said, pulling my cell out of my pocket.

Daddy could fix this.

Claire had no idea, obviously, how to make things happen.

I shot off a quick text to Daddy.

ME: *Had to order a part. AND weather has flight delayed. Can you get me out of here?*

I walked over to one of the sofas and sat down. Beau jumped up to sit beside me.

There was only one other man in the lobby, but his back was to me. A phone was pressed to his ear.

"I don't think you're supposed to be up here," I said, pushing at Beau.

He didn't budge.

He was awfully heavy for a puppy.

DADDY: *Let me see. Hold tight. Be right back.*

Hold tight. He had no idea what he was asking.

Claire was shooting me dirty looks for having Beau on the sofa.

Well, it wasn't like I could do anything about it.

I stood up and Beau followed. We walked over to the window and turned our backs to Claire as I held my cell and waited.

Clouds had gathered around the mountain peaks. I remembered Madison talking about how the mountain peaks would disappear in a swirl of clouds when it was going to snow.

Then when clouds cleared, they would leave a layer of fresh snow.

While waiting for Daddy to get back to me, I checked the weather on my phone.

Wow. According to the projection, this whole area was going to be blanketed by snow in about… three hours.

I needed to leave. Now.

I turned and started back toward the desk, Beau in tow.

Claire saw me coming. I know she did. She stood up and disappeared into the back.

I stood in the middle of the lobby. Beau's leash in one hand. My phone in the other.

My thoughts scattered in a thousand different directions.

There was no way I was getting out of here today.

I had to find dog food for this dog. And a place to stay.

A hotel that took dogs.

I stared at my phone. Willing Daddy to write back.

The phone rang and I jumped.

"Hi Daddy," I said. I had a sinking feeling in the pit of my stomach.

Chapter 2
Wyatt Beaufort

I'D BEEN on hold for far too long.

But it had paid off.

While I was on hold, listening to interminable elevator music, I'd watched the young lady who had come in with her dog.

I couldn't hear her conversation with Claire, the receptionist, but I could tell by Claire's smug expression and the girl's look of distress, that she was stranded here.

I stood up. Stretched. The girl was pacing and talking on her cell. She was one of those dark-haired brunettes that automatically sent my pulse racing.

But this particular dark-haired brunette had the beauty of an angel.

I didn't know who she was or where she came from. Frankly I didn't care.

I shoved my iPad into my satchel and tossed it over my shoulder.

Hanging back, I waited for her finish her call. I could hear her voice, but she spoke low, so I couldn't understand her words.

"Love you, too," she said before ending the call. I flinched.

Didn't matter. There were lots of people she could say that to. Didn't mean she was taken.

Either way, I could still help her.

Claire had disappeared into the back. I'd dealt with her before, so I wasn't surprised.

The girl stood there, looking bereft.

I walked over and stopped a few feet away.

"Hi," I said.

She looked over at me and frowned. Her dog walked over and licked my fingers.

They said dogs and owners tended to have the same personality, so I had hope for this girl.

I nodded toward the receptionist desk. "Having trouble getting out of here?"

"A bit," she said.

"Well, I just got clearance for takeoff."

She was frowning again.

"Must be nice," she said.

"Can I give you a lift?" I asked, scratching her dog's ears.

"I don't know you," she said.

"Your dog likes me," I said.

"He's not—" Her phone chimed again and she glanced at it, then lifted her gaze back to mine.

Her eyes were green. Not hazel. A deep emerald green. Mesmerizing.

I took another step forward, holding out my hand.

"I'm Wyatt," I said.

She hesitated, but then slipped her phone in her pocket and pressed her hand against mine.

She had a professional handshake. That told me a lot about her.

I grinned. "Now you know me."

She shook her head and grabbed the dog's leash with both hands.

"So can I give you a lift?"

Claire walked back out to her desk and watched us.

"I don't even know where you're headed," she said.

"With this weather, I'm thinking it wouldn't matter."

I could tell she was considering it. But she was still wary. A good quality for a girl who looked like her to have.

Claire's voice came over the loudspeaker. You'd think there was a roomful of people and not just the two of us.

"The terminal will be closing in ten minutes."

I'd been in this terminal a hundred times and I'd never even known it to have a loudspeaker.

Probably just for emergencies.

But Claire was being an ass. I'd seen it before. This was different though. She was usually a lot more subtle about it.

She smiled when she saw me looking in her direction. She raised a hand and sent me a smile.

I ignored her and turned back to the girl.

"Well," I said. "I take that as my cue to get out of here." I gave the dog another pat. "Good luck."

I turned and walked toward the door to the tarmac.

Damn. I hated leaving this girl stranded here.

But I understood where she was coming from.

She had no idea who I was.

And had no reason to leave with me.

If she were my sister, I'd commend her caution.

I reached the door and wrapping my fingers around the doorknob, prepared myself to face the air that seemed to be getting colder by the minute.

"Wait," the girl said from behind me.

Keep Reading Second Chance Secrets

Kathryn Kaleigh is the author of seventy novels, over one hundred short stories, and many collections.

kathrynkaleigh.com

www.ingramcontent.com/pod-product-compliance
Lightning Source LLC
Chambersburg PA
CBHW020545120726
47903CB00001B/135